VG 1

FLIGHT INTO FEAR

After years of flying brokendown aircraft for two-bit concerns, John Shaw lands a soft assignment. Go to San Francisco and deliver a brand-new twin-engined Tiger to England. It was a cinch.

But then the nightmare begins. In San Franscisco someone tries to kill him. Then he gets an unexpected passenger: America's most wanted man! When he acquires still another unwelcome guest on the flight back Shaw begins to know what trouble is. What he doesn't know is why this is happening to him. Nor does the reader. It isn't until the final nerve-racking round is played out against the incongruous background of a sleepy English university town that Shaw discovers the identity of the people who are out to get him—and why they want him dead.

DUNCAN KYLE

Flight into Fear

COLLINS
8 Grafton Street, London W1

William Collins Sons & Co Ltd
London · Glasgow · Sydney · Auckland
Toronto · Johannesburg

First published in 1972
This reprint 1988
© Duncan Kyle 1972

ISBN 0 00 221942 5

Made and Printed in Great Britain by
William Collins Sons & Co Ltd, Glasgow

Gratefully,
to M B who gave me
this delight
and A M B who shares it

One

The problem is to stay in the air. In the beginning, of course, it was easy. That was twenty years ago, when the flying bug bit me and I moved into a wonderful world filled by long lines of RAF trainers with full fuel tanks and ground crews swarming all over them; networks of airfields with comfortable quarters for pilots—and no landing charges anywhere. For years I just climbed into the cockpit, switched on and flew. Then one day the taxpayer stopped paying; at least, he stopped paying for John Shaw. That was when I discovered that fuel came only for cash, that maintenance people might or might not accept cheques and that it cost a small fortune to put three wheels on a stretch of concrete.

So nowadays I support this expensive addiction of mine by moving aircraft about for other people. I fly anything. Name the beast and I have clearance on it, however many engines it may have and whatever they are. So, from time to time, my telephone rings and if I'm not there to answer it, there's a little tape gadget that records messages.

That morning I'd been out early. When I returned I pressed the playback button and a voice boomed at me. 'I'll call you at ten-thirty, John,' it said. And laughed. Jimmy Pope's laugh.

Jimmy Pope is Airflo's London Man. He's a great big fat jolly kind of fellow with mean eyes. He laughs all the time and everything shakes: jowls, neck muscles and seven stomachs; but all the time his eyes have a flat, level look and notes are being made, ticketed and filed in the shrewd, sharp mind that hides behind the noisy nonsense. He's got a little double office with a girl in one half and himself in the other in an oldish building in Kingsway.

Airflo is a very neat low-overhead operation. There are two phones on Jimmy Pope's desk and that's about it. Seventy-five hundred miles away, in San Francisco, is the home office of Airflo and the guy who thought it all up: Marion Capote, founder and president. Back in 1945 Capote realized that private flying was going to mushroom, and he made a deal with a small firm of aircraft manufacturers, based in San Francisco, called Stripe. The deal was beautifully simple: Stripe would build and sell, Airflo would deliver. The customer naturally pays. Only Cessna and Piper are bigger than Stripe now, and Capote has this lovely little gold mine. All he does is employ pilots and maintain an around-the-clock guard on his contract. If Mr Hatsumo of Hokkaido, or Mr Sonderburg in Sweden buys a Stripe aircraft, Marion Capote's boys fly it to Toyko or Gothenburg, then jet back to deliver another to Siñor Ramirez in Rio or plain Joe Sochaki in Hackensack. No overheads, no equipment. An elegant piece of thinking.

Even after delivery Airflo stands to collect; often enough an aircraft needs servicing, and that's where a pilot like me—not based in San Francisco—comes in. Normally, Jimmy Pope rings me and says that the good Mr Sonderburg has a deficient something or other and will I please go to Gothenburg, coax the plane into the air and limp to Stripe's European repair centre in Zürich. Sometimes I hang around there until the job's done and fly it back. The return journey is invariably the more cheerful.

Anyway, the phone rang and I picked it up and said with practised briskness, 'Shaw Aviation Services.' One day I'll work up the nerve to say 'SAS' but I haven't yet.

'John? Jimmy Pope. How are you, boy?'

I felt the familiar mixture of anticipation and naked terror. 'Morning, Jimmy.'

'In good fettle, are you, boy? Hands steady?'

I said, 'How steady do they need to be?'

He laughed, a great raucous boom that set the plastic of my handset vibrating. 'Not one of those, John. Not nasty at all.'

'I'd like to meet your nasty one,' I said. Not nasty was a meaningless phrase Jimmy Pope always used and it bracketed trips like one I'd done from Keflavik to Prestwick in a Stripe Corporal that couldn't grunt up higher than two hundred feet. The Atlantic rollers were scouring my toenails for five and a half hours.

'Well this isn't it,' he said. 'This is the nice one. If you're free.'

'Where?'

'San Francisco.' He poured the words out slowly as though they were Lyle's Golden Syrup. Then he laughed again, knowing he'd got me and knowing that I knew that he knew that I knew, etc.

'When?' I said, maintaining the pretence. If he'd said yesterday I'd have run backwards to catch up.

'Tonight. This afternoon, rather.'

I said, 'What's happened? Has Marion got a strike?'

When he stopped laughing he said, 'Pilot shortage, I think. This time we go and get.'

'Returning?'

'She's ready, John. Night's sleep and back you come.'

'What is she?'

'Stripe Tiger. Brand new. Twin Continentals, fuel injection, the lot.'

'De-icing equipment?'

'Half a tick.' You really couldn't trust a bloke like Jimmy. Here he was sending me off to fly the autumn Atlantic, no less, single-handed, no less, and he hadn't checked whether the aircraft had de-icing. The phone clicked as he put it down on the desk and I could hear him whistling under his breath as he rattled paper.

'John?'

'Has she?'

'Of course she has, boy. Big, beautiful kinky rubber boots. They'd clear the Humboldt Glacier. Are you on?'

'Naturally I'm on,' I replied.

'Then shut up shop and slip round,' he said. 'About twelve-thirty, eh boy?'

'Okay, Jimmy. I'll be there.' I was about to hang up.

'By the way,' he said. I knew what that meant. It meant Lennox.

'Oh God, no!'

'I'm afraid so. He's expecting you at eleven-thirty, boy. Clean, bright, and slightly oiled.'

I sighed, audibly I hoped. 'Any idea what?'

He roared with laughter. 'Sophia Loren, boy,' he said. 'Wants her for his collection. How the hell would I know! You know what he's like, boy, wouldn't tell you it's half past nine if he could bloody well help it.'

I said, 'He would if it was eleven-fifteen.'

Jimmy Pope hung up in the middle of the laugh. I wondered lightly if he'd had a sudden heart attack and died, but Jimmy won't die of a heart attack for the same reason that whales won't walk.

I pushed back my chair and put my feet on the couch arm and said damn a time or two. Jimmy Pope's assignments might have sugar coatings but they usually had hard centres. Whenever Lennox was involved they were tungsten-toughened. I wondered what it was that Lennox had ticking over in San Francisco.

I shut up shop as instructed; for me it's not a lengthy process. Years ago I learned that for a man living alone the best investment in the world is plastic cups and plates and a freezer. I took the breakfast plates and cup and slung them in the bin along with the plastic cutlery, then I straightened out my sleeping bag, slung my razor and the other odds and ends in a grip, tucked my passport and my Diners' card in my pocket, and left.

Two

Shown Sidney Lennox, ninety-nine out of a hundred Londoners would identify him as a commuting civil servant. Some trace of never-quite-absent annoyance, around eyes that gleam dully like twin ball bearings in a pool of oil, some fractional mismatch of collar and neck, a touch of bagginess in the knees that careful pressing cannot remove from trousers, a down turn to the right-hand corner of the mouth indicating disapproval and calculation, dust in the welts of the shiny shoes, the well-kicked brief case and the bony nose, marked him as spots mark a leopard. He could create an atmosphere by his mere presence, without doing anything at all, much as a vulture will : the mere fact that he's there demonstrates something unpleasant in the neighbourhood.

He'd rattle in from Orpington in the mornings, exuding disapproval, and take up his favourite face-away position in his lair at the Board of Trade in Victoria Street. His office, at the end of a little spur corridor on the fourth floor, hasn't a door of its own; you go in through two other offices and find yourself staring at Lennox's back. He doesn't turn. Until his visitor is in front of his desk, he doesn't even look up. Eventually, though, he stops reading or writing or whatever it is he's doing; you expect to hear a click as those eyes swivel upward.

'You should knock, Shaw.'

'I did.'

'More loudly.'

He looked at me, and I looked at him. Considering that

in any dealings we had, I was the one doing favours, he adopted a pretty arrogant attitude. Perhaps it's something endemic in the withdrawn corners of Intelligence, but I wouldn't know; Lennox is the only Intelligence manipulator I've ever met and it isn't really likely that Lennoxes roll off production lines.

'I have a small duty for you, Shaw.' He spoke exactly as unpleasant schoolmasters speak, selecting words and tone carefully for their offensive qualities.

I said, 'Is it dangerous?'

The corner of his mouth ran downward. 'How characteristic that you should ask.'

'And how sensible,' I said.

He breathed in slowly, through his nose, as though inspecting the air and finding it wanting. 'The duty of which I speak is entirely without hazard, Shaw.'

'Is it also, as usual, entirely without payment?'

'As a reserve officer, you should be ready for duty.'

'Patriotism is not enough,' I said.

Lennox looked at me. 'I cannot understand why Pope regards you so highly.'

'It's because I get there and back. The day I don't, he'll stop.'

'Yes.' He looked down at his fingers, as always when he gave orders. I suppose it was because he hated looking anybody unnecessarily in the eye. I remembered other days when we'd gone through similar conversations, other briefings as openly contemptuous. I remembered, too, the things I had been sent from that room to do: the man who whimpered with fear all the way from the little Austrian airstrip near the Hungarian border to the landing field in East Yorkshire; the splash in the North Sea one dark moonless night when three passengers became two and Ivan Skavinsky Skavar or somebody spread ripples wide and far. A small duty for you, Shaw.

Lennox said, 'When you leave San Francisco in the

Stripe Tiger, you will have a passenger. You will fly him back to Britain.'

'One passenger?' At least it meant no rough play in the rear seats.

'That's all.'

'If that's all, fine,' I said. 'Where will I find him?'

'When the times comes for take-off, your passenger will already be aboard the aircraft.'

'All fixed?'

'Certainly. As I said, a small duty and without hazard.'

'Good.' I turned to go, but he stopped me.

'It is necessary to tell you that your passenger is an—ah —employee of this organization. You will wonder why we have such people on the territory of a friendly power like the United States. The answer is that it helps to maintain friendships if there are no secrets.'

'Surprisingly enough,' I said, 'I can understand that. But what's wrong with BOAC and Pan-Am?'

Lennox was still examining his fingers. 'This individual is *persona non grata* in the United States. Capture would be fatal.'

'They really do things like that?'

He gave a small, cold, contemptuous smile. 'Everybody does. It is important that nobody in America should know that you have a passenger or, in this country, that you have brought anybody in. Is that clear?'

I nodded.

'That is all, Shaw. Twenty-five pounds will be credited to you.'

'The economy must be booming.'

'You will be paid by Airflo, too.'

I said, 'The return air fare *to* San Francisco *from* London is at least two-fifty quid, tourist.'

'Yes,' Lennox told his fingers with satisfaction. 'A substantial saving *is* being effected. It has been arranged that you will fly on an aircraft of the United States Military Air

Transport Service.'

'Times *are* hard.'

'You leave this afternoon, from Vicarsheath. And now Mr Pope will be waiting.'

His head stayed down and one hand moved sideways along the surface of the desk to pull a sheet of paper to the centre, beneath the bony nose.

I said, 'Good luck.'

'Mm?' He didn't look up. I had the peripheral attention of about eleven brain cells.

'I thought one of us had better say it.'

The eleven cells about-turned like a squad of guardsmen and I was alone. Lennox was there, but in every sense but the purely physical he had gone.

I went out through the two outer offices, trying to stare down two slender and ambitious young men whose thin watch-chains were draped over thinner stomachs. The look in their eyes was familiar: I've seen it at livestock markets on farmers who measure beef on the hoof. But there was no staring them down. For them I didn't exist as a man: I was as much an implement as a paperclip, just a chunk of ambulant raw material.

I crossed Kingsway short of the tunnel exit, where the cars buzz up the ramp like bees swarming, and walked up to the battered Victorian building that houses Jimmy Pope. The lift creaked and clanked and climbed and deposited me outside the frosted glass door. Even as I closed the lift doors I could hear Pope's laughter belting out. In his outer office a girl looked up at me, trying to show an interest she did not feel. They all went that way with Jimmy; it's like living at the end of a jet runway, sheer over-exposure to high-decibel sound gradually dims the sparks of glowing life.

'John Shaw,' I said. 'He's expecting me.'

Another crashing laugh rolled from Jimmy Pope's office, and she said, 'I think he's on the phone.'

'Not him, he's tickling himself.'

She stared at me, her bruised mind trying to take it in. 'I said he's on the phone.'

'Yes.'

I sat down and waited. When the laughter stopped I got up and walked to Jimmy's door, knocked and began to push it open.

'You can go in now,' the girl said.

'Thanks!'

'John, boy,' Pope shouted. 'Great to see you.'

His face glowed with welcome, but his eyes priced my suit, checked my shave and gave me a quick medical. 'Seen Lennox, eh?'

'I've seen him.'

Pope laughed. 'What a man! We can all sleep soundly in our beds at night, knowing he's there.'

I said, 'It seems routine.'

'Always does, boy. Think back, it always does.'

'What time's the MAC flight?'

'Four,' Pope said. 'Safest airline in the world. You should be pleased.'

'I'm not sold on reheated frozen steaks, but they're better than ham sandwiches,' I said. 'And I like the part where the beauteous hostess brings the Scotch.'

'Yes, they're dry flights aren't they? I forgot.'

He hadn't forgotten; he didn't care.

I said, 'Is the Tiger new?'

He bellowed with laughter. 'Make a change, won't it, John? Flying one without anything wrong.'

'It's a good aeroplane,' I said.

'Your papers okay? Visa and smallpox?'

'I got the visa two years ago. It's virgin but it's valid. Smallpox booster less than a year ago.'

Pope said, 'By the way—'

I groaned. 'Not another by the way!'

The laugh again. 'It really is by the way, John.'

He heaved himself out of his chair and walked over to a folding table that stood beside the window. On it stood a parcel, a small crate, really, I suppose, made with heavy brown paper and a framework of rough hemlock. From the way Jimmy Pope grunted as he lifted it, I gathered it was fairly heavy.

I grinned, 'How do I start it ticking?'

'You'd be bloody clever, boy. Only ticking differential in the northern hemisphere.'

'Differential?' I said. 'Listen, I've got news for you. There's no point in carrying spares. It's not like a car; you can't get out and lift up the cowling.'

'For Marion Capote's Silver Ghost,' he wheezed. 'One differential and a pair of brake shoes. He asked if you could take them with you. Safer than air freight.'

'He's one of those?'

'He's nuts,' Jimmy said. 'Silver Ghost and three engines. Spends ten hours under it for every hour in it. Chromes the inside of the sump. You know.'

'I know.'

'They've been customed at Derby,' he said. 'Rolls-Royce do so much of this they've got special arrangements so you won't have any bother, and it's probably small enough for hand luggage.'

I said, 'Fine. Which way do I come back? North-about?'

There are three accepted ways across the Atlantic for light aircraft: the long hop from Gander to Shannon for those with nerveless bowels and bags of range; south-about via the Azores and Lisbon, or north-about through Greenland and Iceland to Scotland. The hops are shorter going north-about, but there are a couple of hazards: the ten-thousand-foot cliffs in the fiord you fly down to Bluie West One and the bloody great volcano called Hekla that's too near either Reykjavik or Keflavik for comfort if the weather's on the dodge. If you go south-about you kick off with twelve hundred miles of lonely ocean under you to the Azores.

Jets have shrunk the Atlantic to six or seven hours of boredom for most of the people who go across, but it remains a large and formidable piece of water. It's swallowed more ships and planes than you and I have smoked cigarettes and they've affected it a lot less. I prefer to go north-about. The hops are shorter and you're nearer land for more of the time.

'Gander-Shannon,' he said. For once, he wasn't laughing. 'The long hop.'

'For God's sake!' I was horrified. 'Why?'

'It's a new machine,' he said. 'Oddly enough nobody's done Gander-Shannon in one yet.'

'Could it be,' I asked, 'that many have tried and none conquered? I think Mallory was a twit. Because it's there just isn't a good reason.'

Pope was laughing again. 'You'll get your picture in *Flight*.'

'And if I don't, there'll be six tasteful lines in *The Times* and *Telegraph*. How much?'

'Hundred.'

'Good morning,' I said. I meant it, too. I was on my way.

'And fifty.'

'You're as bad as Lennox,' I said. 'Upstick unoffer.'

'How much, then?'

'Four hundred.'

He started laughing again and I began to realize what a powerful weapon that laugh was. I could imagine the effect of prolonged exposure to it.

'John Shaw,' he said, 'you're a caution.'

'Jet captains get nearly that much every week,' I protested.

'They've got shiny buttons on nice blue uniforms and they have to talk nicely to the passengers,' Pope said. 'Two-fifty.'

We settled for three hundred.

'Fee only,' I added. 'Plus expenses.'

He agreed.

'And fifty a day if I have to do any sitting and waiting. I once knew a bloke who was snowed in for a month at Bluie on a seventy-five quid fee. His wife and nine children starved to death.'

'You're an orphan, and single,' he said.

'That's why I have to pay more out in tax.'

We agreed on that and he lumbered to the door with me. I thought the girl cringed a bit as Jimmy Pope laughed his farewells, but maybe she didn't and it was just the way nature made her.

I almost forgot the parcel in my eagerness to get clear of the barrage of sound. It's strange, looking back, to think what that would have meant, but Pope hauled me back and I left with the rough twine cutting a weal into my hand. Just lugging that parcel to the lift was work.

Jimmy had fixed a ride for me to Vicarsheath. On the cheap, naturally. The driver would pick me up outside the Ministry of Defence building in High Holborn, the one that looks like a badly-tied packing case multiplied up a few times; the only condition was that I should be waiting when he arrived. I'd meant to walk up through Lincoln's Inn Fields, but the differential and the brake shoes necessitated a taxi, so I was good and early.

I stood for a few minutes, looking at the recruiting displays in the window. State House, the building's called. Nowadays the services try to lure girls as well as lads, but I didn't notice any interest flickering among the passing popsy population. I suppose if your idea of pleasure is a psychedelic light show in some suitably sound-proofed cellar, the offer of a healthy, tennis-laden life polishing a cap badge hasn't much appeal. I was looking at the pictures of all the happy people hanging out of helicopters and riding breeches buoys when a horn gave a little toot behind me. I turned, saw the car stop at the kerb, picked up my grip and my parcel, and went over.

'Mr Shaw?'

'Yes,' I said. 'Thanks.'

'No sweat. You wanna ride with me or in back.'

'With you. I'll put this stuff in the back if I may.'

'Surely.'

I slung my grip in, then hoisted the parcel on to the back seat, closed the door on it, and climbed into the front passenger seat. The driver was half turned toward me, about twenty-five or so, with red hair. I looked at the nametape on his work jacket.

'Thanks, Mr Conroy.'

'Let's go,' he said.

Three

Conroy pulled the car away and threaded it through the web of streets round the Bank with splendid confidence; before long we were sliding along the Whitechapel Road among the two-abreast traffic, then out to Wanstead Flats, the dual carriageway and on to the A12. They say American cars are built for American roads and aren't suitable for ours, but I've never moved more easily through London traffic than in that Ford.

Conroy didn't talk much, concentrating on driving, but he was pleasant and polite, interested in where I was going and why.

'Sure wouldn't wanna fly a little ship like that across the Atlantic, Mr Shaw.'

I didn't particularly, either, but I made gentle and confident noises.

The Rolls-Royce label on my parcel had caught his eye, too, and he asked what was in it. When I told him, he said, 'Jeez, fifty years old and still runnin'. Think of that!'

'Not likely to happen with this,' I said, tapping the dash-padding of the Ford.

'No,' he grinned. 'Year and a half, maybe. All those guys driving it.'

He was easy and relaxed as we by-passed Chelmsford and rolled out again on to dual carriageway. His left foot was tucked away as his right worked the throttle and brake of the automatic, and the big car floated at an easy seventy towards that hellish bottleneck at Colchester. Suddenly he grunted with annoyance, and a second later I felt and heard the unmistakable sound of a flat tyre being mangled and the back end of the big Ford began to break away.

Conroy controlled it easily enough and brought the car in to the side. He didn't say a word, but as he opened the door and got out I was surprised to see that his face was tight with anger. It wasn't rueful, just-my-luck annoyance, either, but real fury. I got out to give him a hand and I could see that his face was white and his hands trembled as he unlocked the boot. I shrugged mentally; it was his affair and anyone who works regularly with machines that roll, sail or fly needs to become a little philosophical, otherwise madness lurks nearby.

He banged the hubcap off and it rolled clattering in the road; then he started on the wheel nuts. They say anger lends strength but it wasn't helping Conroy because he couldn't begin to turn one of them. Those wheel nuts had been done up sadistically tight by some workshop mechanic with a grudge and a spider. I've seen them do it and you can discern the malign thought in their pigmy brains that if the car ever has a puncture, God will need to help the guy who has to change the wheel. Conroy was struggling with one of those handles that aren't much better than bent wire. Sweat was rolling off him, he was swearing viciously and pretty well continuously and his eyes were moist with tears of fury.

I was amazed. We'd been riding together for more than

an hour and he'd seemed pleasantly relaxed. Now he was literally crying with rage and frustration. I glanced around. A couple of hundred yards up the road there was a big factory.

'Stop worrying,' I said to Conroy. 'I'll go borrow something better.'

He glanced up at me as though he didn't know me and I looked at the glistening eyes and straining muscles in bewilderment. He didn't nod, or stop, he just went on struggling and sobbing with rage.

I jogged gently away up the road and turned in at the factory gate.

The gateman grinned sympathetically. 'Garage mechanics,' he said, and spat.

'Have you a spider I can borrow?'

'Happens all the time, mate. There's one in the workshop, up here and to your right. See the foreman.'

People do still trust people; it's surprising but it's true. A couple of minutes later, I was jog-trotting back to the Ford and in less than five the spare wheel was on. A pale, silent Conroy drove forward and stopped at the factory gate to let me return the spider, then, when I got into the car, he put his foot down to the floorboards and the car hurtled forward, nearly whiplashing my spine.

I looked at my watch. 'Steady, Mr Conroy. We're not too short of time.'

Nothing happened for a moment, then he lifted his foot on the throttle and our speed eased back. After a few more seconds, he glanced across at me. 'Sorry, Mr Shaw. Didn't want you to miss your flight.' He tried to grin, but it didn't work and he didn't try again, just wove the car through the roundabout, then along the road by-passing Colchester, turning off for Ipswich and on to Vicarsheath.

It isn't till you go on to one of those American bases that you realize just how huge is their commitment in Britain. Some of them are good-sized towns, with several thousand men and a lot of families living lives centred on the dull silver machines that go up, come down and fly round and round, all day and every day. Go through the gate and you're emigrating from rural Suffolk to New Jersey or Illinois. Everything changes in a couple of paces : accents, mores, uniforms, cigarettes.

I was checked by the guard on the gate and driven to the MAC terminal, where I went through the routine of checking in.

The clerk looked doubtfully at the little crate. 'Looks heavy, Mr Shaw. Place it on the scale, please.'

I lugged the thing over. It weighed forty-two pounds. 'It's for Mr Marion Capote at Stripe Aircraft,' I said. 'I gather some arrangement has been made—'

He looked at me. 'Arrangement, sir?'

'They're spares,' I said, weakly, 'for an old Rolls-Royce. I'm just taking them over as a favour. My bag's light enough.'

'That's all right, Mr Shaw,' he said. 'Have a good flight.'

I bent to pick up the parcel but he stopped me.

'What's wrong?'

'A heavy item like that, sir. I think it should go in the hold.'

'Fine,' I said. I listened to his grunt as he lifted it on to a waiting baggage trolley.

I went and stood looking out of the window, watching the ground crews working on the big Boeing out there on the apron. I can never look at that plane without awe. Damn it, I'm still under forty, but when I started flying, jets were only for fighter planes and passenger flying consisted of piston-engined hops. Now these Boeings can go to Britain-California in one hop—and they're first-generation jets, getting on towards obsolescence. Behind me in the departure hall, which nobody could describe as a lounge, the rest of the passengers were gathering, families mainly, people going home and looking reasonably happy about it.

'Mr Shaw?'

I turned. Two bars, he was a captain.

'My name's Barnett, Mr Shaw. I'm the captain of the aircraft and I understand you're a pilot yourself.'

We shook hands. Yes, I was a pilot.

'Then if you'd like to come up on the flight deck for a while during the flight, you'll be welcome.'

I thanked him and he went out, walking with his crew across the apron towards the Boeing. I watched a little train of baggage follow, pulled by its tractor, and saw it being loaded.

In a few minutes, the flight was called and I walked with the chattering children and the home-going wives, and took a seat at the rear of the aircraft. All the seats face the rear in every military transport I've ever seen and it's the difference, I suppose, between flying operations that are authoritarian and those that have to attract customers. It also helps to account for the superb safety records of people like MAC and Transport Command.

And then we took off and flew to San Francisco. As simply as that. Below us there was land, then water, then ice, then water, then land again. We ate and talked and the hours passed. I went up on the flight deck over Greenland, and there was Barnett in shirtsleeves and sunglasses with coffee in one hand and sandwich in the other and the Boeing flying itself. I thought about Nansen for a moment : frostbite and dogs and ten miles a day; then I sipped my coffee and decided this was better. I thanked Barnett and he said he'd take a drink from me at the officers' club when we landed. Then I filled in the Customs form and that's about it.

While all those exciting events were happening, we went nearly a quarter way round the world, but such are the joys of standardization that the place we landed at looked exactly like the place we took off from.

I said as much to Captain Barnett when I joined him in Customs, after passing immigration.

'Joys of travel,' he said, grinning. 'There's another just like it in Hawaii. Or maybe you prefer Greenland.'

'Smashing,' I said.

'If you're complaining,' Barnett said, 'you're the wrong nationality. I've seen Chinese boys playing cricket and Indians playing bagpipes.'

I said, 'Who's complaining? I like Coke and export gin. I'm looking forward to staying at the North Pole Hilton.'

I put the little crate in front of the Customs man and my grip alongside it. He asked me to open the grip and went over my hairbrush and spare socks pretty carefully. Then he pointed.

'What's that?'

'Parts,' I said. 'There's the declaration from Rolls-Royce.'

He looked at me grimly. I suppose it's his job to look awesome, but he was doing it unnecessarily well. 'I could have you open it.'

'I know,' I said. My heart was light and my conscience clear.

He stared at me for a moment and I was tempted to be bright and cheerful but I resisted. Whenever I'm tempted to be amusing with Customs men, I think of Tony Bell, an old chum of mine, who was shown the list at London Airport and didn't resist. He had, he said, opium in his underpants, diamonds in his teeth, and a howitzer in his fundament. The Customs man said had he really and his colleagues would be most interested and would sir come this way. They stripped him, probed him and prodded him, unfastened every seam on his clothes, took his suitcase and his shoes to pieces and dismantled his razor and his wrist-watch, then told him he could go. It wasn't their responsibility to put things together; just to search.

So I said nothing, and he reached out a hand and chalked something on both the grip and the crate, and I was through.

'Martooni time,' Captain Barnett said. 'Airman!'

'Sir.' The lad hurried over.

'Take these two things from Mr Shaw and bring them over to the officers' club in a jeep. Okay?'

'Right, sir.'

'Thanks,' I said.

'We're in a hurry,' he said. 'That's the club over there. This chile sho' don't want nuthin' holdin' us byack.'

We stood at the bar for the first one, relishing the edged cleanliness as the icy Martini slid soothingly down. The second we carried across to deep, easy chairs. We chatted for a while, drank the Martinis, then got up to go and when we strolled into the big, carpeted hall, a woman came forward, examining her watch irritably. When she saw me she smiled faintly and kissed Barnett quickly on the cheek.

He introduced us. Her name was Helen and she was a walking illustration of how women have come to own two-thirds of everything in America.

'How do you do, Mr Shaw. Darling, the car's outside and we're having dinner over at the Freuhafs so we'll have to hurry if I'm to have time to change and I've got to get some new shoes on the way. So nice to meet you, Mr Shaw.' I've put a couple of full stops in, but she didn't.

I said, 'You ought to take care of him, Mrs Barnett. He's a very good pilot.'

He grinned. 'Well, thanks. Have a good trip yourself.' Then to his wife. 'Mr Shaw's flying a light aircraft back to England.'

She glanced rapidly from him to me and back again.

'How very interesting excuse us Mr Shaw we really must be going.'

I waved to his departing back and strolled across to the desk.

'Yes, sir?'

'My name's Shaw,' I said. 'A grip and a parcel should have been brought here for me.'

'A grip and a parcel. Yes, sir.' He leaned back to glance

under the counter, then turned to look in a little room behind.

I said, helpfully, 'The parcel's a small crate, really. It was
brought across from Customs.'

'One moment, please, sir.' He went into the little room,
came back a moment later. 'Well, I'm sorry, sir, but it really
doesn't appear to be here.'

'That's funny,' I said, 'Captain Barnett told one of the
jeep drivers to bring it over here.'

'Then it should—' he paused. 'Would you know the
driver's name, sir?'

'No.' I thought for a moment, but I knew I hadn't really
looked at him. All that remained was a vague impression of
very dark hair and sunburn. 'No, I don't know.'

'If you try the baggage bay, sir,' he said, 'it's maybe been
taken there.'

'And where—?'

'Out the door and make a left. It's about three hundred,
three-fifty yards on your right.'

'We couldn't telephone, I suppose?'

'Wouldn't do much good, I reckon, sir. Hell of a lot of
stuff over there and they're good and busy.'

'All right,' I said. 'Thanks.'

I made that left and set off, aware that every step I took
was another step I'd have to carry that damn crate back.
I found the baggage section, went in and told the tale to a
sergeant.

'Which flight was that?' He wasn't very interested.

'MAC from Vicarsheath,' I said. 'It landed just short of
an hour ago.'

'An hour?' He shook his head. Anybody whose baggage
was unloaded an hour ago was clearly in trouble.

I told him about Customs, and Barnett's instructions to
bring it across to the officers' club. 'Listen, bud,' he said,
'there's people here'd lose it just because it's going to the
officers' club. Best thing is, have a look around.'

I began to search the place, with its piles of boxes and bags and little trains and tractors moving around, and finally I found them, hidden underneath a couple of massive hold-alls. I picked them up and told the sergeant all was well.

'You're just lucky,' he said.

'Yes, well thanks all the same.'

I set off back towards the club, and the crate grew heavier with every step, the weight dragging at the tendons in my arm and the string cutting into my hand; after a while I stopped and transferred it to the other hand. I was about half-way there when the loudspeaker system gave a click and a voice said, 'If Mr John Shaw, M A C passenger from England is still on the base, will he please report to the main gate. I will repeat that—'

While he was repeating it I put down my luggage and looked around wondering where, among all those buildings, the main gate might be. Various vehicles went past me at various speeds, but nobody except me seemed to be walking. I picked up my gear and marched on to the distant oasis of the officers' club. The dim but helpful airman was still behind the counter.

'You got them, sir?'

'Yes, thank you. And now I'm being paged over the loudspeaker. I'm to report to the main gate. Could you tell me—?'

'Well, sir, I'm afraid it's back the way you've come. About a half mile, then you make a left—'

I interrupted. 'Perhaps if you telephoned the main gate.'

'Sure thing, sir.' He looked mildly surprised for no reason that I could envisage.

'Officers' club here, Pfc Hines. You have a call out for a Mr—?' He looked at me, eyebrows raised in inquiry.

'Shaw. John Shaw.'

He nodded. 'For Mr John Shaw. Yes. Yes.' He looked at me. 'It's a car, sir.'

It was also a relief. 'Tell them I'll wait here for it.'

He told them. A moment later he told me that the car wasn't allowed into the base without a pass.

'Does that mean,' I asked, 'that I have to carry this lot all the way?'

'Oh?' He hadn't thought of it. Doesn't everybody have wheels? Even people who've just stepped off aircraft? 'I'm sure we can arrange something, sir.'

'Thank you,' I said.

A pick-up materialized in a couple of minutes and took me to the front gate as though the hounds of hell were baying at its exhaust, and there, parked just outside, was a very large and very shiny Lincoln, long, low and wide. The window glass, like the paintwork, was green. As the pick-up halted, a chauffeur sprang forward, and I'm using that word deliberately. He seemed to cover the distance from Lincoln to pick-up in two bounds.

'Mr Shaw, sir?'

'Yes.'

His eyes were on the crate. 'I'm Mr Newton's chauffeur, sir.'

'Mr Newton?' I hadn't heard of any Newtons.

'Mr Newton is a vice-president of Airflo, Mr Shaw.'

'I see.'

'He sent me to meet you, sir, because Mr Capote was hoping to do some work on his car tonight if you have brought the parts.'

'Here,' I said.

He took the crate from me and walked round to the boot of the Lincoln. Carrying it, he was, as my Scottish grandmother used to say, away to one side like Gourock. He closed the boot lid and rubbed his hand where the string had bitten.

'Heavy,' I said unnecessarily.

'I know Mr Capote is most appreciative, Mr Shaw.' He grinned. 'He's likely to work all night here on these. I was instructed to ask whether I can drive you somewhere?'

I hauled Jimmy Pope's bit of paper out of my pocket and looked for the name of the hotel. 'I'm staying at a place called the Pickwick,' I said.

'I know it, sir. At Fifth and Mission.' He took my grip and opened the door of the limousine; he didn't put the grip inside with me, maybe because it would have looked tattyish against the beautiful green upholstery. He put it in the boot, then climbed into the driving seat. The Lincoln didn't make a sound as he started the engine and eased it forward.

I peered out through the green glass as he headed towards the city, hating the power lines draped everywhere, but relishing the clear, cool-looking evening light.

Half an hour later I got out at the Pickwick and he carried my grip in for me, declining my proffered dollar politely. 'I'm told to tell you, sir, that when you are ready to come to the field tomorrow, you are to call this number and a car will be sent for you.'

I thanked him, checked in and went up to my room. Considering that it was, by now, about two in the morning, London time, I wasn't too tired. I took a shower, though, to freshen myself up a bit, and went out to have a look at the city. The doorman at the Pickwick told me to have a drink at Top of the Mark, the bar on top of the Mark Hopkins Hotel, to ride a cable car, and to try the crab on Fisherman's Wharf. I reckoned they'd see me through what waking hours I had left.

The climb up to the Mark Hopkins about pulverized me, but the view was worth the effort: all San Francisco is spread out below, while you sit comfortably with a drink in your hand. I didn't spend too long there, though. I was now three Martinis to the good, and it's plenty. I rode a swaying, jerking, cable car almost to the wharf, and that too was an experience. I was then comprehensively robbed for a plate of seafood at a tourist clipjoint on Fisherman's Wharf. It was pleasant but not worth that kind of money. Then I rode the cable car back again and went for a walk into Chinatown that was prophetic if only I'd known it. The only thing that interrupted my even pacing was a topless shoeshine parlour which was rather like the seafood; interesting but overpriced.

By now I was bone weary; my legs ached and my eyelids had to be kept hoisted by a conscious and considerable effort of will. I'd meant to walk back to the hotel, but a beautiful, tempting taxi slid close to me and won my heart. I got out, took three deep breaths, collected my key, and went up to my room. It must now be about seven a.m. in London and the thought of those clean, cool sheets was as inviting as a Muslim's dream of heaven.

I slid the key into the lock, pushed the door open and walked in. I just had time to notice that my grip had been emptied on to the bed, before a voice said, 'Keep still.'

I started to turn.

'Very still,' the voice said. Something cold was pressed below my ear.

Four

I kept very still while a hand slid over me searching, presumably, for a gun.

'Wear these.' I looked down. A hand held a pair of sunglasses. I took them and put them on. The frames were the wrap-round type designed for people with big, oblong eyes, but the lenses were opaque : the blindfold of the 'seventies.

I said, 'I don't understand. You must have the wrong—' I might as well not have spoken.

'Walk just ahead of me. Keep your hands in your pockets, turn left out of the hotel door.'

I heard the room door open and turned and walked towards it, then tried once more. 'Look,' I said, 'I'm English. I've only just got here. I've had a Martini, a crab dinner and a long walk and I leave tomorrow. You've got the wrong boy.'

He said, 'Keep moving.'

'You heard what I said?'

He dug something into my back over my right kidney. The sunglasses obscured almost all the vision except a faint rim of light at the top and bottom. I lowered my head to peer over them and the gun dug viciously into my back. 'Walk,' he said. 'And keep your head up.'

I tried to squint underneath the frame, and round the sides, but each movement of my head brought another dig in the back. I did as I was told and kept walking : into the lift, which was empty, out again on the ground floor, across the lobby, into the street, turned left. I was blind as a bat, but the whole thing was done without difficulty. The funny thing was that I wasn't particularly afraid. Nervous, yes; aware that the situation was potentially dangerous; but not afraid in the sense of real gut-gnawing fear.

'Walk twenty paces, then stop,' I was told, and I obeyed. I was so sure this was a case of mistaken identity that I didn't think of resistance or flight; I suppose I thought, naïvely, that someone, some time, would realize I was the wrong man and let me go.

There was a scraping, sliding, rattling sound quite loud and quite close by, then the voice said, 'Turn and take three paces to your right.' After the third, I stopped and a hand took my elbow. 'Shuffle forward, then climb in.' As he spoke I heard a starter motor spinning and an engine igniting and roaring on a blipped throttle. They were putting me into a van. I moved until my knees pressed against something, then fumbled my way aboard.

'Sit on the bench over there.'

I found it with my fingertips, turned and sat down. The van started forward with a jerk.

'Hold on tight,' the voice said.

In a few moments I knew why: the van was climbing one of San Francisco's hills: unbelievably steep and relieved only by the occasional flat ledge of an intersecting street. I clung grimly to the edge of the bench to stop myself being hurled around the back of the van.

We went up one hill, then down one, then up another, then along the flat. Finally, the van slowed and did a slow, tight, right turn, ran on for a few yards, stopped and reversed.

'Move when I tell ya,' the voice said.

I waited, then the noise came again and by now I thought I had it identified: a roller shutter running up and down. The engine died and I heard something that could have been a big door closing. A hand took my elbow, propelling me forward.

'Okay, forward. Then sit down and ease yourself out. Don't move any other way.'

I did as I was told, feeling forward with my feet for the open door, then finding it, feeling down for the floor, standing up. Again the hand took my elbow. I obeyed its pressure and walked forward, turning right up a couple of steps, along a passage and down maybe half a dozen more steps.

'Walk forward three paces.'

I did. Behind me a door closed and I heard two bolts being shot. Then receding footsteps. Then silence.

I was in total darkness and I'd left my lighter behind in my room. But where? Obviously it was a cellar or basement of some kind. I sniffed and thought I caught the smell of food cooking, but I wasn't sure; the smell was faint and elusive and the room I was in, whatever it was, had a negative, flat kind of smell. I stretched out my arms and moved cautiously forward, sliding my feet over the concrete and keeping my weight on the rear foot in case stairs or some other hazard lay ahead. After four paces the tips of my fingers touched something and I stopped and tried to discover what it was. It didn't take long. The wall was fitted with wooden shelves on which large cardboard boxes of various sizes were stacked. I tried to lift one and it was fairly heavy.

I began to feel my way round the walls. All seemed to be fitted with shelves of the same kind, and on some of them cans were stacked. I picked up one or two and shook them, listening as fluid gurgled inside. It seemed likely this was a food store and the thought occurred to me that a tin would make a more than useful weapon if I needed one. Most of them, though, were big tins and I had to search for quite a while before I found one small enough to hold. I don't know how long it took me to discover that it was a four-sided, roughly square room lined with shelves everywhere except the door. However long, it was a total waste of time because I was standing against the shelves on one side of the room when I heard the sound of the bolts sliding. The door opened and the beam of a powerful torch hit me between the eyes. I swore and spun away from it, watching the dazzle-lights flash on my eyelids.

'Come towards me,' the voice said.

I opened my eyes and saw the shelves: plain pine and with the goodies stacked high. My eyes were beginning to focus as I turned.

'Put on the glasses,' he said.

I felt in my pocket for them, meanwhile glancing downward at the tin in my hand, still shielded by my body. The label said this was a product of the O-Joy Canning Company of Hong Kong and contained preserved ginger in heavy syrup. I hoped, as I hurled it at the flashlight, that it was very heavy syrup.

There was a thud, followed by a satisfying grunt of pain and the flashlight fell to the concrete and went out. I flung myself in the direction of the door, but it slammed and before I could grab at the handle, a bolt was rammed home on the other side. A moment later the second bolt was secured and I heard feet going away. I was left alone for a few more minutes and armed myself with a couple more cans, just in case. I had a feeling that throwing the other can hadn't done much to increase my chances of being released.

There was a little click and a beam of light shone across the room. I raised my hands to shield my eyes and it seemed to be coming from a small hole in the door. I wondered if I could hit it first time.

'You will put those cans back on a shelf,' the voice said, 'and this time you will do exactly as you are told, no more and no less, or you will be hurt.'

There was no alternative. I put the tins back on the shelf and heard the bolts being withdrawn.

'Put on the glasses and walk towards the light.'

I followed the light out of the room, a few steps along a corridor and into another room. The flashlight flicked away from me, indicating a chair standing in the middle of the floor.

'Sit down.'

There was a little click as the overhead light went on. When my vision had cleared a little, I realized there were three of them.

And they were all Chinese.

Two of them stood at the door. They looked tough but impersonal. The third, who came slowly towards me, looked as though he didn't like me; I assumed he was the one who'd been hit by the tin.

He stopped in front of me, looking down, then backhanded me viciously across the mouth. I felt as though my jaw had been dislocated; I could taste blood from a cut where the lining of my mouth had been slashed by my teeth. Then his hand swung again and his palm smacked hard against the other side of my jaw.

'Now perhaps you will think before you throw things.'

I said, 'Don't be bloody ridiculous! I don't know what

this is about, but it's damn all to do with me. I only got here tonight. I've got no money.'

'I know about you,' he said, then turned to the others. 'Hold him.'

They grabbed my arms and bent them up while he removed my passport.

'John Shaw, pilot. That is right.'

'I know it's bloody well right,' I said.

Again he back-handed me. Rod Laver could have taken lessons from him. My face felt both numb and agonized simultaneously.

'You will speak correctly.'

I ran my tongue round my mouth, trying to assess the damage. There was a fair amount of blood and it was very sore, but my teeth seemed all right.

'You landed today at Travis Air Force Base on a Military Airlift Command flight from England?'

'Yes,' I said.

'Then where is it?'

'Where is what?' I said.

'You brought a parcel with you.'

I nodded. 'I don't know how the hell you know, but yes I did.'

'Where is it?'

I said, 'For God's sake, it was only spare parts. I gave it to somebody's chauffeur at the airport.'

He pointed. 'Look over there, Mr Shaw.'

I turned and looked. Then I stared. In a corner of the room, unwrapped and coated in a dull sheen of good oil, were a differential and a set of brake shoes, surrounded by the wreckage of the little crate and the brown paper.

'That's right,' I said. 'Differential and brake shoes. That's what I brought. It even says so on the label. May I go now, please?'

Again I got the murderous back-hand. 'I told you to speak correctly. You will now tell me exactly where you obtained these . . . things . . . and precisely what happened to them afterwards.'

There didn't seem to be any reason why I shouldn't tell him, so I started with Marion Capote and his motor mania and went on to describe the flight to Travis and the drink with the pilot. I didn't mention the captain's name. With a wife like Helen, he'd got all the trouble he needed, and in any case, the Chinese didn't ask for it.

'What happened to the crate at the airport?' he demanded.

'Vicarsheath or Travis?'

'At Travis, Mr Shaw.'

'It was supposed to be delivered to the officers' club, but it wasn't. I found it eventually in the baggage dispersal shed.'

He punched his palm with his fist and said something angry and sibilant in a language which was presumably Chinese. He leaned over me and suddenly, for the first time, I was scared. There was something in his face that told me I didn't matter except as a source of information. When next he spoke, his voice was pitched deliberately low.

'For whom do you work, Mr Shaw?'

Why he persevered with the mister, I can't imagine.

'For myself,' I said.

His open palm hit my cheek.

'The truth, please.'

'It's true.' I was having difficulty in enunciating the words. My face felt numb all over and the hinges of my jaw ached abominably.

'Explain.'

'I'm a freelance pilot. My own boss. Other people hire me to fly their aircraft. I just fly aircraft.'

'And carry parcels,' he said.

My stomach clenched inside me. I thought of Lennox's agent who was to fly back with me. Illicit passengers were sometimes referred to as parcels. I must have winced.

'What is it, Mr Shaw?' he asked , softly.

'My tooth,' I lied, 'I think I've a broken tooth.'

'You carry parcels, Mr Shaw.'

'Just this trip. Pope asked me to.'

'Just this trip. This trip when it disappears! To whom did you give it, Mr Shaw?'

I stared at him. 'Disappears?' I said incredulously. 'You've got the bloody thing there!'

'To whom did you give it, Mr Shaw?'

'I gave it to the chauffeur.'

'Earlier, Mr Shaw. When you came from the Customs shed and gave it to somebody else.'

'Just an airman,' I said. 'He was to take it to the officers' club.'

'Describe this man,' he said.

I thought about it. I'd already tried to describe him once before, to the desk clerk in the officers' club and I could remember no more now than I had been able to remember then. 'I don't know. I barely looked.'

That earned me another blow on the face.

'Tell me what you remember.'

I said, 'He was sort of sun-burned, dark-haired.'

'How dark, Mr Shaw?'

'Dark. Very dark.'

'As dark as me?'

I looked. My interrogator had the shiny blue-black hair of the Chinese.

'Something like that,' I said.

His face was very close to mine. 'It will not have escaped you that I am of Asiatic origin. Was this man also Asiatic?'

'I didn't look,' I said.

'Think, Mr Shaw.'

'Sorry, but I didn't notice.'

His face moved away from mine as he straightened. He stood looking down at me for a few moments.

'I find it difficult to believe, Mr Shaw, that you bring a

41

parcel from England to San Francisco, then hand it to a man you have never seen.'

'He was an airman,' I said.

'And you do this without even looking at the man's face?'

'I was staring round like a tourist,' I said. 'I haven't been here before, but I've seen a million airmen.'

He opened my passport quickly and began riffling the pages. There were almost as many visas and entry stamps in there as Mao has minions, but only one was for entry into the United States, and that was dated the same day.

'Nine days ago, Mr Shaw. Where were you nine days ago?'

I tried to think. There'd been a dirty old Dakota one of the freight outfits had sold to some Greek pirates and I'd flown it to Athens. Was that nine days ago? Days and times telescope a bit in flying.

'Greece, I think. Or maybe coming back. There'll be a stamp in my passport.'

He checked and I assume he found it because he stood looking from the passport to me and back again.

I remembered something. 'I flew BEA from Athens,' I said. 'Afternoon flight at around four-thirty. The pilot happened to be somebody I know. Ted Kingsbury. Lives at Ewell, Surrey. Phone him and he'll tell you.'

'For you, no doubt, your friend would lie.'

'For God's sake,' I said, 'don't tell him my name. Ask him who flew back from Athens with him last week.'

'All right, Mr Shaw. I accept that you were in Athens nine days ago. But you are also here today. You brought with you a parcel, a very important parcel, which has disappeared.'

I jerked my head towards the components in the corner. 'Those are what I brought with me. Look at the declaration on the crate. One differential and two brake shoes.'

He looked down at me. 'No, Mr Shaw. Those are what you *thought* you brought with you.'

Five

They tied me to the chair, switched the light out and left me to think. There was so much to think about that my mind couldn't begin to grapple with it, so I decided not to try; I put off any speculation about Jimmy Pope and Barnett and Newton and Marion Capote and Uncle Tom Cobley until I was somewhere more comfortable, and concentrated on trying to get out of whatever it was I'd got into.

The only things in the room, I knew, were myself, the chair and the spares. It wasn't promising. My mind went back to advanced flying training and the instructor who said assemble the data, then correlate it, then examine the results and then, and only then, make your decision.

I started with myself. I was wearing a suit and leather shoes. The suit contained nothing of any use, but the shoes were strong and feet are formidable weapons. Mine are more formidable than most because I'm a solid sort of bloke, five eight and fourteen stones and shaped like a thickish wedge.

Next the chair. I tried to visualize it as I'd seen it. It was plain, ordinary, sit-up-and-beg, fairly low, with a drop-in leathercloth upholstered seat. Struts joining legs side-to-side and front-to-back. Fairly old.

I was tied to it with a rope passed around my chest and my knees. My hands, as far as I could tell, were tied together but not to the chair. My feet had been bent back round the front legs of the chair in a position nicely calculated to induce cramp.

Finally the spares : the brake shoes didn't offer much prospect, but the helical gearing of the crown wheel in the differential assembly was a useful bit of metal. If I could get to it.

I rocked the chair experimentally and found that when

I leaned forward, I could put the soles of my feet flat on the ground. There was also a small but encouraging creak from the chair frame. I flexed my arms and shoulders to see what kind of pressure I might be able to exert and heard the same creak again. Or maybe it was a different creak. I hoped it was.

I leaned forward so that my whole weight rested on the front legs, took it on my toes, then bounced it back to the chair legs. It was clumsy and not very effective; all the shock was absorbed by the timber. I tried to force my legs forward and my back backward, exerting two lots of leverage against the seat, but my own weight, pressing the front legs downward, was defeating my effort. I wriggled round a bit more, listening to the creaks of the chair and trying to assess, through my bottom, where any weakness might be. It's not a thing I recommend. You hear lots of people say they drive, or fly, or make their decisions by the seats of their pants. If that's so, I don't want to drive or fly with them or live by their decisions, because you can take it from me that at least in any tactile sense, it's a pretty damned insensitive area.

In the end, if you'll forgive the expression, I found the most satisfying creaks and groans came when I took the weight on my toes, lifted all the chair legs precariously clear of the ground, twisted my trunk one way and my thighs the other. It was exhausting and I felt as though knives were slicing at my calf muscles, but I persevered and after a while the little creaking noises became little cracking noises.

Now I wriggled it round some more, feeling the chair begin to rock, hoping that the joints and the glue were going. Sitting there in the clammy darkness, I tried to swing my buttocks from side to side as hard as I could, rocking that timber frame until the stays came clear. At first it moved a quarter of an inch, a dozen more exhausting swings made it half, then three-quarters. Each swing now was carrying the chair seat further from side to side, but still it held together.

It must have been made by a craftsman of an older and more conscientious generation.

I stopped rocking and tilted forward and sideways, balancing my weight on my toes for a moment, then forcing down as violently as I could on the right front leg which I suspected might be the weak point. After a few efforts, the cracking noises grew a little louder. I tried the same thing then on the left front leg, with the same result. Then I resumed the side to side swing. By now the whole frame had become fairly loose and I tried to imagine how much the dowels or mortises might be moving.

I breathed deeply for a minute or so, trying to recover some of the strength I had lost in the murderous muscular efforts I'd been making, and tried to think what might be going on outside. It seemed likely that my captors either thought I was carrying something other than the parts, or had arranged that I should do so. Whatever it was that I was supposed to be carrying must be extremely valuable: drugs or diamonds probably. And my Chinese interrogator, having found out what he could, must now be seeking advice from above. That, at least, was the only explanation I could see for the abrupt end to the questioning and the prolonged absence.

I took a deep breath and rocked forward, balancing on my toes and the two front legs of the chair. Now, holding my breath deeply and tightly in my expanded chest, I exerted all the muscle power I could manage to bring my knees and chest together. The strain on my stomach muscles was tremendous and even as I concentrated on holding that murderous pressure, I knew it couldn't last for long. I counted slowly to ten, tried to increase the pressure and then tried to increase it again. At twenty-five I'd just about had it and my breath exploded out of me as I rocked back. My heart was thumping like a drum but I felt a wild surge of excitement. At the last second, in the last fraction of the time I had strained at that frame, I thought I had felt it give.

As my breathing returned to normal, I began to rock the chair again and there was a definite increase in the movement. Hating the exertion, even afraid of it, I began to work my body up to another huge effort and at last, with my lungs filled almost to bursting, exerted every bit of strength I had to force my knees and my chest close together.

And it worked! The chair frame creaked and groaned, and then it gave, the seat and the front legs bending away from the back at the pivotal point at the rear of the seat. I was now bent over almost double and held there, but the strength of the rigid frame had now been shattered and it came in two as I straightened my back.

In a way I was now worse placed than I had been before, still tied to the shattered frame in the darkness of the cellar, but now at least I could move my feet and use my heavy shoes to bend apart the bits of the frame that impeded my legs. That didn't take long; but nothing I could do would dismember the upright half of the chair that was still fastened to my back. My feet could now move easily but my hands were held as tightly as ever. There must, somewhere, be a knot that maintained the tension, but I had no idea where it was and even had I known, could have done nothing about it.

I stopped struggling for a moment and stood listening, wondering whether the racket I'd made had been heard, expecting the door to open and the three Chinese to reappear.

I was listening to silence. Intensely relieved, I turned towards the corner in which the parts lay and shuffled slowly and carefully towards it. The whole differential assembly, I knew, was lying face upwards, with the crown wheel flat on the floor. If I could just get my hands to the edge of that, it would cut in seconds through the ropes that tied me.

The frame of the chair prevented my sitting down and I had to lie awkwardly on my side, searching for it with my fingertips, but at last I touched the machined smoothness of the metal and my fingers felt the gearing with its precision cuts and perfect, geometrical formation. I edged my body round to bring my bound wrists against the metal rim.

It was impossible to move my wrists back or forward more than an inch at a time, and at first, with each sawing motion, I tended to knock lumps out of my hands on the wheel. I got the hang of it fairly quickly, though, and soon the rope parted. The remnants of rope and chair came away easily, and then in the darkness I fumbled round until I found one of the chair legs to use as a weapon and a length of rope that could be useful. The rest I moved into the corner of the room farthest from the door.

Which way did the door open? I tried to remember, then flattened myself against the wall beside it. The smash, smash, smash of that hand against my face had made me determined to pay back a little of the pain I had felt. Putting my ear against the timber of the door, I listened for the sound of movement in the corridor outside, but there was only silence. I waited, wondering what to do. If three of them came back, they were almost certainly more than I could handle, even allowing for my improvised club and the unexpectedness of my attack. I would need a lot of luck to get away with it, but very occasionally a man does have a lot of luck, and the alternative in my case, was to sit and take another beating.

Then I remembered the door of the other cellar, with the peephole trap in it. Maybe this door had one too? I ran my hands carefully over the timbers of the heavy door, but either it fitted too well to be detected by touch, or it didn't exist.

The tips of my fingers were still on the wood when I heard a tiny sound, like the light scuff of a shoe on the corridor floor. I waited, holding my breath. Long moments passed and then I heard the thin scrape of metal on metal. A pause, and there it was again. I knew that sound! One of the bolts that held that door on the corridor side was being withdrawn. But why so slowly? Why so quietly, even furtively?

Why, when I was tied to a chair in the middle of the room, would anybody take such trouble to be undetected? Tensely I followed each tiny scrape as the bolt slid back. When it was done there was a pause and then the same sounds began to come from the bottom of the door.

A minute, two, even three or four, dragged by. I don't know how long it took, but finally my straining ears told me that the second bolt, too, had been withdrawn. In the darkness I positioned myself with care, the fingers of my outstretched left hand resting lightly on the door so that I would catch its slightest movement, my right holding the chair leg high, ready to smash it down on the first thing to come through.

Then the door moved. Slowly and gently it opened into the room with the dim light from the corridor creeping in a widening triangle across the floor. Hidden behind the moving door, scarcely daring to breathe, I waited, my heart hammering. The door moved again, the angle increasing, and by now it was open perhaps thirty degrees. In some further corner of the building I suddenly heard quick, pattering footsteps on a flight of stairs, and drew farther back into my corner, wondering how many of them there would be.

There was a sudden flash of movement and the door closed quickly, plunging the room into darkness again. But someone else was in the room. I could hear quick, shallow breathing a few feet away. It had all happened very quickly and the light had been almost non-existent, but I was sure there was only one man. My heavy shoes were a hindrance now, but a lifetime of controlling the rudder bar has given my feet more delicacy than you'd imagine and I managed one silent step forward. Again I paused, listening, and again I heard that rapid, nervous breathing. Now I knew where it was : against the wall to my left and four or five feet away. One thing was certain though; he didn't know where I was. And that was the one tiny advantage I had. He might have a gun, a knife, anything, and I would have only one chance, could strike only once with surprise on my side, so the blow must be made solidly, accurately and hard. With infinite slow care I took another step forward and listened again, knowing I was near, concentrating on slow, even breathing.

I had my target pinpointed now. My grip on the chair leg tightened and I swung it hard, downward, and nearly broke my wrist. I must have become somehow disorientated in the darkness, and the chair leg crashed into the wall. Pain shot along my arm and the leg fell from my numbed fingers. Beside me there was a gasp and I didn't wait. I hurled myself in the direction from which it had come.

The fingers of my left hand grasped material of some kind and I held on to it tightly, falling, dragging us both to the floor. Then fighting, rolling, struggling desperately for the upper hand.

I stopped fighting very suddenly. The body I had thrown to the ground was small and soft and in my nostrils there was a light floral fragrance.

'What the hell?'

She gave a little grunt of pain, then whispered fiercely, 'Quiet. You must get out of here.'

I picked myself up. I couldn't see, but all my other senses told me she was young and beautiful.

Her hands found my arm and something cold and metallic was pressed into my hand. 'Here is a gun. I was going to cut you free.'

'Who are you?' I whispered.

'It is not important. Just go. Quickly.'

Beautiful girl or not, I had no thoughts about staying. I whispered my thanks into the darkness.

'It is all I can do,' she said.

I found the door at the second time of asking and opened it slowly. She came silently up to my shoulder and in the dim light I saw the perfect oval of her Chinese face, the frame of blue-black hair and the wide almond eyes. I had not been wrong; she was very beautiful indeed.

'Give me one minute,' she whispered. 'Then go to your left. Up six stairs and to your right at the top. Up three more stairs and there is a door which leads into an alley. At the end of it, there is a taxi waiting.'

I nodded and she slipped past me, pausing to glance along the corridor, then vanishing softly and silently. Slowly, baffled but determined that I would act now and leave the thinking till later, I counted off sixty seconds. Then I cocked the gun and moved forward into the corridor.

Six

Imagine a mouse of exceptionally timid disposition who lives in an exhibition hall and discovers that a Siamese cat show is being held. Imagine how he'd stick his nose through the hole in the skirting, the beady-eyed, whisker-twitching, dry-mouthed care he'd take before he moved one paw one milli-metre. That's how I went out into that corridor.

I peered round one side of the doorway, then the other, seeing with relief the bare brick of the empty corridor. On tiptoe I stepped out to the left, past the door of the other cellar with its sliding trap, and on to the steps. Before I turned up them, I went through my mouse act again, but the whole place was quiet. I tiptoed up the sides of the stair treads, placing my feet carefully to avoid making a stair squeak. At the top, I paused again; still the silence every-where. To the right, up the three stairs she'd told me about, was the door with bolts at the top and bottom, but none fastened. I looked round cautiously, but nothing was mov-ing against the greyish-yellow brickwork. My hand went to the door handle and turned it slowly. The lock was off and the door opened easily and silently.

Outside, the alley was dark, a mass of dark shadows and dustbins, unlit anywhere along its length except where its mouth opened on to the street, I could see cars going by and people walking, only twenty-five feet away. Somewhere to my left there was a quick flash of movement as a stray cat sought the deeper shadows, but otherwise the alley seemed deserted. I stood for a moment or two with my back to the door, allowing my eyes to accustom themselves to the light out there.

By the time I moved, I knew the alley was deserted. I stepped quickly out and hurried to the street. At two o'clock in the morning there were still plenty of people about, the lights still shone, the traffic still moved. The cab she had told me about was parked a few yards away to my left. I hurried over to it and began to climb into the back, then stopped as I realized that I should at least know where I'd been held. Looking back I saw a neon sign in silver and blue : the Lotus Garden. Up and down the street there were Golden Bamboos, and Dragon Wings, South Chinas and Hong Kongs. It was a street of Chinese restaurants.

I climbed into the back of the cab and told the driver to take me to the Pickwick. Two in the morning here meant mid-morning or thereabouts in London and I'd now been awake for nearly thirty hours and felt like it. My face and teeth ached from the blows they'd taken, my arms and ankles bore the marks of the ropes, I felt weary and filthy and angry. I lay back against the cushions and tried to decide whether to go to bed or have a bath and go to bed. Maybe call the police first? It probably wouldn't do a lot of good. By the time I'd persuaded them I wasn't either drunk or a liar, and they'd got a warrant, there wouldn't be a thing left at the Lotus Garden to show I'd been there. And they might keep me in town and stop me flying off. Bath and bed it was, then, with doors and windows locked and the gun under my pillow. Already I could feel my leaden eyelids aching to thud down and my mind turning to cotton wool. Even getting out of the cab would be an effort.

The cabbie was talking into the horizontal arm of his radio, and I listened idly. 'Cab Ninety-three. Fare to Pickwick Hotel, Fifth and Mission, ETA three minutes.'

'OK—uh—Roger,' his controller said. These days everybody thinks he's Mission Control at Houston. The driver set his module down gently beside the Pickwick and I was all ready to undertake the extra-vehicular walk across the lobby, when my mind, which I had forbidden to ponder the whys and wherefores, disobeyed instructions and asked me a barrage of questions.

Why, it said, did those spares you gave to Newton's chauffeur wind up in the possession of some necessarily criminal mob in the basement of a Chinese restaurant? Had the chauffeur been robbed? Or killed? If Marion Capote had been as keen to get those parts as everyone from Jimmy Pope onward seemed to think, wouldn't he be rather angry? If, that is, he wanted the parts. There were so many imponderables and my mind's a very strange object. Once it starts speculating it goes on speculating quite independently of what I may wish. Tired as I was, I knew there'd be no sleep for me until I could answer a question of two to my own satisfaction.

I looked at the Pickwick, and then at the cabbie. What the hell? It wouldn't be the first time I'd missed a night's sleep.

'Cabbie,' I said, 'can I get either whisky or coffee in this town at this hour?'

'Coffee's easy,' he said. He had a big flask beside him.

'Give me a big cup,' I said, 'and you can drive me out to the airport at Ignacio.'

'Long way,' he said. 'Cost you.'

I grinned. 'It's only money.' In any case, I'd have the cost of it out of somebody's hide, either Lennox's or Jimmy Pope's. I climbed back in and the module blasted off.

I sat back comfortably, drinking his coffee and smoking

his cigarettes and wondering if I'd ever see my passport again. It is always pleasant, driving in those hours that are neither late nor early, the limpid hours when almost everything stops, almost everywhere, even the endless jamming of traffic.

The cab ran on to a long climbing ramp, and I realized suddenly where we were and where we were going : up ahead was the Golden Gate Bridge, and as we climbed on to its gigantic span, the scene below was a breathtaking sea of light shining into the air and out of the water of the bay. I couldn't drag my eyes away. People argue about the world's beautiful cities and usually the same names come up : Sydney, Rio de Janeiro, San Francisco, Vancouver, Hong Kong. I've seen them all, but I've never seen a sight like the one that burst upon me then.

The driver didn't look, he was talking into his microphone again. 'Same fare to Ignacio airfield. ETA twenty minutes. Fare changed his mind.' I was glad he didn't talk space talk all the time.

Control did, though. 'Uh—Roger.'

The cabbie paid the toll and we swished along through the night, along Highway 101 until the unmistakable lights of the airfield showed up. The cabbie turned in his seat.

'Ignacio. Where d'you wanna be?'

'Outfit called Airflo,' I said. 'Know it?'

'I think so,' he said. He swung the cab through the airport gate and on to the access road. 'Somewhere along here, I think.'

We were both peering out at the darkened hangars and offices, looking for a sign that said Airflo, and finally I saw the capital A with wings which they, with a proper public-relations-sense-of-the-dramatic, doubtless called a flying A. A little paved path led from the access road across the grass to a single-storey brick building with a hangar behind it.

'Wait here,' I said.

I climbed out of the cab and walked towards the building. If you think I was mad arriving there at three o'clock in the morning, then I should tell you that the world I live in is pretty mad. Every airfield you go to will have somebody around at that hour and I remembered Newton's chauffeur saying Marion Capote might work all night on his Rolls. What, I ask you, could be madder than that?

There wasn't a light of any kind in the single-storey building, but that was to be expected. Even in the aviation world, you don't catch the office staff around after five-thirty unless something very exceptional is happening, like the outbreak of a world war, or a new millennium. If there was action anywhere, it would be in the hangar, among the boys who get their hands dirty.

I skirted the office building and began working my way round the side to where the hangar loomed black against the deep sky. That penetrating early morning chill caught me and I shivered as a grey goose, somewhere, strolled across my grave. The hangar seemed to be in darkness; no light at the windows, and the big main doors closed. I tried the doors but they must have been bolted and locked because they wouldn't slide and the little through door cut into the big ones was locked too. At the back of the hangar it was the same story. Airflo might be busy, but no one was losing any sleep. Except the pilot of course. It's always the pilot.

I walked across the rear of the hangar and came back down the far side, then crossed to the lee of the office building, walking on the damp grass. There were potted plants on windowsills and pin-up calendars on walls; plenty of evidence of people, but no people.

Or were there? I stopped and listened. Somewhere up ahead was the sound of voices, low voices, talking in tones that I could catch only because, in the hour before dawn, everything is magnified by the stillness. I smiled at myself as I suddenly realized it could be the cabbie's radio, and smiled again when the magnetic, amplified tone confirmed it. I was about to move on when I caught the words.

54

'He's nosing around the Airflo hangar.'

The controller's voice replied but I couldn't catch it. I hurried silently forward and slid in behind a row of bushes that separated Airflo's space from the next fellow's.

'Yeah,' the cabbie said softly, 'but what if he don't wanna go back to the Lotus Garden? What then?'

'He doesn't know this town. Never been here before. He won't know where he's going until it's too late. Just bring him.'

'Okay,' the driver said. 'You're the boss.'

I slid quickly back behind the office block and began to whistle: softly, but loudly enough to be heard, and then sauntered along the path to the cab. He was feigning sleep, drooping in his seat with his cap tipped forward over his eyes.

I tapped him on the shoulder and he grunted and snorted and generally tried to behave like a man who has dozed off. Only the Robert Newtons of this world can get away with that kind of overacting, but I let him think he had.

'Home,' I said.

'Pickwick?'

'The Pickwick,' I said.

'Nobody ain't here, huh?'

'Nobody,' I said. I sat back in my seat, smirking, as the car moved off the airfield and out on to US 101, back to San Francisco. I smoked and contemplated the satisfying prospect of one-upping the man who sat so unsuspectingly in front of me, the viper in my bosom, the bloody little treacher. Treachers are people who are treacherous.

I said, 'Is there anywhere on these roads where you can stop?'

'Sure. Pull-offs every coupla miles.'

'Pull off at the next one.'

'Okay-ay. Roger.'

We sang along the highway for a while, then he pulled over, braked, turned. I got out of the car and opened his door. He was not quite so startled as I thought he might be at the sight of the gun in my hand.

'Get out.'

'Take it easy, bud. I've only about five bucks. Take it and leave me alone.'

'Don't play the bloody innocent with me,' I said. 'I overheard you on the radio.'

'Uh-huh.' He was watching the gun in a way I didn't like, a confident kind of way. He began to reach for his pocket and I jerked the gun.

'Hands up.'

He reached unhurriedly into his pocket and brought something out that lay dark in the palm of his hand. As his thumb touched it, a spring clicked and a long blade swung over.

I said, 'Sit very still or I shoot.'

'Go right ahead.' He was smiling. 'I took the bullets out myself.'

'What? When?'

'Before you got it, bud.'

I pointed the gun at the ground and pulled the trigger. The tiny pointless click confirmed what he'd said: the gun was empty. The cab driver came sliding out of the front seat like a snake, knife held low before him, blade up. It was ready for knife-fighting, not for knife-throwing.

I threw the pistol at him as hard as I could. We weren't standing more than six or seven feet apart and a couple of pounds of metal makes an effective projectile. It hit him where his shoulder joined his neck and he gave a long deep grunt of pain; his hands flew to his injured throat and the knife fell on the concrete, forgotten in the sudden agony. I snatched it up quickly. Knife-fighting isn't a speciality of mine, but as with violins, I do know how to hold the instrument.

'Get in and drive,' I said.

He got in, but it was several minutes before he could drive. He spent them sitting slumped in the driving seat, whimpering as he tried to soothe the savage pain in his neck. After a while, when I thought he'd got over the worst of it, and was just overacting again. I told him to move.

I sat in the back seat, with the tip of the knife blade touching the hairline at the back of his neck. 'In case you've got thoughts about sudden braking,' I said, 'remember that any violent forward motions are going to propel this thing into your brain. So drive carefully.'

We had gone a mile or two when his short-wave radio came alive. 'Control to Ninety-three. Your location, please.'

I hissed, 'Tell him you're still waiting at Ignacio.'

When the message had been passed, I wondered suddenly whether the channel remained open and the controller could hear us. I told him to switch on the ordinary radio and keep it on loud.

It was loud, all right; the final crashing bars of a pop record blasted into the car. Then Sinatra sang 'Granada' and we were into a newscast. The announcer sounded excited. 'During processing of film taken during Sunday night's student riots at the Berkeley campus of the University of California, it has been discovered that a murder was filmed as it took place. The killing was that of Patrolman Michael J. Kowalski of the Berkeley force, and the film has been copied and prints supplied to police departments. The incident takes place in one corner of a crowd scene, but is entirely clear. Patrolman Kowalski is first roughly handled by several young men. He steps back two paces and raises his nightstick. At this point one of the young men throws a knife which hits Patrolman Kowalski in the throat. The young man has not so far been identified, but police and photographic experts are hopeful that further enlargement of the film will result in identification and an early arrest. In Vietnam, thirty-eight Vietcong are reported dead in heavy fighting in the Mekong delta. US losses were two dead and five wounded. West Germany's Federal Chancellor, on a visit to the US has said that he believes prospects for strengthening friendship between East and West Germany are growing stronger. And that's the news.' Then we were back to the records, in particular to a little higher moral philosophy from the Rolling Stones.

This time as we approached the bridge, I didn't move my eyes to admire the scenery; I kept them on the cabby and the unwinding road.

As the car ran on into San Francisco, however, I started looking round. I was looking for an all-night, multi-storey car park and I found one.

'Drive in here.'

He half-turned in his seat, looking scared.

'Go ahead,' I said. I touched his skin with the tip of the knife and he edged gingerly up the ramp and took the ticket from the machine.

'Top floor,' I told him.

We went round and round, climbing up through nine levels; the top floor was likely to be empty and it was. I directed him across to a corner by a fire-escape where one of the strip lights had gone, and told him to back the car into the corner. Then I ordered him out. I tied his hands behind him with his belt, his feet with my belt and linked the two tightly; I opened the massive boot, ripped off some of the rubber sealing, then put him in and closed the lid.

I left the car park using the automatic lift to street level and started walking down the hill outside. The Pickwick might not be the healthiest place on earth at the moment, but it *was* where Lennox would be expecting to find me. Also there was bed and bath. I'd been awake too long and it's no sort of preparation for flying; what I needed now more than anything else was for the rest of the world to get on with its private affairs and leave me to sleep. I strode on down the hill, wondering where I was. I could see the Bay Bridge ahead and to the right, so I wasn't far from the right spot. At last I came to Market Street, and then Mission, walked toward Fifth. The Pickwick was still there.

I walked towards the entrance, too tired for my step to be jaunty, but dwelling on the beautiful thought that hot water and a bath were only a few feet away.

'Hey.' The voice was not loud but the command in it was clear.

I turned. A blue saloon stood by the kerb. The window was down and a Negro wearing a light coloured hat over a very black face was looking out at me.

'Sorry,' I said. 'I'm going to sleep.'

'For a long time,' he said softly. 'If you don't step this way.'

Something came into view; something bluish and metallic; something that pointed at my stomach.

'Get in the car,' he said.

Seven

I really didn't believe it. Since yesterday morning I'd had so many shocks that reaction and sheer weariness combined in something akin to hysteria. Involuntarily, I laughed, though maybe giggled would be a better word. He looked surprised and I don't blame him, but he recovered and swung the rear door open. I climbed in.

'Please,' I said. 'Put that away. If you want to knock me over, just breathe out hard and I'll fall.'

'Where's your partner?' he said. It jerked some sense into me and the adrenalin glands went to work again. Partner, to me, at that moment, meant Lennox's boy, the *persona non grata* spy I was to fly back to Britain, starting quite soon. But nobody was supposed to know about him.

'What partner?' I said.

He said, 'You drove in over the Golden Gate Bridge and went into a car park. There were two of you. When you came out there was only one. Where is he?'

'I hope he's asleep,' I said.

'Okay,' he said. 'Gimme your wrists.' He was big and quiet. His voice had a weary quality.

'Why?' I asked.

He held up the handcuffs. 'Because I'm not going to be stupid enough to drive you to the precinct house with your hands free.'

'You're arresting me?'

'The wrists.'

I said, 'What's the charge?'

'We'll find one,' he said. 'Something to hold you on. Suspicion, maybe.'

'Suspicion of what?' I said. I held out my wrists and watched a precise black hand snap on a handcuff. I realized there was something else I should have asked. 'Who are you, anyway?'

'Suspicion of narcotics smuggling,' he said. He fished a little wallet out of his pocket and showed me a badge. 'Federal Narcotics Bureau,' then put the wallet back and snapped the other handcuff on.

'Is that what I've been doing?' I said. 'I'm glad somebody told me.'

'Wise guy.' He grabbed the chain between my wrists and fastened it to a spring shackle on the back of his car seat. 'Don't fool about,' he said. 'Don't give me any chances. Don't make me want to kill you any more, because I want to already. And I might be tempted.'

'Look,' I said. 'I'm British and I only landed in your lousy bloody country yesterday afternoon. I'm going back again today, I hope—'

'Not you,' he said. 'Your partner in that car was a guy I just know is distributing drugs in San Francisco. If you're driving with him in the early hours, you are, too. Two questions: where is he now, and where had you been? Unless the answers to those and a lot of others are good, you're

60

not going to Britain. You're not even going to leave California. You'll just spend the rest of your life in San Quentin. It's right up the bay there.'

I thought of Lennox and his man, of the eight o'clock phone call I had to take. They must remain secret. The rest this man was entitled to hear.

'All right,' I said. 'What do you want to know?'

He stopped the engine and turned to face me. 'I told you.'

'I'm sorry,' I said. 'I'm dead tired and a bit stupid. I've been out to Ignacio. To the airfield.'

'And who was the guy you were with?'

'He started out as a taxi-driver,' I said, 'then he pulled out a knife—Look,' I said, 'I'd better start at the beginning.'

'Go right ahead,' he said.

I suppose it must have taken about twenty minutes to tell him the story, suitably edited. He just sat there, his dark face impassive, listening. At the end he took a key out of his pocket and unlocked my handcuffs. The longer I talked to Rafer Hayes, narcotics agent, the more I liked him. I didn't have to be psychic to know he was in the Narcotics Bureau because he hated drugs; the hate shone out of every pore and glittered in his eyes. If ever I saw a man with a mission in life, he was the man. But it didn't stop him being human, having humour.

Finally he grinned and said, 'What're you gonna do about your passport?'

'I'm a law-abiding citizen,' I said, 'I'll apply to the British Consul for another, and tell him I lost it.'

'You can't call it lost if you know where it is,' he said.

'Meaning?'

'I'm going to have a look at the Lotus Garden. Only I get lonely.'

'I don't hold men's hands,' I said.

'And I won't be able to identify the cast. Not of this show.'

'It's what they call a happening,' I said. 'Nobody sells programmes.'

I went with him all the same, not because I'm bright and brave and ready for any adventure but because I'm not. I'm a professional pilot making a living in the rough end of the flying business and I'm still alive because I try very hard not to take any risks I don't know about.

If I succeeded in getting into that Stripe Tiger some time later that day, I wanted to do so with a reasonable knowledge that it hadn't been tampered with. Aircraft are vulnerable; it doesn't take much to convert them into coffins : just a saw cut here, or a loosened nut there. All the pre-flight inspections in the world aren't proof against sabotage. And if I had any suspicion the Tiger had been got at, I'd take Lennox's lad by the hand and walk home. If Hayes was going to do any interrogating this night, I'd like to be listening.

As we drove he told me a little, but not much, about his job, about the war against drugs. He believed he was fighting a rearguard action; that in a few years the whole world would be high; he was losing but he meant to go down fighting.

'Listen,' he said. 'A few years ago they were just trying marijuana in college. Heroin was a long way along the line. Now we've got twelve-year-olds in this country mainlining on heroin. Before you know where you are they'll package it for toddlers.'

'Where does it come from?' I asked.

He shrugged. 'Turkey. They grow the poppy legally there, and in Mexico. The opium's refined as often as not in France. Hell, it grows in a lot of places. There's so much dough to be made. And oh brother, have we got an epidemic. Listen, a kilogram of morphine base is worth maybe three-fifty dollars in Turkey. By the time it's been refined into heroin, it's worth ten times that. Unloaded in New York City or here or Los Angeles, it's worth maybe twenty thousand bucks. By the time it's gone through the distributors, pushers and peddlers it's made maybe a quarter of a million.'

He stopped the car. 'California and Grant. I reckon we're not far away.' We got out and left it at the kerb and walked off into Chinatown. There weren't many people about now : just a few determined revellers assuring one another that the dying night was still young.

We found the Lotus Garden in darkness, though above it the blue and silver neon sign still blazed. I looked up at the windows but the glass served only to reflect back at me the multi-coloured lights of other and higher neon signs. Opposite the mouth of the alley we stopped, lighting cigarettes, checking that the alley looked empty. The cigarettes were stamped out a few seconds later as we slid into the darkness. Those shadows were deep and black and welcoming and we slunk into them like a pair of old tomcats. Easing along on tiptoe, we came to the door I'd used to get out, moved rapidly past it and came to the end of the alley. It wasn't the end, though. There was a big brick wall across that made the alley appear blind, but in fact it turned to the right and then to the left, leading back to an old cobbled street. Here the wall was perhaps four and a half feet high, enclosing a concreted yard at the rear of the Lotus Garden. Built into the wall was the entrance to a large, flat-roofed double garage that projected back into the yard.

We looked up at the face of the building. The ground, first and second floors were in darkness, but light fanned upward from the basement windows; light that flickered a little, as though people were passing between the source and the window.

Hayes leaned towards me. 'No lights anywhere else, you'll notice.'

I looked round, shivering a bit in the early chill. People were where people ought to be at that hour : in bed. But not at the Lotus Garden. Either its proprietors were inefficient restauranteurs, tardy with the washing-up, or something else was going on. I noticed a big square shape on top of the garage roof : a tank, probably. I pointed.

'Give me a leg up,' I whispered. 'I should be well hidden behind that.'

Hayes nodded and bent, lacing his fingers together, like the trainer putting the jockey up. I sailed almost silently to the roof and slid quickly into the shelter of the square shape. There was no question, for anybody with nostrils to sniff with, what it was : the tank contained paraffin.

I started by looking carefully at all the upper windows, to make sure that nobody was spying on the spies, but all they did was reflect back at me the silver of the moonlit sky. Raising my head, I looked down at the basement windows : there were two of them, both wide, and between them stood a door with a flight of steps leading down to it from the yard. Inside the cellars were long wooden tables and stoves, obviously the restaurant's kitchens, and work was still going on : two men in chef's white trudged backward and forward with that unmistakable enthusiasm people always show when they're clearing up. Listening, I could hear faintly the rattle of plates and the jingle of pans. It all looked very innocent. I turned and keeping that tank between me and the yard, crawled the few feet to the edge.

Rafer Hayes looked up at me. 'Well?'

'Looks normal.'

'Okay, come on d—' His head turned sharply and he raised a finger warningly to his lips.

I listened too. The sound was faint, but clear enough, a knock on a door that seemed to come from the alley. In a moment it came again, more loudly this time. There was silence for a while. Then footsteps.

Hayes just vanished, I don't know where, and I moved rapidly back into the stinking shadows around that tank. Whoever was coming was hurrying. The steps clicked briskly out of the alley round the back of the garage, and in through a gate on the far side, the hinges squeaking as he went through. As he crossed the yard and went down the steps to the door, I could see he was holding his right arm in an odd kind of way, and when he came out into the light I knew why. It was the cabbie I'd dispossessed. I wondered how he'd escaped.

He tapped on the door and it was opened by a white-clad Chinese, presumably one of the cooks.

'Is Mr Wong here?' the cabbie asked.

'Wait,' said the cook.

The cabbie remained obediently on the doorstep. A moment later another man appeared. He first came into vision as a pair of black shoes, then the trousers and the jacket, and finally the face. It was the man who'd given me the working-over.

'Sorry, Mr Wong. I've lost him,' the cabbie said.

'Lost him?' Wong raised his hand, then remembered he was out of doors and checked the blow.

'He threw the gun and—' the cabbie began.

Wong interrupted him. 'Inside. Where is he now—?'

The door closed on them and I could hear no more. I slid back to the edge and called softly.

Hayes crept forward below me.

'Did you hear? That was my partner. The cabbie.'

'And the other?'

'The one who asked the questions? He seems to be called Wong.'

'Watch a bit longer.' He faded away again.

I began to feel cramped as I crouched there behind the tank, inhaling that paraffin smell. My body ached for a cigarette but my muscles just ached; my head felt as though it were full of wet cotton wool and my eyes as though they were full of gravel.

In the cellar, the cabbie sat miserably on the stool, smoking. Wong seemed to have disappeared into some other part of the house and I found myself glancing nervously

65

from time to time at the upstairs windows.

Suddenly I saw the cabbie's head jerk round. He stood up quickly and put his cigarette out in the familiar sequence of actions that means the CO or the sergeant major is on the way. The interior door that the cabbie had turned to face was out of my line of vision, but I saw the cabbie begin to speak and knew somebody had come in. The cabbie spoke, then listened, then spoke again, but I couldn't see to whom. I took a deep breath and moved out of my hiding place, out on to the flat, exposed area of roof to my left, and lay full-length on the tarred felt. Raising my head, I looked cautiously down into the cellar.

Talking to the cabbie was a tall, thin Chinese: fiftyish, maybe more, wearing a dark, formal overcoat, gold-rimmed glasses and a Homburg hat. Wong stood beside him and both of them were giving the cabbie a dressing down; it was noticeable, though, that Wong was number two boy; the older man's mouth had only to open for Wong's to close deferentially.

I wished desperately that I could either hear or lip-read. It's astonishing, though, how much one's eye can pick up: mine told me for instance, that somebody else was joining them from the way they all turned their heads at a sound I couldn't hear. From the expression on their faces, I had a good idea who it was, too: the older man's expression had softened to a small smile of pleasure by the time the girl came into the room. She was pale, slim and beautiful and it was obvious that the older man had a mental barbed-wire fence built around her; even talking as he was with subordinates, his manner bespoke jealous protectiveness. He spoke to her for quite a while, then suddenly they all began to look at their watches and look expectant. Occasionally one or other of them would glance towards the door that led into the yard.

The general air of expectancy was so strong that it seemed

sensible to move from my exposed position. I crawled carefully backward, making a little more noise than I cared to, but hoping there wasn't anybody except Hayes to hear it. Within a couple of minutes I was crouching again in the comparative safety of the tank's shadow. I probably smelt like the underside of a sump heater.

'Stay where you are!' The hair stood up and tingled all over my scalp, but it was only Hayes, stage-whispering. 'Something's coming.'

And something was. Away to my right, I heard the sound of an engine, fairly low but approaching, growing louder. Headlight beams waved as a suspension system bounced on the rough surface of the back road. When it stopped and began to turn, I could see what it was: a large, pale yellow van with SUN LAUNDRY painted on its side.

I hoped that Hayes was well hidden as the door to the kitchens opened and Wong hurried out with one of the cooks, crossing the yard to what I thought was the wall of the garage but turned out to be another set of doors. The doors opened, then I heard their footsteps pass beneath me as they walked through the garage to the street end and began to open the doors there. The van swung forward and round, there was a crunch as the driver banged it into reverse with the revs over-high, and began to back it into the garage, then it ran out of sight and stopped, the engine was cut and the headlights switched off.

Wong and the cook stood waiting in the yard. I heard the door of the van slam as the driver got out; he walked round to the back and opened the doors.

Wong said, 'All right?'

The driver grunted something.

A moment later, the three of them appeared carrying a big laundry hamper which, from the way they were grunting must have been heavy. As they got to the stairs leading down to the kitchens, the older Chinese spoke, the second cook hurried forward and the four of them carried the

67

wicker hamper down the steps. The door closed quickly behind them.

Whatever was happening now was happening beyond my view. Crouching low I moved out on to the roof, forward and to my left, to try to see into the kitchens. I had to move further and further diagonally across the roof, my heart hammering, my mouth dry. If one of them should look out of the window I would be clearly visible, silhouetted against the sky.

I flung myself flat as something moved in the yard below, then breathed deeply in relief as I realized it was Hayes. He must have walked through the open doors at the end of the garages. He, too, was moving forward to the windows.

In the cellar, padlocks were being unfastened on the laundry hamper, then the lid was lifted and I cursed under my breath because it partially obscured my view. But only partially.

I saw a man climb out of the basket.

Eight

I saw his back and his dark, straight, Chinese hair, his dark trousers and his shoes, but I didn't see his face. He didn't turn, either, after he climbed out of the basket; just hurried through that inner door into some other part of the house.

I looked down at Hayes. He was waving me back towards the street and I crawled obediently away, so I didn't see what happened. I heard it, though: a sudden grunt of pain and a clanging noise. Instantly the kitchen door flew open and men poured out into the yard: Wong, the two cooks, the cabbie and others. There were guns everywhere and even if Hayes had had time to use his own pistol, he'd have been mad to try.

'Who are you?' It was Wong's voice.

Hayes said, 'I'm an agent of the Federal Bureau of Narcotics.' It seemed a strange thing to do, somehow, to say it like that. I suppose he was relying, as law enforcement people do, on ingrained and long-established respect for law and order. In any case all they had to do was search his pockets to find that identity card.

Wong said, 'Have you a warrant? These are private premises.' He laughed. 'Turn around.'

I shrank back, trying to become invisible. But I wasn't invisible: I was still out in the middle of that roof and anybody looking out of an upper window would see me.

Below me there was a thud and a grunt; then a soft, authoritative voice which could only belong to the older Chinese, said, 'Take him with the other.'

Wong protested: 'We don't know how much he saw, or heard. We ought to find out.'

The other voice said, 'It is of no importance. But we can find out there, as easily as here. Guard him well. Make sure he does not get away as the other one got away.'

'He's a Federal agent,' Wong said.

'They die, just as easily.'

I lay flat, praying that all their attention was focused on the yard and on Hayes. Then small, scuffling, scraping noises began to come from below. I was ten, maybe twelve yards from the tank, but somehow I had to get back there; somehow I had to remain undetected. Two lives, my own and Hayes's, depended on that.

I raised my body slightly, taking my weight on elbows and knees, keeping my trunk and my toes from any contact with the roof, and moved a cautious, experimental step back. The strain on my muscles was awful, but it worked and it was quiet. I tried again and gained another silent foot.

Wong said, 'Is there another basket? Then bring it. And get him inside quickly.'

I waited. The awkward crawl was not going to be necessary. The whole gang, presumably carrying Hayes, vanished into the kitchen. I raised my head to look and I could see Rafer's feet on the kitchen floor, and a certain amount of activity going on around him. I rose and moved swiftly back to the tank, then to the edge of the roof, peered over and lowered myself quickly to the ground. Facing me was the bonnet of the van, and through the windscreen I could see right through from front to back.

I knew what I should do : I should go marching into that kitchen with the gun I had in my pocket, hold them up and get Hayes out. The trouble was that the gun was still unloaded and at least one of them knew it. The only alternative was to go wherever the van was going and the only way to do that was to travel in it, or on it or under it. Hayes's car was parked too far away, and in any case the keys were probably in his pocket. I dropped quickly to my knees and looked under the van. No prospects there : total road clearance probably wasn't more than a foot and there would be nothing to hang on to except the roasting-hot exhaust pipe. The top, I knew already, was flat : no chance of hanging on to that with the van moving. That left only one possibility.

I tiptoed forward and opened the door of the van, climbed quietly up and across the driving seat. The rear doors were wide and if anyone opened the cellar door, I must be seen. I got my feet into the space between the seats and climbed into the back. There were several large laundry baskets, full, and a pile of brown-paper-wrapped parcels. Immediately behind the passenger seat, however, lay a large tarpaulin. It was the only hiding place there was.

Quickly I lay on the floor, forcing my body into the angle so that the upper half of me lay along the side of the van and my legs across it, behind the seats. With a bit of luck, and provided nobody trod on my legs in climbing from the back of the van into the cab, I might be all right.

It seemed like an age before anything happened and it was stuffy, dusty and uncomfortable under the tarpaulin.

My hip bone pressed awkwardly and painfully against the metal floor, and I knew that as soon as the van moved, my ribs and elbows would be bruised.

I stiffened as the sound came and light spilled from the opening door. Footsteps, then the creaking of the wicker hamper, a thud as it was half-thrown into the back of the van, then the footsteps retreating. A minute later they returned with another hamper and that, too, was tossed into the back. I prayed desperately that whoever was riding in the van would not go to the cab via the back: the tarpaulin covering my legs stretched half-way across and it would be a reflex action to kick it out of the way.

The doors of the van were closed and the voices outside were muffled. If only they'd walk round the side—please, please, please!

A moment later I heard the door open on the driver's side and the van rocked on its springs as he took his seat. I waited, and the other door opened. Nobody was in the back! I almost sighed with relief, but sighs make noises.

The motor started and the van moved off, jerking a bit as it bounced along the pitted back street, then turning, picking up speed. I felt for my gun. In a moment, I could crawl out, hold them up and set Hayes free.

'Who's gonna do it?' asked a voice from the direction of the passenger seat. I could have wept with disappointment: the voice was the cabbie's, and he knew my gun wasn't loaded.

I clung with one hand to the tubing of the driving seat as the van lurched, tilted forward at thirty degrees or so down one of San Francisco's incredibly steep streets. Every time we crossed one of the intersecting streets, the van levelled and I was banged against the hard, metal floor, but I daren't move; I could only hang on and hope they wouldn't hear my body bouncing and that the journey would be short.

'He will,' the driver said.

'Just like that?'

'Shaddap.'

The van bounced on, for hours, it seemed, while my body was flung this way and that and my bones collected bruises from floor, walls and a loose sharp-cornered parcel that slid endlessly round the smooth interior. But finally we stopped. I lay aching, feeling as though somebody had put me in a great cocktail shaker and shaken hard.

The driver got out, and I heard his footsteps go away, then return. The doors at the back were opened and the cabbie climbed out to help. They were grunting as they pulled the first of the wicker baskets across the floor. When I felt that they had lifted it clear, I raised my head. The two men, watched by a third, an elderly Chinese, were dragging the hamper across the pavement and through open double doors. As they disappeared and the older man followed, I dragged myself out from under the tarpaulin, and into the driving seat and began to open the door. Their returning footsteps stopped me. I cringed down in the seat, not breathing, not moving, not doing anything except pray that I wouldn't be spotted. The silence was unbearable as I waited to be found; but it was brief, too, and it was broken by the sound of the second hamper sliding across the van floor. They hadn't seen me! As the footsteps receded, I slid out of the van, my bones and muscles alive with aches and twinges, and into the shadow of a doorway twenty yards down the street.

As the van moved away I took a deep, shuddering breath of relief. I was bathed in sweat but shivering, too, aching in every bone and muscle and wearier than I have ever been in my life. I realized, with sudden, agonizing horror, that it might not have been Rafer Hayes they'd unloaded; it could have been a straightforward delivery of laundry! If that were so, Hayes was as good as dead!

I waited a few minutes, hoping my body would begin to feel less like a stranger's and more like my own, then moved slowly out of the doorway's reassuring shadow and back along the street to the double doors through which the hampers had been taken. They were black doors, not too wide, and they fitted well. There was no handle on the outside and the surrounding brickwork ran close to those doors; they could be opened only from the inside. An expert burglar might, perhaps, have done it from outside, but those aren't my skills.

No one was moving in the deserted street and I stood looking around me for a little while, hoping for inspiration. I realized, suddenly, that it was a cul-de-sac and then, as I looked more closely, that its real purpose was to service the two-storeyed buildings on either side, which meant, in turn, that it was likely these buildings had business fronts in another street.

I hurried along the pavement, counting the buildings as I went. At the intersection, about eighty yards away, I turned left. Sure enough, there was another street facing me, wider and lined with shops. I counted the shops carefully as I worked my way along the street; fourteen would bring me to the one I wanted. There were antique dealers, shops selling fruit and artists' materials, a camera shop and a small dispensary. Then I came to number fourteen: the front of the premises, like the rear, was black-painted and a small, discreetly-lit sign was visible in the otherwise draped and darkened window. It was an undertaker's, a funeral parlour!

I looked at the little sign. 'Night and day service,' it said. 'Please ring the bell.' I took my empty gun out, hoping it looked as though it might be bursting with bullets, and pressed the bell. There was a pause, then the slow shuffle of footsteps inside; another pause, and the door opened. The same elderly Chinese I'd seen at the back stood there, face professionally set in an expression of interest and concern which changed rapidly when he saw the gun, to narrow-eyed wariness.

'There's no money here,' he said quickly.

I waved the gun about a bit, gesturing him back into the shop or parlour or whatever it was. He backed away and I followed, squinting quickly from side to side. We were in a carpeted room which held only three or four armchairs. Relatives doubtless sat there making final arrangements. Another door led from the room, back into the building and as I moved on, he backed towards it. The door opened on to another room, also carpeted, but bare of furniture. Off it, behind a curtain, was the coffin room from which, presumably, the empty boxes were wheeled out on a trolley for inspection.

We worked our way back. On the other side of the corridor from the room we had just left was a door with a large cross on it and gilt lettering read : Chapel of Rest. The chapel was empty.

He backed away down the corridor. A staircase climbed away to my left and I stopped at the bottom, listening to the silence from the upper part of the building. I'd just have to hope there was nobody up there, but I didn't have too much confidence in the hope; people don't live alone in funeral parlours if they intend to stay sane. Another door led to a small office that was empty. That left one more door, which could only open on to the back of the building, and it was into the back of the building that I'd seen those two baskets go.

'Open it,' I said harshly.

'There is nothing here,' the old man said, 'except the dead and the equipment I use in passing them on to where they are going.' He made it sound as though he was in steady personal contact with Heaven.

'Open it.' He nodded gravely and I began to wonder whether those hampers might not, after all, contain freshly-laundered undertaker's outfits or whatever it is they use. He reached behind him for the door handle, turned it and began to pull the door open to reveal a room in total darkness except for a small red light glowing brightly, low down to the left.

'In,' I said. I took a step forward, motioning with the gun and he turned to go through the door. In that second he seemed to dive for the floor, kicking backward at the same instant with both feet. The gun went spinning from my hand and I staggered back in time to watch him perform something between a somersault and a roll, that carried him through the door and into the room beyond. I dived after him, kicking the door back and racing through, then stopping abruptly.

He had disappeared. It was ridiculous, but that room didn't just look empty, it felt empty. The light from the door I'd just come through showed me that I was in a large store-cum-reception room. One or two coffins stood against the walls and there were those silver and gold things, whatever they're called, that coffins stand on. On one wall was a rack of shelves and on another, grey steel cabinets. It was here that the red light glowed. Facing me were the double doors. I looked carefully round the room, searching for the wicker hampers I'd seen carried in.

At first I couldn't see them, but as I moved further into the room, I saw that they lay partly hidden by a big screen made of brass and velvet. I hurried towards them and my weary mind realized, too late, that the screen had begun to topple. I tried to jump back but the falling screen caught me a painful blow on the shoulder and instantly the Chinese was coming at me, a woodworker's mallet held ready to smash my skull.

I did the only possible thing, grasping at his raised right arm with my left. I got it too, but he was stronger than he looked, that old man, and almost wrenched it clear again, meanwhile aiming vicious blows with his knees at my whole abdominal area. I turned my side to him, but it only needed one of those blows to land and I'd be done. His left hand was clawing at my face now; he was going for my eyes. Incredibly, he was winning. I lifted my right foot off the ground, stamped down forward and hard and was rewarded by a crunching feeling and a howl of pain as my heavy heel crashed on his instep. The fight went out of him instantly and he staggered back, moaning. When I went after him he tried to swing the mallet at me, but I got him with a left-handed punch to the jaw and he hit the floor in a heap. It wasn't any great achievement; he must have been nearly seventy.

At the door, I found the light switch, turned it on, then crossed to the hampers. Each had a bolt securing it and held in place by a padlock. I had started to look for something to use as a crowbar, when it occurred to my dim and ponderous wits that somebody, and probably the old man, must have the keys.

They were in his jacket pocket.

I bent over one of the hampers, listening for the sound of breathing, but there was nothing. I moved to the other and there I thought I heard something.

Feeling was coming back into my right arm, now, but my shoulder was aching abominably and my hands were shaking. It took a long time to find the right key and open the padlock, but I managed it, slid back the bolt and raised the lid. Rafer Hayes lay in the bottom, tied tightly into a kind of foetal position. A wide strip of plaster was taped across his mouth, but his eyes were open wide in apprehension. When he realized who it was, his eyelids lowered and his eyes tightened in a long moment of relief.

I hunted round for a knife, found a chisel instead and cut the rope carefully. Hayes tried to rise but couldn't : his muscles were knotting with cramp and the pain of blood flowing back into his hands and feet must have been intense. Eventually, though, he managed to stand and I helped him climb out. He promptly collapsed to the floor again with murderous cramp in calves and thighs and it was several minutes before his muscles recovered.

The old man still lay where he had fallen and Hayes jerked his head inquiringly.

'That who you were fighting?'

'Yes,' I said. 'Came for me with a mallet. Not to mention knees and elbows.'

He grinned and I was glad to see him grin : 'Yo' po' ol' thing,' he said. 'Did you kill him?'

'I don't know.'

Hayes looked lazily around. 'If you did, he's placed right handy here.'

I said, 'Let's forget the comedy.' I was so tired now that I could barely stand.

There was a coffin lying on the floor beside the unopened hamper and I sat down on it, hoping I wouldn't ever have to stand up again. 'Here are the keys,' I said. 'Open the other hamper.'

'Right.'

He took them from me and I watched idly as he fiddled with the lock. 'If a raiding party of Sioux come galloping out,' I said, 'don't expect me to be surprised.'

'Okay.' He found the key that turned the lock, slid the bolt back and lifted the lid. After a moment I looked up at his face, then I had to get up and look, too.

The man inside was lying in a position no man alive can get into; legs bent strangely, head thrown back. He was young, maybe about twenty, and he was Chinese.

We stood looking at him for a moment and then, on the periphery of my vision, my eye was caught by some tiny movement. It was a label, fastened to the coffin on which I'd been sitting. 'Pathology Laboratory, University of California Medical School, Berkeley, Calif.'

I bent and pulled it off, held it so Hayes could see.

He shook his head slowly from side to side. 'I thought I knew all the ways to get rid of a corpse, but a dissecting room's a new one on me.'

Nine

I felt as though I'd been asleep for one point nine eight four three seven seconds give or take a nanosecond, when the bell rang. I thought at first that it signalled the start of the fifteenth and final round of the wrestling match with twenty-eight flame-coloured soft noodles in the nightmare I was having. It kept on ringing, though, and finally, it pierced the armoured shell of my sleep.

I picked up the telephone and said, 'Hello.'

In a moment, and with a little click, a girl's voice was on the line. 'Is that Mr Shaw?'

'Who is it?' I asked, dopey but suspicious.

'Long distance, sir. I have a call for you from London, England. Mr Lennox.'

I reached for my watch, groaning. It was eight o'clock, all right, and Lennox was giving a demonstration of his precision staff-work.

'Put him on.'

'Shaw?'

'Yes,' I said.

'There's a change of plan. Your-ah-partner will not be where you expected to find him. Instead it will be necessary for you to go and collect him. Understand?'

'Yes,' I croaked.

'There is a yacht with the name *Sunrise*. *Sunrise*, have you got that?'

'*Sunrise*,' I muttered.

'You sound half-asleep, Shaw.' Lennox said irritably. 'Write it down or you'll forget it. *Sunrise*.'

Obediently I opened the drawer, took out a ball-point pen and a tariff card, and wrote *Sunrise*.

'It's at the Marina east of the Presidio,' he said. 'Write that down, too.'

I wrote.

'Apparently,' Lennox grated on, 'she has a white and pink hull and is tied close to the quayside. Go aboard.'

'All right,' I said.

'At noon.'

'Thank God!'

'What was that, Shaw? My God, you sound stupid. Are you drunk, or something?'

'Tired,' I said. 'It's the change of rhythm we flying men have to suffer.'

'You've got it all? *Sunrise*, pink and white, Marina east of the Presidio, noon. Got it? I'm told she's easy to identify.'

'You're bloody well nagging,' I said. 'If I'd wanted to be nagged I'd have found a nagging wife.'

'Don't make a mess of it,' Lennox said. Not good-bye, or good luck or *bon voyage* or anything. Just a final, contemptuous phrase to hang up with.

I jiggled the receiver up and down a bit until the operator came on the line, told her I intended to sleep till eleven and would she please call me then. After that I turned over and fell happily into that beautiful big, black pit.

Promptly and courteously the operator awakened me. She told me it was a fine, bright day, 'A little cold perhaps, sir, if you're not used to it.' I asked if breakfast was possible and she told me how to get to the coffee shop.

I showered and then shaved and dressed with one eye on the television set. I'm not sure whether I'd like breakfast-time television as a regular diet; spreading marmalade over *The Guardian* is a lifetime's habit, but it's pleasant now and again. As promised, they showed the film of the murder at the University of California campus at Berkeley, running it through the first time just the way it had been taken, but with a little white square outlining the incident. Then they showed that area blown up and in slow motion and there it was, clear and plain : murder. The students were roughing the policeman up at first; they knocked his cap off and he stepped back and lifted his stick. Then one of the students threw a knife, and the film was so clear the knife was actually visible, flying through the air. It hit the cop in the throat and he made a kind of clutching gesture and began to fall. Immediately the student turned and began to make off, but in doing so he turned to face the camera. The film had got a perfect portrait of him and I stared at it: the student was Chinese. Was everything in this damn country (a) Chinese and (b) violent?

I switched off the set and went and had some eggs shirred with ham strips which turned out to be bacon and scrambled egg as near as makes no matter. When I started eating it I felt eighty per cent retarded; by the time the second cup of coffee had vanished downstairs, the revolutions were starting to pick up and my mind was beginning to go through certain reflex motions; the third cup, and a big lungful of cigarette smoke, plucked my conversation with Lennox from the memory bank and played it over to me. I looked at my watch; there was still a reasonable amount of time. And then I realized something: I hadn't told Lennox anything, not one single damned word, of what had happened. He didn't know somebody had been using me as a courier, he didn't know half the underworld of San Francisco had been and probably still was trying to kill me. It was his own fault; he'd been, as always, so damned keen to get the conversational upper hand that he'd squashed the possibility of two-way communication. All the same, he should have been told. Come to that, he should still be told. Eleven-fifteen . . . eight hours behind . . . seven-fifteen. He'd have elbowed his bony way through the crowds at Charing Cross an hour and a half ago, and Lennox did not run the kind of organization you could ring and leave a message. Oh, well, I'd just have to tell him later.

I paid for my breakfast, went back up to my room, slung my gear into the grip, paid the bill, took a cab to Hertz and rented a car. They gave me a map of San Francisco to go with it and I spent a couple of minutes getting my bearings and working out a path through the one-way system, then I set off.

When I found her, *Sunrise* was, as Lennox had said, pink and white. I'm no sailor, but I have a long acquaintance with the colours people paint their carriages, particularly cars and aircraft, and I can say with absolute truth that *Sunrise* was among the two or three foulest confections I've seen. She was not, as you might imagine, pink to the water-line and white below, or vice versa; she was white with pink applied in horizontal, irregular stripes like the low, flat clouds in a dawn sky. Except that they weren't; they weren't like anything but the phoney daubings of a real nut. Lennox had said she would be easy to identify and he had been right.

I parked the car and walked towards her. *Sunrise* was a big cruiser, maybe forty feet long, and I thought she probably had a pair of thunderous diesels lurking somewhere under all that icing. I've never understood the principle of buying an object that's beautiful precisely *because* it's functional and then wrecking it with paint and presumption. I once saw a little Cessna at Shannon with huge lace-frilled pink panties on the undercarriage struts. The pilot, naturally, was an amateur, an underwear manufacturer from Texas, and the whole thing fitted together. You have to be nuts to do the long hop to Shannon single-engined, and you certainly have to be nuts to put pink pants on the plane.

Sunrise was tied up alongside, her deck about four feet lower than the harbour wall. I stood looking down at her for a moment or two. To tell the truth, I was just a little bit ashamed to be associated with her.

'Hello,' I called. Then repeated it. Nobody answered. I looked down at decks that could have done with a scrub and peered through the glass to see what was there. All that was inside was the inside of a boat.

A few other sailing enthusiasts were busy nearby, painting

and scraping and scrubbing, fitting new gubbinses and removing old ones and I didn't want to attract too much attention, so I stopped shouting and did as Lennox told me. I went aboard. She rolled very slightly and my feet made a substantial thump as I jumped down to her deck, but neither movement nor sound brought any response from below decks. I stepped to the wheelhouse door, tried the handle and rather to my surprise it opened immediately. Inside, it was more like the flight deck of a Boeing than the wheelhouse of a yacht. There were dials and vacuum tubes and banks of switches, a big padded seat with a lap strap, a green glass visor to slap down over the forward windshield and one of those splendid little tables with holes cut in them to take glasses so your drinks won't spill.

Behind the helmsman's seat, a door led below. That, too, was open and I followed my nose into a little corridor with three cabins opening off it, plus what estate agents call the usual offices. Nobody anywhere. Out came the cigarettes. I went back to the wheelhouse and sat in the padded seat. With no other means of contacting my boy, I'd simply have to sit and wait. What puzzled me was that *Sunrise* obviously hadn't been used for a while and it wasn't just the seagull signatures; you can tell when a machine's in regular employment and this one wasn't. There was dust pretty well everywhere, and undisturbed dust at that, yet the doors were open and nothing was locked; beds weren't made up, ashtrays were empty.

I sat smoking for a while, rather enjoying myself. The scene was that nice combination of Nature at peace and other people at work that most of us find so soothing. Occasionally some tourist would stroll aimlessly along the quay, or somebody else would hurry off to buy the new and much-advertised anti-luffing quadrant sensor from the chandler, but the scene was blue and clean and quiet. It was disturbed by the car.

A Volkswagen. The little grey bug came chuntering

round the corner a bit more quickly than it should have done in that kind of place and it stopped with a couple of nasty jerks when the driver saw *Sunrise*. I could see only the top half of the car and that half included somebody's head, but my vision through the boat's windshield and the car's was hardly clear. There was a longish pause and I began to wonder whether the car's approach had, after all, any connection with my own presence.

Then the door opened. I wish it hadn't. I wish she'd turned the ignition key and put that little grey bug into gear and driven away. But that wasn't what happened. The door of the Volks opened and the sun glared at me from the window-glass for a moment and by the time my eyes belonged to me again, she was out of the car and walking towards me. I was looking at her through a layer of glass and at a distance, but hers was a kind of beauty that murdered distance.

For a moment I did not move; surprise kept me rooted in my seat. But then I came out quickly, through the door and up on to the stone quay, and there I stood still, watching as she glided towards me, remembering the tall Chinese the night before with his protectiveness, his nervousness about her. Not blaming him at all.

She was still eight or ten yards away when she spoke and her voice was like her skin, smooth and somehow golden; the sound was as graceful as the walk, a low vibrating pitch that strummed at my backbone. Yet all she said was, 'Please, out of sight. Go back.'

I didn't move.

She hurried over to me, put her hand on my arm. 'Please, Mr Shaw. We must talk. You must understand.' She stood looking at me.

I looked her over, wondering.

'Why?' I said.

'It is important.'

'So important that you tricked me and almost got me

killed last night. And another guy. And you *did* get the third one!'

She shook her head; the clear, wide eyes shone at me like a pair of medium-brown searchlights. 'Aboard the boat, Mr Shaw. Please.'

'The hell with you and your damn drug rackets,' I said. 'I don't want to know.'

The tiny gun came quickly out of the tiny handbag. 'I am sorry, Mr Shaw. We must talk. Go aboard, please.'

I was getting pretty blasé about guns in this particular twenty-four hours of my life. I turned and jumped down to the deck and she followed me, floating down like blossom on a breath of air. I went into the wheelhouse, contemplated slamming the door on her, but decided that for all her fragility, she gave off too powerful an air of competence.

'Into the cabin.'

So she knew the boat, too! I went through and stood against the bulkhead at the far end. As I turned she was already through the door.

I said, 'Go ahead. Tell me.'

'Mr Shaw, do not be too sceptical. It is very important that—'

'It is very important,' I said, 'that I get out of here today. So tell me who you are and why you're here. Et cetera.'

'Very well.' The little gun still pointed at my heart, but her eyelashes, I remember, were going like big black fans. They were real, too. You can tell real eyelashes with real eyes. 'My name is Jasmine Yang. I—'

Her eyes widened suddenly, and went on widening. Then she sort of fell to one side and collapsed on to the bunk and slid to the floor.

'What the—?'

I stepped forward quickly and grabbed her shoulders, but she was already gone into the brief limpness of death. As I lifted her, I saw the knife sticking out of her back and looked up in a sudden, desperate chill of fear and shock.

He stood looking down at me, laughing. 'Can't have any-one killing the pilot, can I, Mr Shaw?'

I knew him. I'd seen his face before. It took me a moment to place him, but then I did: it was the man I'd seen kill the policeman, Kowalski, on television, not two hours earlier.

Ten

I must have remained where I was, kneeling beside the girl's body for quite a long time, because he spread his hands and said, 'It's all right. Don't worry!'

I blinked up at him and then looked down at her. Jasmine Yang, she'd said. Even death could not immediately destroy the petal texture of the skin, the ivory complexion.

'It was necessary.' His tone said he was surprised that I was surprised; his words were a flat statement without regret.

'Who are you?' I said slowly. I hate death in all its forms and most of all I hate unnecessary death. I could feel anger rising inside me, growing and boiling; anger that this ex-quisite creature, so beautifully alive just a moment ago, should now be finished totally and so uncaringly. 'Who the hell *are* you?'

'My name is Chao Li,' he said. 'You are John Shaw who is to fly me to England. Or so Mr Lennox has instructed.'

'You killed that copper—cop, too?' I said.

He shrugged. 'Nobody likes killing. When it is necessary, it should be done efficiently and then forgotten promptly.'

'Forgotten?' I looked down at Jasmine Yang lying there with the pathetic little gun hanging from her limp hand and knew I would not soon forget this scene.

'Do you know her, Mr Shaw?'

'I've seen her before.'

'Ah, then you must know that she is—was—the mistress

of one of the most unpleasant criminals in San Francisco or, indeed, in California.'

'Tell me,' I said.

He sat casually on the edge of the bunk. 'She was a woman of great beauty, as you see, and of great treachery.'

I thought of the way she had given me the gun last night, of the elaborate performance that had made my escape seem genuine, but with the cabbie waiting outside.

'I can see you know that,' he said.

'What's your name again?'

'Chao Li.'

I rubbed my hands across my eyes. All at once I felt a terrible weary languor. 'I landed in San Francisco,' I said, 'late yesterday afternoon. Ever since, I have been beaten by Chinese, hunted by Chinese, betrayed by Chinese. Now I have a Chinese girl dead at my feet and I'm talking to a Chinese who did it. Why?'

He laughed. 'There are very many Chinese.' The fact that he had just killed, that the body lay at his feet, affected him not at all.

'If you go on this way, there won't be for long.'

'You are forgetting already,' Chao Li said. He bent and picked up her handbag and spread its contents on the bunk to his left. There was a slim, blue-bound cardboard book which he turned over then threw across to me. I wondered why she'd brought it.

'Never trust a woman who has your passport in her hand-bag,' he said.

I said dully, 'What do we do with her?' I can handle some kinds of emergency, but getting rid of bodies is not one of them.

'Leave her here,' Chao Li shrugged. 'If Lennox arranged for us to meet here it must be safe.'

'Whose boat is it?'

'I don't know.'

'Look,' I said, 'if she's found soon and there's anything at all to link her with us, we're in trouble. We're not in a jet, you know.'

'What do you mean?'

'The Stripe Tiger,' I said, 'the plane you're flying in, has an economic cruising speed of one-forty miles an hour and it's around three thousand miles coast to coast. Work it out.'

'Economy isn't important,' he said.

'It's a matter of petrol consumption, not money.'

'We can't go faster?'

'Never mind,' I said.

'No, you must explain.'

There was no must about it, but as I discovered over the following day or two, he didn't like not knowing. I told him about the relationship between speed and range which is, after all, simple enough : you just use more fuel when you cover the same distance faster; and since there's always a limit to the amount of fuel an aircraft can carry, the way to go further is to go more slowly, which means the econ-omical cruising speed. Except at the start, but—well, it's roughly that.

'So we can go as fast as we like over land where fuel is available?'

'Yes, I suppose so.'

'And it is only over the sea, from Gander to Shannon, that this equation arises?'

'Yes.'

He looked at me reprovingly. 'That is not what you said, Mr Shaw.'

'No,' I said slowly. 'It isn't.'

'I wish to be kept informed.'

'Wish away,' I said. Curious how Lennox's man should have the same Lennox-like ability to rub the wrong way and should do it through the same arrogant, almost con-temptuous mode of speech. My mind ran swiftly over the journey we were to undertake : three thousand miles plus to the eastern seaboard to begin with; a solid day's flying time

87

and more up to Newfoundland, another to Shannon. Then on to England. I was likely to spend four days or more with this character in my hair and I was beginning to think it wouldn't be a particularly attractive experience.

'Can you fly?' I asked.

He shook his head.

'Right.' I tried to say in that one word : leave it to me and don't interfere. One tries, always, to avoid setting up unnecessary tensions inside aircraft, and if this uppity guy would take the hint and back down a trifle, it would be better all round.

'You brought a car, Mr Shaw?'

'As instructed,' I said.

'Then—?'

I nodded, but there was one thing I wanted to do before we left *Sunrise*. Jasmine Yang's body lay sprawled awkwardly and unprettily on the cabin floor and I wasn't going to leave her like that. I bent and took her shoulders to lift her on to the bunk but I hadn't lifted a body before; she was limp and it was strangely difficult. I looked up at Chao Li. 'Take her feet.'

He was watching me with an air of puzzled amusement, as though he could not understand this waste of time and effort.

'Take her feet,' I said again.

'Very well.'

He bent and took her ankles and together we hoisted the body on to the bunk.

Chao Li looked relaxed and confident. I felt ghastly. Strangely enough, I have always lived a reasonably law-abiding life and this kind of thing grated and grated again. Then there was fear. As I walked across to the car with Chao Li it felt as though a million accusing eyes were boring into my back. Also I began to realize what a hell of a position I was in.

I speeded my pace. 'We'd better move.'

'No need to panic,' he said.

'No? Look around. See all these people painting boats? They saw two men and a beautiful girl go aboard *Sunrise*. Now they're watching two men leave.'

He said, 'They will not approach yet. And soon it will be too late. We shall be gone.'

'Look,' I said angrily. 'You were on TV this morning. The whole damn world saw you throw that knife into the policeman's throat. All it needs is for somebody to take the car number.'

'I see,' he said softly. 'I did not know about that.'

We hurried towards the car, opened the doors and climbed in. I'd got the key in the ignition when the idea hit me.

'Hand me the map,' I said.

I spread it out and looked at the bay. We might very well get out to Ignacio, but every mile of the way I'd be expecting somebody to spot Chao Li; every minute I'd be expecting to see the flash of recognition or hear the wail of sirens. What a situation to be in! Leaving a body behind to be found by the first guy who felt like talking to a girl, and then setting off to drive through a metropolis with a wanted murderer whose picture had been televised that morning into every home in the place!

I stared at the map of the bay, checking the positions of the marina and the airfield. 'There's another way out to Ignacio,' I said.

'How?'

'Can you handle a boat?'

Chao Li shook his head.

'We'll just have to be careful,' I said. My finger traced the route up there, across the bay. 'At least, nobody will see us.'

'And when we get ashore?'

'We'll face that when we come to it.'

We got out of the car and went back to the boat. I

skipped down to the deck and into the wheelhouse, wondering about fuel and about the motors. Marine diesels aren't my territory and I wasn't sure how to start them. Then there was a question of fuel.

But nowadays they make everything easy, even for thieves, and *Sunrise* had a self-starter. If you've been around engines any length of time, even the absence of an ignition key doesn't present much of a problem and I was underneath like a rat down a rope, completing the circuit.

'See if there's a manual,' I said.

We found it tucked into a little padded pocket on the forward bulkhead, and I set the throttles as per instructions. When I touched wires and completed the circuit the motors swung over then stopped with a thunk. I tried again with the same result. I wondered how long those diesels had sat there getting cold all through. I gave it a third go, kept the starter motor spinning and listened with my fingers crossed and a little prayer on my lips. It's a vile noise. You know every spin is draining your battery and if it doesn't start soon you're flattened. With diesels it's worse, because the starter motor has that murderous compression to contend with.

But she fired, first on one engine, then on two; throttled back a bit she still roared healthily. The needle of the fuel gauge crawled slowly over the dial and stopped. It was well short of the quarter mark.

'What's the fuel capacity?' I asked.

'It says the range is six hundred miles,' Chao replied.

'Give it to me.'

She used four gallons an hour at low throttle settings and had a tank capacity of ninety. I wondered how accurate the gauge was. If there were ten gallons, two and a half hours' fuel, everything was fine because it wasn't much more than twenty miles across there. If the gauge was on the optimistic side, however, and fuel gauges often are, there was an excellent chance of running out of diesel oil out in the bay.

I said, 'We'll have to get fuel.'

'That's crazy,' Chao said. 'Let's change it. Go by car.'

'We're going by water.' Something inside me said I should stay out of the car and when that particular voice speaks, I listen. 'We'll just have to get fuel.'

'Where?' he said.

I looked round the marina at the endless boats, the forests of masts pricking the pale sky, wondered for a panicky moment whether perhaps *Sunrise* was the only power cruiser and all the rest got their fuel from the air. But then the familiar Esso oval, flying on a high flagstaff, caught my eye. I skipped up on deck and cast off the forward line, then the after one, and pushed *Sunrise* clear of the wall with the boat hook. Maybe it wasn't very seamanlike, but she moved obediently away, the gap increasing slowly until it was seven or eight feet wide. Back in the wheelhouse I moved the lever and *Sunrise* began to chug slowly ahead. I spun the wheel to take her out into the little channel and, keeping the engine revs low, took her gently round to the fuel pontoon. As I came close I cut the drive and let her coast in gently and bump alongside the rubber fenders of the pontoon. A touch astern and she settled. If I hadn't been so frightened I might have felt proud.

A boy came running over. 'Yessir?'

My back was suddenly clammy with sweat. I hadn't the faintest idea where the fuel tank was, and I had precious little cash left. There was probably one last ten-dollar bill in my wallet, but I wasn't sure. Then I breathed a sigh of relief: I had my Diners Club credit card. I could fill her till she burst and pay later.

'Do you take Diners?'

'You name it, we take it,' the kid said.

'Okay. Twenty.'

Then the hair stood up on the nape of my neck. Body— Diner's card—John Shaw!

The kid said, 'Haven't seen *Sunrise* out for quite a while, sir.'

'No,' I said, 'well, you know—'

He looked up at me. 'Yeah. Shame. I hope his leg'll soon be okay, sir. Shame to see a boat like *Sunrise* just sitting. Would you give the fuel cap a turn?'

'Sure.' Deliberately, I pretended to trip as I rose, kicking the bulkhead noisily. 'Damn,' I said. 'My ankle. I've turned it over.' I winced with pain.

'Tough,' he sympathized, coming up like a gymnast on one arm and turning the tank cap with the other. 'Hope it won't bother you.' He passed up the fuel hose and I obediently placed the nozzle in the pipe.

Chao had ducked out of sight into the cabin where the girl's body lay. I took out my wallet; the ten wasn't there. There was a five and a couple of ones. I'd forgotten using the ten to pay for breakfast.

I leaned out of the wheelhouse window.

'Make it ten,' I said.

'Ten, sir?' He looked surprised, then puzzled.

I forced a grin. 'Haven't got my wallet—cash or Diners! All I have is loose change.'

'Sure.' He still looked puzzled. He watched the pump clock come round to ten and stopped it. 'Four-fifty.'

I gave him the five. 'Thank you.'

'No sweat,' he said. He still looked puzzled though, staring up at me as I started the engine.

I went gently astern a little, then brought *Sunrise*'s head cautiously round. The fuel gauge now showed a quarter full: we'd probably have been all right anyway without going through that little nightmare.

I turned *Sunrise* towards the entrance to the marina, went through slowly, then headed out on to the waters of San Francisco Bay. My hands were wet with sweat as I advanced the throttles and *Sunrise* picked up speed. I turned and looked back. On the fuel pontoon, the boy was still looking after us. And he was still looking puzzled.

Eleven

I don't know what the sailing boys would call it, but to me
the water was rough. It wasn't choppy. There wasn't a little
lop from the west, old boy. Waves ran about five feet, crest
to trough, and they smacked against *Sunrise*'s side with the
kind of thud you hear when a boxer digs his fist into a heavy
punch bag. The wind was in the west and blowing at fifteen
to twenty knots and the boat was beam on. We rolled and
pitched a good deal.

The little map they'd given me at Hertz was out on the
wheelhouse table and I was trying to place the local landmarks for a heading; not that it was difficult, but I'm a lot
more accustomed to navigating looking down.

A mile or so off my starboard bow, a garishly painted little
steamer was heading out towards a hog-backed island that
lay dead ahead, and above the thump of *Sunrise*'s diesels I
could hear distant brassy music. I looked at my map and
saw what was happening : the boat was a pleasure cruiser
and the island—I swallowed at the realization—the island
was called Alcatraz! With the wheelhouse window open I
could make out the tune, Sousa's 'Liberty Bell,' and even if
the island is a prison no longer, it seemed a strange choice.

Hertz's map, not unnaturally, was a road map. It showed
the water in a pretty shade of blue, but wasn't informative
about tides, rocks, currents and the rest of the hazards of
water travel. And dimly I remembered a broadcast I'd
heard; one of those hypnotic Alastair Cooke stories, about
Alcatraz and the men who had tried to escape from it. Bits
of it had taken root in my mind, as bits of Alastair Cooke
often do, and I remembered his phrases, about rip tides and
whirlpools running at eight or nine knots, pushed by the
Sacramento River and I reckoned if I was not to be pushed
on to the unfriendly rocks of Alcatraz, I'd better either make

a generous allowance to the east of it or pass to the west. Caution said west and I brought *Sunrise*'s nose round and advanced the throttle a bit more.

She may have been ugly, but that pink-and-white monstrosity was powerful and efficient. With the diesels thumping she tucked her tail down a little tighter in the water and began to hurry, bumping into the wave troughs and riding the crests in a brisk, out-of-my-way manner.

There was a leather loop hanging from the bulkhead by the wheel and when I gathered that it was a kind of sailor's 'George' I clipped it in position and went to the cabin door to dig Chao out.

He was bending over a long roll of bedclothes on the bunk and looked up, grinning. 'Burial at sea, Mr Shaw. One, two, three, swoosh.'

'Leave her,' I said.

'At least, that way we get rid of her.'

'Listen,' I said, 'listen and remember. Wherever there are machines that move, there are eyes watching them. There are eyes everywhere. They're glued to binoculars and telescopes and cameras and they never stop watching.'

'How do you know?'

'Because that's the way the world works,' I said. 'People watch things that move. And in a place like this you'll have every retired sea captain for miles around checking every turn of every screw.'

He said, 'Nonsense. One little boat like this?'

'Try it,' I said. 'You'll have a police launch alongside in ten minutes flat, fishing her out and carting us off to the gas chamber.'

'Then where do we put her?'

'When we get there we leave her on the boat and the boat on a mooring, and we pray nobody comes investigating until we're over the ocean. Clear?'

Chao wasn't happy. Since he believed in efficient killing, he must also believe in efficient disposal of the body and he wasn't getting that. It made me think, though, of the funeral parlour and Rafer Hayes and the label that read 'Pathology Laboratory'. I wondered how Hayes was doing. He'd left me to go straight over to Berkeley.

We swung west in an arc beneath the grey-green rock walls of the island prison where the invading Red Indian demonstrators now sat. I pointed to them and their banners, high on a metal bridge. 'Now they've got this back from the white man,' I said, 'I wonder if they'll get the rest?'

Chao didn't answer for a moment. He was staring at the island and at the people on it, and then his eyes swung round in a slow arc, taking in half the bay. He turned to me. 'I do not think so.'

I looked round, too. Behind us, San Francisco climbed up its hills, sharply white and handsome in the sunlight; to the right the Bay Bridge, all eight miles of it, arrowed across the water to Oakland; to the left, the bright vermilion of the mighty Golden Gate Bridge spanned a mile of the Pacific. All around us man had been at work, building, building, building. I knew how those Indians must feel, but theirs seemed a forlorn cause.

We came out of the lee of Alcatraz, bow lifting, and the whole thing nearly ended there and then. We were making a goodish speed : eighteen to twenty knots. To be truthful about it, my eyes were still glued to the Golden Gate Bridge and I wasn't looking where I was going. I nearly died of shock when the hooter blasted about two million decibels into my ear from a range of about nine inches. I swung round to find that the pleasure steamer I'd seen earlier must have gone the other way round the island and was now bearing down on me hard. She was only about twenty yards away when I saw her and not exactly crawling.

The rule of the road at sea is : pass to the right. I didn't know that, then, however; all I knew was that in a couple of seconds I'd have the bows of that steamer half way up my nostrils. My hand flew to the throttle levers and I gave

95

her all the gun that was going, at the same time spinning her off to port as fast as I could. It didn't help. The skipper of the cruiser, following the rule of the road, went to starboard and once again we were going to meet. This time there was nothing either of us could do about it, but wait. *Sunrise*'s twin propellers bit hard into the dark water, urging us forward in a sudden surge of bright, white foam, but above us the bows of the slower-answering steamer loomed.

'He's going to hit us,' Chao said, his voice low, almost a whisper. He grabbed at the boathook, ready to leap up and fend him off. There wasn't a hope and even a landlubber like me could see it : either we'd crash, or we'd miss by a hairsbreadth.

Those great bows drove remorselessly on, and as the two vessels closed it seemed that in seconds we must be plunged into the icy waters of the bay. Agonizingly the seconds ticked by and I watched her stem, blunt but sharp enough, sheering through the water towards our beam.

Inch by painful inch *Sunrise*'s head came round and the racing propellers forced her forward and round in a fast, tight curve. There wasn't more than inches in it as our stern passed beneath the overhang of the steamer's bows.

Her captain opened the bridge window to bellow at us and we heard him plainly because he'd still got his loudspeaker system switched on and his passengers, male and female, got an earful. As we pulled away, I glanced at Chao Li : he didn't even seem to have been scared. I was lathered in sweat but he was smooth and cool. He was even laughing at the steamer captain's blushes. This, I thought, was a formidable boy. Anyone who could kill as he could, face death as he could, and still stay cool and controlled—I'd rather have that kind on *my* side !

'Keep your eyes skinned,' I told him. 'You never know what may be coming our way after a do like that.'

'Okay.' He nipped up on deck and took a swift look round. One knew instinctively that Chao Li had the same kind of eyes as a seagull : the beady kind that miss very little. He popped his head down again and said, 'All clear so far. Any binoculars?'

A hunt through the wheelhouse cupboards unearthed a powerful pair of Nikkons that would make a police cutter look like the Q.E.2. I left him up there, looking, while we battered on across the bay waters. I have the usual non-sailor's total inability to recognize landmarks from the sea and I kept my eyes glued to the Hertz map, trying to identify everything as we passed it. It may sound easy, but it's not. When you're on the water, all land looks alike and there's a two-dimensional effect that's highly confusing, even to experienced seamen. Sir Francis Drake sailed right past the Golden Gate without realizing it was the entrance to a bay, so you'll gather what I mean.

'Anything stirring?' I looked up to where Chao Li was perched.

'Not sure,' he said. 'I'm watching a boat that's going our way.'

'Is she? Let's see if she changes course.' I spun round the wheel until the bow of *Sunrise* swung through ninety degrees and we were heading out towards Berkeley and showing him our beam. 'Well?'

'Wait a minute.' Chao Li was staring through the binoculars. 'Yes. She's changing direction.'

'Following us?'

'Heading us off.'

I slung the leather loop over a spoke and climbed up. 'Give me the binoculars.'

When I'd found her and brought her into focus, I knew we were in trouble. She was bigger than *Sunrise*, and she sat in the water in that pointed, purposeful way MTBs have : it bespeaks big, powerful engines. She was plain white and though she doubtless had a name somewhere on her bow, I couldn't read it. But I could see people aboard her, several of them.

I clambered swiftly into the wheelhouse well, took the loop off and swung the wheel until *Sunrise*'s bow came round to our original heading, then I opened the throttles wide, feeling her surge beneath me.

'She's turning after us.'

'Who the hell is it?' I said. 'Who the hell would be after us? And who the hell would know where we were?'

Chao Li jerked his thumb in the direction of the cabin. 'She knew.'

'She followed me,' I said. 'She knew where I was staying last night, and she followed me.'

'That's probably how she knew. Do you know who she was?'

I said, 'I'd be glad if somebody would tell me.'

'I told you she was the mistress of a notorious Chinese gang leader in San Francisco,' he said. 'So if you're wondering who *they* are . . .'

'Are they gaining?' I said.

'It's hard to know. Yes, they're gaining.'

'You know this bloody place,' I said. 'How do we get away?'

He slid suddenly in beside me. 'I have an idea. Steer left.'

'Left?' I said. I spun the wheel. Any talk about port and starboard could wait. 'Where are we heading for?'

'The Golden Gate,' he said.

I stared at him. 'But there's nothing the other side, nothing except five thousand miles of ocean.'

'You're wrong,' he said softly. 'There's escape.'

Sunrise swung rapidly round and I pointed her bow at the more northerly of the bridge's two soaring towers.

Then I saw it. 'You're crazy,' I said savagely.

Thick fog was rolling through the Golden Gate.

Twelve

The twin diesels thumped beneath our feet as *Sunrise* forced her way through the water, towards the white wall of vapour that was already shrouding the bases of the towers. I began to swing the wheel again, but Chao Li stopped me.

'Don't be a fool,' he said. 'It's the only chance we've got.'

'Do you realize what it will be like in there? Everything from liners to tugs milling about hooting and tooting and ringing bells. It's suicide!'

I stuck my head out of the wheelhouse window, staring back at the white boat that was now so obviously on our tail; she was going like a dingbat. While we had behaved like a sheep, dashing this way and that, she was playing the sheepdog. We'd sailed along two sides of a right-angled triangle: she was cutting along the hypotenuse.

I shook my head. 'Okay, but—'

'There's a strong current out here,' Chao Li said suddenly.

'I know,' I said, 'we've been fighting it.'

'No, that's not what I meant. It comes from the Sacramento River so it should help us going this way. Move a bit to the left.'

Obediently I nosed *Sunrise* over; within a few seconds I was feeling the difference: the pick-up in speed was readily apparent, and with the kind of power we'd got, the current under the stern didn't make handling any more difficult or make her respond less quickly to the rudder.

'Better,' Chao Li said.

I nodded. 'How far away are they now?'

He bobbed up and looked. 'Four, perhaps five hundred yards. Distances are difficult to judge.'

'Take the wheel,' I said. I went up into the top decking, looking aft. The boat behind us was going like the hammers of hell, twin quiffs of white climbing away from her bow.

And somebody was balanced, crouching, on her bow.

Near me something splintered and I jumped in surprise and turned : a chunk of the cabin roofing had been torn away. Then I heard the thin, high crack of a rifle shot. Quickly I ducked below again, but another bullet smacked into the bulkhead beside me.

'They're gaining fast,' I said grimly. Ahead, through the screen, the white vapour rolled nearer, but it was moving slowly. We'd a good half mile to go.

Chao Li stuck his head out for another look and a bullet bounced off *Sunrise*'s forward decking, whining off into the advancing fog. *Sunrise* raced ahead making the better part of thirty knots, including the help the current was providing, but he said the other boat was closing the gap quickly.

'Rocks?' I asked.

'I don't think so.'

'Think's no good,' I said. 'Try to remember everything you've heard. And what you've seen.'

'It's a wide span between the headland and the first tower,' he said. 'Three hundred yards or more. I remember seeing boats go through. Lots of them.'

'We're about to trust your memory.' The fog wall loomed closer now, a great hill of swirling white that crept inexorably forward. Four hundred—three hundred—two hundred —the first swirling fronds of vapour reached out towards us as *Sunrise* plunged at full speed into the dense fog bank, still a hundred yards clear of the other boat.

'Tell me the moment they're out of sight,' I snapped.

Chao Li climbed up and promptly ducked as a bullet sang past his head. I was half-turnèd, watching him, as he raised it again more cautiously. He waited, tense and still. He said 'Now!'

I counted slowly to five to make sure I was deep into the fog and not about to run out of it into a sudden clear patch, then looked upward. Dimly in the heavy vapour I could still see the massive steelwork of the bridge tower climbing to the sky just off my port bow. The other boat, unable to see me, must follow my wake. On top of that, the current would be carrying my wake, whole and entire, along at eight knots. At the speed I was going it was a lunatic trick but there would be only one chance and I took it.

I spun the wheel hard to port and for a sickening moment I thought *Sunrise* was not going to answer. The tower loomed terrifyingly close as her bow moved a little, then steadied, then moved again, inching round with agonizing slowness. But it *was* coming round and *Sunrise* was heeled a few degrees over as she slewed across the current in a skidding turn.

I stared skyward again, but even the massive bulk of the bridge tower was now swallowed in the fog. All I could do was to pray and wait, with my stomach taut and my nerves singing like A-strings. Then rearing out of the fog, huge and terrifyingly close, came the great wall of the concrete fender that guarded the tower's foundations against the powerful currents. It was only feet away. *Sunrise* was fighting her way round, her screws racing, dragging herself across the massive curved front of the fender, and the air was full of the hiss of water and the thump of the motors. For long seconds I was sure we were going to smash head-on into the wall, but then *Sunrise* gained movement across the current.

We almost made it, too. We missed only by inches; the current shoving against *Sunrise*'s beam stopped her bow coming round enough to take us clear, and with a dreadful grating noise, her stern swung against the fender and the starboard propeller fouled the concrete. You could hear the blades stripping.

And then, naturally, as the port screw bit, our bow was flung round against the fender. There was a splintering crunch, then *Sunrise* floated free. I swung her wheel, to try to straighten her, but nothing happened. The rudder, too, must have been damaged when the stern smacked against the fender. *Sunrise* was completely disabled.

Now everything depended upon the caution of the man at the wheel of the following boat. I could imagine what was in his mind as he plunged into the fog bank, lost sight of us and raced on with only our wake to follow. Then, when our wake swung sharply to port, the question of whether to follow : a question that had to be answered the moment it was asked. I stood there, my hands on the useless wheel and looked at Chao Li. His head was a little to one side and he was listening as the seconds, the fractions of seconds, inched by.

We heard it then, sudden and sharp and amazingly near : the great crashing of smashed wood and tearing metal as the following boat smacked at full speed into that fender. She couldn't have been more than fifty yards away, but the rearing walls of the fender were between us and we couldn't see. We heard, though : we heard yells of distress that were faint and grew fainter. I knew what had happened : with her bow smashed in she would have filled with water in seconds and gone down like a stone. As *Sunrise* drifted in the swirling water beyond the fender, somebody floated by unseen but screaming for help, afloat but carried helplessly by the current.

There was nothing we could do. *Sunrise* was unmanageable now, swinging and swirling in the current with one screw racing and her rudder gone and the main stream whipping us out to the Pacific.

'The boat,' I yelled to Chao Li.

He climbed out of one side of the wheelhouse well, I out of the other; together we went to the stern where *Sunrise*'s surprisingly large tender hung on davits. The oars were tucked inside her, but though the transom showed the marks of the outboard screw clamps, the outboard wasn't there and there would be no hope of rowing in a rip tide of this strength.

'It must be somewhere,' I said. 'Search.'

'Maybe they take it away every time.'

We found it stowed in an upright housing in the after well, along with a tool kit and a five-gallon can of petrol: it was a forty-horse Johnson that would fairly blast the dinghy through the water. Thank God *Sunrise*'s owner either liked water-skiing or had girl-friends who did. While Chao Li held the motor steady, I sloshed in the petrol, and together we struggled with it across the whirling deck to the davits, while *Sunrise* spun in the racing water, and clamped it in position. Then I did what I should have done before: I went forward and cut the engines. When I came back, Chao Li had the dinghy's bows tilted down at about thirty degrees and her stern was in the air. Davits are always tricky, they say, and these were murder, but I finally unjammed the lowering mechanism of the port davit and we got her into the water and leapt in after her.

I reached and cast her loose forward, then aft, and the dinghy whipped instantly away from *Sunrise*. In a second a big gap had opened and we couldn't have got back if we'd wanted to.

Now I had to get that Johnson started before the current took us half-way to Pago-Pago. The dinghy was flung about as I hauled on the rope. No response. Another pull. Again, no response. I pulled and pulled until sweat ran off me, but that damned engine stayed dead and there's nothing in this whole world half so inanimate as an engine that won't fire. I had a feeling somewhere deep in my guts, that it would come down to carburettor trouble and it did. Thank God for those tools! While we tossed and swirled on the increasingly high wave crests that grew where the current met the ocean water, I had that damned thing out and dismantled it on my knee, wiping out the float chamber with my handkerchief, putting it together, having a quick gander at the plug, which seemed to spark well enough when I turned over the engine on the starter rope. I put the carburettor back, took a deep breath, and pulled. Nothing. I pulled again. Nothing. The third time she roared like the start of a Grand Prix. I lowered the shaft into the water and engaged the drive.

Suddenly there was control again.

It felt wonderful, after all those minutes of fear and despair, to be able to turn the dinghy and point her.

I grinned at Chao Li and swung the dinghy round, across the current, almost capsizing her in the process through sheer carelessness, and began to head back for the bridge.

'The other way, I think,' Chao Li said.

'Why?'

'Our friends may have friends.'

'So?'

'Land up the coast, then cross to Ignacio.'

I remembered something. 'Airflo promised to send a car.'

'All the better,' Chao Li said.

I turned the dinghy round again and pointed her nose at the coast of China.

'What's the ocean like out there?' I asked.

For the first time he smiled. 'Very big,' he said. He didn't know then, and neither did I, but we were to learn very soon. Before long, the bow of the dinghy was lifting and smacking down again as the incoming waves came pushing underneath, but I kept her pointing out to sea for several minutes, until I judged there would be enough water for manoeuvring room. Then I swung her northward.

It was uncanny, sitting there among the Pacific rollers in a little boat in the middle of a fog so thick that visibility wasn't much more than ten feet. Uncanny and frightening. It was stupid, too, to be going so fast. I turned the throttle down, staring forward, hoping for a break in the fog; hoping too that I hadn't been turned, without my knowledge, by the swirling currents, and was now heading out to sea.

I crouched in the stern with my hand on the tiller trying to spread out my senses like a defence line, listening and staring. I was tasting, too; tasting the coppery flavour of fear that filled my mouth. Anything could be happening within feet of us and I hadn't any way of knowing whether a rocky outcrop was about to rip the bottom out of the boat or a ten-thousand-ton cargo ship was going to run us down.

'Get up in the bow,' I told Chao Li.

He moved forward, crouching on the little forward seat and staring over the plunging bow.

I could hardly complain; the fog had saved us when nothing else could, but how ironic if it had swallowed us not, as I had thought, temporarily, but in some dark and implacable way, permanently. But please let it lift now! Please!

We must have run for a couple of miles when Chao Li suddenly leapt forward in the bow, staring forward like some huge figurehead in the tiny boat. Then he turned.

'Back! Get back!'

I didn't ask why; just twisted the throttle grip and swung her to port as a great wave lifted under us, combing towards massive rocks that reached suddenly out at us from the fog. We must be almost ashore!

The dinghy hung poised for a long moment on top of that massive, rising sweep of water, then slid back into the trough as the Johnson bit, turning us harder, sweeping us into the face of the next wave, carrying us back, away from the rocks.

It had been near, but not too near; dangerous but not desperate. But as we hit the faces of the oncoming waves, I realized I was completely disorientated. It was probably true that the waves were rolling in from some generally westerly direction, but they might not be. They could be rolling up the coast, or down it.

We were lost. And unless we were either lucky enough to be heading for a nice sandy shore, or the fog lifted soon, we were in bad trouble.

Thirteen

For twenty minutes we'd been cruising ahead on half-throttle and we weren't any wiser. The fog still lay all round us, dense and cold; it was like being packed in clammy cotton wool. On top of that, neither of us had the faintest idea which way we were heading.

'How much do you know about this coast?' I asked.

Chao Li shrugged. 'Very little. There are beaches a bit farther north.'

'How far north?'

'Ten, twelve, fifteen miles. I'm not sure.'

'What about here?'

'I don't know,' Chao Li said simply. 'Most of this coast-line is army, or navy or something. I think it's rocky, though. How much petrol have we?'

How much indeed! We'd sloshed it merrily into the tank from that jerrycan, but how much had we poured in and how much had we spilt? I picked up the jerrycan, shook it and heard the unmistakable sound of a little liquid sloshing about in a large vessel.

'Not so good,' I said. 'And these big outboards guzzle the stuff.' I reached over and cut the engine. The moment I'd done it, even while the last spluttering drops were still being blown out of the cooling system, I knew I'd made a stupid mistake. Another ten seconds confirmed it. It's one thing to ride a heavy, rolling swell in a small boat: it's not pleasant, but it's not terrifying; when the boat has neither sail nor engine to keep it up to the sea, it's a very different matter. The dinghy was suddenly being lifted, turned, spun, tilted and toyed with like one of those spinning cars at fairgrounds. She wallowed, beam on to the rolling ranges of water, and several times came close to capsizing as the boat broadsided into a deep trough and rolled dangerously up the oncoming wall.

Immediately I set about starting her again, struggling to hold my balance with one knee on the bucking seat while I heaved on the rope. The trouble was that I couldn't get a decent tug at it: every time I began to pull the handle, the boat went helter-skeltering down into the greasy depths of a trough and I had to switch all my strength to keeping my balance and staying aboard. I was like those pictures you see of rodeo riders sitting on the necks of bulls for a few seconds. Finally, though, I did manage to get a decent pull at that rope and the Johnson roared. I kept the revs at not much more than tick-over, turned to put my bottom on the seat, and felt my stomach thud down against my pelvic bones. Chao Li had vanished!

I raised myself as high as I dared and looked round through three-sixty degrees of rapidly undulating ocean. Nothing in sight, and already the boat must have moved yards from the spot where he'd fallen over. I thought quickly, trying to decide which way the ocean could have moved the boat, and which way it would be taking Chao Li.

'Chao Li-i-i!' I shouted his name a dozen times, knowing that in the endless swishing of the water, any answering shout would be lost, but hoping. There was no answer.

The only other way was to circle. I brought her round in a tight turn, then set the rudder so that the boat would make a circle about a hundred yards in diameter, and went along the curve slowly, searching every visible inch of the sea. It was precious little; fog still kept visibility down to twelve or fifteen yards and I knew I could easily go past Chao Li without seeing him or hearing his shouts. He could even be in the middle of the circle without my knowing.

'Chao Li!' I called repeatedly, pausing after each shout to listen, but only the sounds of the ocean and the steady rhythm of the Johnson motor came to my ears. I had no idea when I completed that first circle and when the next one began : I didn't know where I was facing! I only knew that if I didn't find Chao Li soon he'd be dead. Then I thought I saw something floating and perhaps I did; maybe a chunk of driftwood or something that went floating away into the fog. By the time I had turned the boat and gone after it, it had vanished and I was in despair, no longer knowing that I was even close to the spot where Chao Li had vanished. I brought the boat round and tried to retrace its wake, but the bubbles had been dispersed instantly in the vast movements of the ocean water.

I called and called. I kicked the jerrycan endlessly, hoping the hollow thud would carry farther through the fog than my now-hoarsening voice. I enlarged the circle a bit, widening the area of search, chug-chugging round, knowing that I might be passing close; that he might see me or hear me and be too weak either to swim towards the boat or make me hear his cries.

I did hear, though. It was very faint, and it came only once and I think I must have been on top of the humping curve of one great swell while he was on another. I tried to pinpoint it and took the boat in the direction from which I thought I had heard it come.

'Where are you?' I shouted. 'Call, for God's sake, call!' After a hundred, a hundred and fifty yards, I began to circle again. 'Chao Li! Chao Li!'

He shouted again, closer now; I took the boat carefully towards the sound, banging the petrol can with my shoe. Then I saw him, at a point away to my right where the fog and the water met and sight ended. His arms were raised high in the air and he was trying to shout, but even that half-glimpse of him was enough to tell me he was exhausted. The boat, however, was facing the wrong way and as I struggled to turn it, he was being swept away into the fog. I grabbed the jerrycan, swung it back and forth, and hurled it as far as I could after him, then brought the boat round. He was clinging to the can when I found him, strength gone, but with the buoyancy holding him up.

Eventually, and with difficulty, I dragged him into the boat, where he lay on the bottom boards gasping and grunting with the pain of aching lungs and weary limbs. I got the petrol can, too, before the sea slid it away out of sight.

About ten minutes later, we ran, quite suddenly, out of the fog into the pale gleam of autumn sunshine. One minute, I could see a few yards, the next the horizon was clean and clear. Aglow with relief, I looked round the heaving sea. Behind us the thick white vapour of the fog still clung to the surface of the water. Ahead lay the coast : rocks and hills as far as I could tell, the ground rising towards the distinct rearing shape of a mountain.

'Are you all right?'

'Thank you,' Chao Li said. 'I'm very—' he coughed deeply and wearily.

'What's the mountain over there?' I interrupted.

He turned awkwardly to look. 'Mount Tamalpais,' he said. 'Other side of the Golden Gate. A few miles north.'

I headed the boat towards the shore. We seemed to be about three miles out, which was about two and a half miles too much. I brought her to a heading roughly north by west, looking for one of the beaches Chao Li had talked about. We were still being buffeted by the water, but now it was exhilarating, rather than frightening. I wound up the motor, increasing our speed. A glance at my watch told me it was now nearly two-thirty and if I didn't get to the airport soon, there'd be no flying time left.

Chao was recovering a bit now. He dragged himself to a sitting position on the bottom boards and sat there for a little while, still coughing up the sea water that had reached his lungs. He looked lousy, but I think that may have had something to do with his Chinese skin : instead of looking pale and foul, he looked pale yellow and foul.

Ahead I saw a headland and a line of rocks and had to swing sharply out to sea to go round them, but I kept boring on to the north and as we came round them, twenty minutes later, Chao Li, by now sitting in the bow, pointed. 'Over there.'

My eyes followed the direction of his pointing arm and as a wave hoisted us high in the air I saw a pale gleaming line at the water's edge. 'What is it?'

'Sand,' Chao Li said. 'It's silver.'

He was shivering hard but, by now, more or less all right. What he needed more than anything was the feel of land under his feet and a change of clothes. Riding up on another swell, I saw the silvery, sandy beach more distinctly : it was long, maybe two or three miles altogether, and fringed with trees. Part way along there seemed to be a village of sorts.

Chao Li said, 'I think its name is Stinson Beach. There's another place called Bolinas. I think it's Stinson, though.'

'Don't you know?' I said.

'I told you. I believe it is Stinson Beach.'

'Is there a road?'

'I don't know.'

I looked at him. 'You don't know a hell of a lot for somebody who comes from San Francisco.'

'I don't,' he said shortly.

'Then where?'

He turned and looked at me; the dirty yellow colour of his skin was less dirty and more yellow. 'It is not your business, Mr Shaw.'

I said, 'Okay. I suppose people like you become *persona non grata* in more places than one.'

He didn't answer, but a moment later he was pointing north to where a forest of high antennae pointed like latticework trees at the sky. 'That I know,' he said. He waited, making me ask.

'Martian?' I said.

'It's the RCA Pacific communication station,' he said, staring at me for a moment. Then, 'Why Martian?'

I kept my face straight. 'Just wondered.'

Chao Li frowned and a little while later I was frowning, too, as the realization sank in that I would have to take the boat in among the surf that rolled into Stinson Beach. A mile out it was a high swell rolling towards the land, but it became pretty savage surf closer to the beach and, although I couldn't see it, I was pretty sure the waves landed hard.

'Better be ready to swim again,' I said grimly as we came nearer and the little boat began to fly on the wave tops with the sea beneath her stern. There was precious little control then; all it needed was a flick of the water and we'd have been tumbled in a second into the flying waves. In the back of my mind an idea had formed that I could take the boat in by waiting for the right wave and gunning the engine so that we rode in on it. I tried it and damn nearly killed us as the powerful motor tried to tilt us off the crest and into the trough ahead; after that I sat tight, tried to keep her straight and hoped. And as it happened, the ride was more frightening than the landing. At the last, the boat was carried along quickly, canting hard to one side and with her bow slewing round. The wave towered above us and smashed down and put us down reasonably gently on the silver sand. Thankfully I cut the motor before the sea had the chance to have second thoughts and spin the racing propeller into us. I even managed to get out without the water coming up over my shoes; and then together we dragged the boat up the beach a few yards. She'd done well for us, that little boat, and it seemed a shame to leave her, but we dumped her on the sand and walked away.

But not unobserved. I imagine Stinson Beach is a pretty popular spot in the summertime for surfers and sun bathers. It was certainly pretty, with a line of willows, of all trees, facing the ocean. And from one of the houses somebody was hurrying towards us, wanting to know if we were in trouble.

He was in his sixties, lean and wiry and lined, skin darkened by prolonged exposure. 'Been watchin' ya,' he said. 'Saw you was in trouble.'

I made myself grin at him and lied hard. 'Rougher than we thought,' I said. 'I guess—'

'Where you from?'

I tried to remember the name of the other place Chao Li had mentioned, somewhere just up the coast, but for the life of me I couldn't, and I didn't know any other names. 'San Francisco.'

'Knew you did,' he said. 'Gotta be crazy to come out through the Golden Gate day like this.'

'I'm afraid so,' I said. 'We didn't realize.'

Chao Li hadn't said a word; he was being as self-effacing as any man can be who is one of only three and dripping wet into the bargain.

The old man turned to him. 'Can tell your partner's a stranger here, but you ain't, I reckon. Shouldn't let anybody out here, day like this.'

'I didn't know,' Chao Li said. He didn't say it apologetically, just rather flatly as though he couldn't really be bothered with the conversation.

The old man looked at him. He was puzzled, and not hiding it; but I didn't think he was connecting Chao Li with the telecast. It was Chao Li's attitude that surprised him.

'Oh well,' the old man said, 'nobody's dead, I suppose, so it's okay.' He looked up at me accusingly. 'But you'll know better next time.'

'I certainly will,' I said heartily. 'It was a very nasty experience, Mr—?'

'Boorstin,' he said. 'Been watching you through the glasses and gettin' ready to call the coastguard.'

I said, 'I'm John Shaw, and this is my friend, James Young. What we really need now is dry clothes and a phone. Even just a phone.'

'C'mon.' He strode off up the beach.

Chao Li held back a bit, nudged me and spoke very softly. 'Don't get involved.'

'You'll die of pneumonia,' I murmured back. I was hunting in my pockets for the note the chauffeur had given me of Airflo's number.

The old man turned. 'C'mon. I can maybe find you somethin' dry while you get these damp things off.' We followed him up the beach, our feet sinking into the soft, fine sand, towards the line of willows. 'Unusual, but pretty,' he said. He was pointing to the trees.

'Oh yes,' I said.

'Yeah. Reckon I can find you some dry clothes.'

'The phone,' I said.

'Sure. Up there. You go call while I take your partner. That's where I live,' and he pointed to a grey-washed cottage nearby.

I hurried to the phone and called Airflo.

'Where the hell have you been, pal?' Newton said.

'It's a long story.'

He chuckled. 'Yeah, it's a great town for broads. Tell you the truth we thought they must have shanghaied you off the Barbary Coast.'

'They tried,' I said. 'They really did. What about the Tiger?'

'All ready. Where are you?'

'Stinson Beach.'

'And you need a car?' He paused. 'Stinson Beach?'

'Yup.'

'I'll send,' he said. 'And I won't ask. My driver should be with you in a half hour or so.'

'Thanks. I appreciate it.'

'Oh, John.'

'Yes.'

'Marion's tickled to death.'

I said, 'Is he now?' wondering why. Marion ought to have been furious, because the precious parts for Marion's precious Rolls had vanished into the depths of Chinatown. 'Why?'

'The new differential,' Newton said. 'It's a hell of a story, but I'll tell you when you get here.'

I put the phone down. The parts had reached Marion Capote after all!

Fourteen

Old man Boorstin turned out to have a wife of similarly straightforward manner, and she, too, thought it was plumb crazy to come out through the Golden Gate in a boat like that. She went on about it at length. Fortunately she was one of those women who work while they talk. There should be more of them. While Chao Li sat hunched over his mug of hot coffee, she rinsed his clothes through in fresh water, then set them drying on hot-water pipes. And all the time she kept talking, which was useful because it meant we didn't have to. She felt strongly about the cost of the Apollo programme and Medicare and she hoped the police would catch the man who killed the cop over at Berkeley.

'He was Chinese, too,' she said. 'Did you know him?'

Chao Li said, 'No.'

'Okay.' The woman shrugged pointedly. This was how some people repaid kindness. 'I wondered. That's all.'

'The Chinese community in San Francisco is the largest outside Asia,' Chao Li said.

'Okay, okay. I only asked.'

I looked at my watch and at Chao Li's trousers steaming gently on the water pipe. 'Nice here.'

'It was,' Boorstin said.

'Was is the word!' His wife took up the tale of invasion and litter and noise and a general destruction of the beauties of the place by all the week-end riders from San Francisco. 'Shouldn't never have built that bridge!'

'Golden Gate Bridge?' I said.

'Yeah. Blasted thing. Knew it wouldn't do no good. Time was it was peaceful out here. Just a few folks and the mountain.'

'It doesn't look exactly busy now.'

'You should see it in the summer—' she was away again. By the time the monologue ended, Chao Li's clothes were stiffly dry and I had seen the green Lincoln slide by the window.

I said, 'Our car's here, I think,' and went and opened the door, waving until the chauffeur saw me, and began to back towards us. When I turned Chao Li was dressed and ready behind me, rumpled but recovered.

We thanked the Boorstins and were warned solemnly about coming out through the Golden Gate again in small boats.

'I won't,' I said. 'I promise.'

When we were in the car, Boorstin rattled something against the window and I opened it.

'Your boat.'

'My God,' I said, 'thanks for reminding me.' I had forgotten, so the surprise wasn't entirely feigned.

'Thought you had.'

'Look,' I said, 'could you keep an eye on it for a day or two. I'll be in touch.'

'Don't forget now,' he said.

'I won't.' They were very kind, those two, and I treated them shabbily. I must write one day, and explain, but I wonder if they'd believe me . . .

Newton's chauffeur eased the Lincoln on to the road. Had sir been boating?

Sir had. Sir also noticed that the edge of a patch of sticking plaster stuck down below the chauffeur's cap. 'Been fighting?' I said.

'Somebody slugged me,' he said.

'They wanted the differential and the brake shoes?'

I watched his eyes flick up to the mirror. 'That's right,

sir. You **knew**?'

'Mr Newton told me. What happened?'

'Just after I left you I stopped at some lights. Guy slid in beside me with a gun and grabbed my keys. Handed them out through the window to another guy, then slugged me. When I woke up the parts were missing. Nothing else.'

'But they turned up this morning?'

'Yes, sir. The parcel was at the main door.'

I said, 'Any ideas?'

'None, sir, except—well, they must have thought it was something else they stole.'

'That,' I said, 'was how I saw it.'

We drove on in silence for a bit and it was then that I suddenly realized I was in trouble again. I'd been told it was important that I shouldn't be seen to have a passenger, yet here I was rolling up at the airfield not just with a passenger but with a Chinese passenger. The original arrangement had been that I'd find Chao Li aboard the aircraft, but the original arrangement had been cancelled and I'd been told to collect. Well, I'd done that; but did it mean I was now able to take him aboard? The answer, if only from the point of view of my own security, had to be no. Yet somebody at the airfield knew about Chao Li. Somebody, indeed, in Airflo knew about him and had been busy, overnight, chatting with Lennox.

I glanced at Chao Li, who was sitting quietly in the corner of the vast rear seat, watching the countryside go by. He seemed totally unconcerned. I reflected savagely that he could be as unconcerned as he bloody well liked—I'd finished. For this little perisher's sake I'd been kidnapped, interrogated, beaten, chased several times and damn near killed more than once; and I was an accessory either to or after the fact of murder. Then there were the little matters of theft and of damage to boats, attempts to dispose of bodies, etc. I'd agreed to fly him and I would fly him, but somebody else could get him aboard the plane.

I said to the chauffeur, 'You might let my friend off when we get to the airport gates. He's being picked up there.'

'Okay, sir. I was wondering whether you had a passenger.'

I laughed. 'Nobody's that crazy! You have to be nuts to do it for money.' I didn't look at Chao Li.

'Yeah.' The chauffeur grinned.

'Mind you,' I said, 'if he was about thirty-six, twenty-two, thirty-four, I might squeeze him in somewhere.'

He said, 'That kind either go Pan-Am first class, or by private jet. Planning on taking off now, sir?'

'I think so. Make a bit of distance tonight.' I tried to be casual. As far as this chauffeur, or anybody else I talked to was concerned, I'd been a bad lad in San Francisco and was now heading home, tail between legs, and trying to make up time. It was the kind of story people believed. 'Makes sense?'

'Well, sir,' he pondered for a moment. 'There's an awful lot of high ground in the Sierra Nevadas.'

I said, 'Be positive. Go, or not go?'

'Not go,' he said. 'Not unless the fuzz was on my tail.' Through the rear view mirror I could see his grin.

'We-e-e-ll-ll you see,' I said, 'there's this little girl in Denver.'

'That's different, sir. No time like the present.'

A couple of minutes later, the car stopped at the airport gates and Chao Li got off, murmuring thanks. We left him there and rolled round the approach road to Airflo's building. As the car stopped, a tall man whose fair, brushed hair was greying fast, came striding towards the building from the tarmac, saw the car and came across.

'Mr Shaw? Don Newton.'

I got out and shook hands. 'Thanks for sending the car, Mr Newton.'

He took my arm, turning me, and pointed. 'There she is. Like her?'

The Stripe Tiger stood on the tarmac two hundred yards

or so away, obviously brand new, her paintwork shining. 'Very nice,' I said. She had an unusual configuration : high-wing monoplane, twin-engined but with an engine at each end of the cabin, one pushing and one pulling. The tail structure had the twin boom set-up of the old wartime Lightning.

'Wait till you fly her,' Newton said enthusiastically. 'She's quite a baby, I'm telling you. Marion reckons she's about the best Stripe have made.'

I grinned. 'Praise from Caesar !'

'Yeah, but it's not just opinion. That Tiger has beautiful flying characteristics, I'm here to tell you—' he rattled on as he whisked me along a corridor into an office and pointed to an arm-chair upholstered in soft pale green leather. The office was executive—a page from *Playboy*, costly but characterless. You see offices like that all over the world : they cost the earth to furnish, but they never reflect the personality of the occupant, and are merely to confer prestige. That's because the occupant is expected to change fairly frequently. Newton clearly loved it, which told me a certain amount about Newton.

I sat and sipped coffee when the girl brought it. Booze wasn't going to be offered and I'm not very sure whether I'd have drunk it, but at that moment I wanted whisky. As I sat and listened to Newton's easy flow of executive chatter, I was not thinking of the massive hunt for Chao Li that was going on in San Francisco, or wondering whether *Sunrise* had yet been found with Jasmine Yang's body aboard. Another and nastier thought had hit me : the people who coshed Newton's chauffeur and grabbed me could, if they had wished, have got at the aircraft. Airflo was certainly being used by Lennox and it was also either used or watched closely by somebody else. A large air ferry outfit will always be a natural for intelligence operations; why, therefore, should Lennox be the only one who'd got in? Which left me thinking about slackened nuts and rotten soldering and worn control cables and the nastiest kind of death there is : the one you have to wait for as the aircraft takes its time going down out of control. Twice I've heard men going through it, listened to their voices on the radio. One was a pal. He said, very calmly but with infinite sadness, 'If anyone's listening, goodbye.' I've had occasional nightmares about it ever since.

'When did the Tiger come over from the factory?' I asked.

'Yesterday morning,' Newton said. 'To give us time to bolt the cabin tank in position and so on.'

'So it's been standing out ever since?'

'No,' he said slowly. 'It was in the hangar last night. Something bothering you?'

I looked at him, wondering. I didn't know a thing about Don Newton except that he talked a lot and was a bit too proud of his office and his car. Better not to rely on him. It was a feeling, really, not a judgement.

'No,' I said. 'I just like them better when they've flown a few hours. Anybody had her up yet?'

He nodded. 'Took her myself, this morning. Only half an hour. Sweet, though.'

'Fine,' I said. It was anything but fine, I didn't like the smell one bit, but short of telling them to take the Tiger to bits and put it together again, or refusing to fly, there was nothing to be done. I put down the coffee cup. 'Okay. I'm ready.'

He looked surprised. 'You're leaving now?'

I said, 'There's still a bit of light left.'

'Come on, then. I'll do a couple of familiarization circuits with you.'

We walked out of the building towards the aircraft with Newton still chattering.

I said, 'Funny about the Rolls-Royce parts.'

He simply switched monologues. 'Yeah, unbelievable. I mean, sapping a guy like that to steal them, then sending the parts back here. I mean, it's crazy.' I could imagine him telling the story again and again without ever stopping to think about it.

He switched again as we climbed into the cabin of the Tiger, describing overthoroughly its instrumentation and its sundry charms. He could fly, though. When he lifted her off, it was admirably smooth and easy and if I'd been less worried about its mechanics I'd have admired the Tiger too.

I watched him fly her for a few minutes, then took the pole. 'I have control,' I said.

I flew her in a couple of tight turns, just getting the feel of the controls. She had nice light well-balanced ailerons and elevators. Then I brought her in for a roller landing.

'Lands short, eh?' Newton shouted.

He was right, too. She could have stopped inside a hundred and fifty yards if I'd really been trying. I kept the roller going and eased her up. 'Pretty.'

'You don't even need a nickel,' Newton bellowed at me, 'you can land on a dime.'

'Fine.' I took her round again while Newton described the various functions and showed me where everything was stowed, including the rubber dinghy. When he'd done that, I brought her in for another landing and taxied on to the perimeter track.

'Okay?' Newton said.

'Yes, I'll come and sign now.'

We climbed out and went back to Airflo's block. 'You fly well, Mr Shaw,' Newton said.

'I've done a certain amount,' I said. 'You're not so bad yourself.'

When I signed the provisional acceptance paper which said nothing was wrong when I took her over, I was praying it was true. As I straightened, he smiled. 'Flight plan?'

'Sorry,' I said. 'Haven't had time.'

He glanced at me, then at his watch. 'Normally we like to feed the flight plan in an hour before take-off.'

I said, 'So do we. There just wasn't time. And from a field like this—' I didn't finish.

'We're in the San Francisco high density area,' he said.

'Let's do it and feed it verbally to the tower,' I said. 'Somebody can take the form over later.'

We went back into the office and he hauled out a great flat file of charts. This should have been, and was, child's play to him. Airflo must have briefed plenty of pilots taking Stripe aircraft to Europe.

'Right,' he said, his finger tracing the route. 'Across the bay to Oakland VOR, then outbound on Victor two-four-four to Stockton. That's where you leave the high density area, okay?' I nodded.

'Then it's up to seventeen thousand,' he said, 'still on two-four-four to Hanksville, Utah.'

'Seventeen thousand!'

His finger came down on the chart. 'The Sierra Nevadas are high, the White Mountains go over fourteen thousand and you're up to thirteen or fourteen in the Wasatch area. Not to mention the Rockies.'

'Fuel,' I said. 'Are we talking about Denver in one hop?'

'Right. You can make it.'

I said, 'Look. She's going to use a hell of a lot getting to seventeen thousand. If there's any question of fuel shortage I'll stage somewhere.'

'You won't run short. She carries a hundred and twenty-eight gallons. Even if you use forty getting up to seventeen thousand you'll still have the better part of seven hours' fuel.'

'At one-four-one cruising speed?' I said. 'Unless there's a hell of a nice tail wind, I'll be running out just as I get to Denver. I don't want to be a glider when I come to Minturn Peak.'

Newton grinned. 'Relax! There's a forty-knot tail wind up there and the weather prog is that it will hold or increase for a further twelve hours. You'll reach Denver with two-fifty miles' fuel left. Twenty per cent.'

I said, 'Okay.'

'Then on from Denver—' He showed me the route across the United States, into Canada and up to Gander, Newfoundland, filling in the flight plan form as he went on. Finally, 'Agreed?'

'Agreed,' I said. What he'd shown me was a long, dull, simple route. High, but easy. Gander-Shannon, when it came, was the same thing, really. Long and dull if you didn't think of the hairy aspects.

Newton picked up the phone. 'Get me the tower, please.' Then he grinned at me. 'You'll enjoy the trip, I promise— Oh, hello. Er, Don Newton at Airflo. We're flight-planning a Stripe Tiger through the airways from here to Gander, Newfoundland.' He read out the details of the flight. 'Accepted? How long? Okay.' He hung up. 'They'll call back on acceptance in a few minutes. Anything else you want? Oxygen?'

'I'd better,' I said, thinking quickly about Chao Li. My own ceiling is around eighteen thousand. Higher than that I begin to get anoxic. But Chao Li hadn't spent several thousand hours in the air : at twelve or thirteen thousand, he'd be in trouble. 'Listen, Don, I'll need plenty aboard. Sixteen thousand's my ceiling these days.'

'You can help yourself. Hey, but you're lucky. Still sixteen?'

'When I was a bright and healthy kid, I could scream around all day at twenty thousand,' I said. 'It's age and bad living.'

Newton nodded. 'I'm about thirteen now. I'd be anoxic at sixteen.'

Looking at him, I could believe it. His nose was veined and his skin had the light flush that looks like rude health and is the beginning of the opposite. I said, 'I'll get the oxygen. Fuelling finished?'

'I imagine.' Newton went to the window. 'Can't quite see from here.'

I had, somehow, to let Chao Li get aboard. If the tanker had been fussing round, he'd have had to stay in hiding and if Newton walked out with me to the aircraft, Chao Li would really be scuppered.

'I'll get the oxygen,' I said, 'if you'll wait for the call.'

I left his office, walked round to the stores bay in the hangar, helped myself to half a dozen oxygen bottles and a couple of mask sets, then staggered off to the aircraft and dumped them in beside the big cabin tank. There was no sign of Chao Li, and as soon as I'd climbed down, Newton was hurrying across towards me.

'Fifteen minutes,' he said. 'Take off sixteen-fifty. You're cleared all the way as per flight plan.'

'Good,' I said. 'I'll have a close look at things at Gander.'

'Don't worry,' he said. He was walking towards the aircraft. 'This Tiger will go to Shannon like shelling peanuts.' He opened the door, put one foot on the step and looked into the cabin. It was a very natural thing to do, but I wondered all the same. 'You're ready, then?'

'Apart from the Operating Data Manual et cetera,' I said.

'Christ! The ODM. It's on my desk.'

'I'll come with you.'

We walked back into his office and picked up the manuals and performance charts and were just leaving when the door was flung back and a white-haired old man came bouncing in.

'Mr Shaw! Glad to meet you. Say, thanks for that differential.'

'My pleasure, Mr Capote.' I recognized the face with no difficulty.

'No, mine,' he said. 'Crazy the way that crate vanished then turned up again! When's Mr Shaw leaving?'

I said, 'Ten minutes.'

'Why, that's a shame. I'd have liked to show my thanks. Wish you'd told me he was here, Don.'

'Sorry,' Newton said. 'I thought you'd already left.'

I patted the pile of papers, picked them up and tucked them under my left arm to leave my right free for shaking hands, shook hands and left. Both Newton and Capote seemed to want to walk with me, so I told them I was superstitious about goodbyes, left them at the door, and walked across to the Tiger wondering which of them was involved. It could be neither. Or both. Half-way across I turned and waved; the two men still stood in the doorway, watching. But there had been that short conversation in Newton's office when both Newton and Capote had been with me. I hoped Chao Li had got aboard then. I'd left the Tiger parked as conveniently as I could, but it's difficult to cross a large area of tarmac unseen.

I got to the aircraft and opened the cabin door. The Tiger was ready to roll : she had fuel and oxygen, she was flight-planned and fitted out. All she lacked was the passenger who was the purpose of the trip.

Fifteen

I thought about it for perhaps two minutes. While I got the twin Continentals started and adjusted the earphones, I tried to put myself in Chao Li's place. He was somewhere on the airfield; no doubt about that because I'd brought him myself. If he hadn't been arrested, which seemed unlikely because there appeared to be no commotion anywhere, then he must be awaiting his chance. The one going through predictable procedures was me, so I'd better continue to go through them and let Chao Li make his move when he could. Looking ahead round the perimeter track there seemed to be one or two points where parked trucks or piles of junk provided hiding places. I got out my documents. What were the registration letters of this bloody thing? When I found them I switched on the radio.

'Golf Alpha Lima Zulu calling tower,' I said.

'Okay, Lima Zulu.'

'Lima Zulu, flight-planned to Denver, Colorado. Take-off sixteen-fifty.'

'Roger, Lima Zulu. Clear taxi-runway zero-nine. QNH one-zero-one-three. There is one aircraft ahead of you, a DC Three now turning from the perimeter on to runway zero-nine.'

'Roger.' I took off the brakes and taxied slowly forward.

'Lima Zulu cleared at twelve repeat one point two thousand feet to Oakland VOR on one-zero-three point seven.'

'Thanks, tower,' I said.

I kept going, slowly, round the perimeter track. Where the hell was Chao Li? The whole place seemed deserted, which must be making things more difficult for him. If cars and people had been dashing about, he'd have had no problem. I taxied slowly past the first of the parked trucks : not a sign of him! There was another, maybe thirty yards on, but he wasn't there, either. Then there was the stack of wooden crates, but he didn't come out from behind those. We were running rapidly out of hiding places. The DC3, elaborately painted out in some business outfit's tarty livery, had begun its run and I watched it because I never can resist. I wondered how old it was and what it had done in its long and reliable life. Some of those crates are thirty years old, now.

Watching the Dak's tail lift, I nearly missed Chao Li. He came strolling out from the far side of a little hut exactly as the Tiger shielded him from sight. He broke into a run. I opened the door and he swung in quickly, his hair bunched into spikes by the slipstream.

'You left that a bit late.'

'I had to.'

'Lima Zulu!' The tower sounded mildly irritated.

'Lima Zulu. Sorry.' I said contritely. 'I'd tied my shoe-laces too tight.'

'You'd what?'

'Permission for take-off?'

His voice hardened. 'Lima Zulu clear for take-off. Starboard turn when airborne.'

'Roger and thanks.'

I brought the engines to take-off boost and two and a half thousand revs, took off the brakes and felt the little Tiger roll powerfully forward, letting her gain plenty of ground-speed before I hauled the pole back and she slid easily into the air. I banked her gently into a long turn to the right, climbed to twelve hundred and looked out. There, spread below me, was San Francisco Bay. I leaned over and switched the radio on to Oakland VOR's frequency, watched the needle come round to point the way. Oakland came up and I talked to them and they turned me towards Stockton at two thousand three hundred.

I said, 'Thank God!' It was seventeen-o-five and I was going home.

'You are pleased,' Chao Li said.

'Pleased! I need to get off the ground to heal up. There are eight hundred and ninety-five cuts all over the inside of my mouth, I'm bruised and battered and weary. Shouldn't I be pleased?'

'I understand.'

'You don't, my lad-oh!' I said. 'You haven't the faintest, tinkling bloody notion. I've wanted to come here all my life. Thirty-nine years I've waited. And then—'

'You don't like the Americans?'

I said, 'They're all right. It's you lot.'

'Us? The Chinese?'

'Six hundred million of you,' I said. 'Are you all as rough as that?'

I looked at him, smiling to take the edge off it, but he was stony-faced. The days are past when you can make jokes out of race.

He said, coldly, 'Ours is a very old culture. You should respect that.'

'Simmer down, I'm just sore.'

He didn't reply and we rode on in silence while I levelled her off and flew on to Stockton, cleared the high density area and began the long climb, still on Victor two-forty-four flight-planned for Hanksville, Utah. Beneath us the land climbed sharply into the foothills of the Nevadas and I checked the instruments again, then began a bit of sight-seeing. Sonora was down there and I began quietly to hum the song, while I looked at the names on the chart and rubber-necked out of the cabin windows. Carson City and Virginia City were away to port : I couldn't see them, but it was fascinating to think they were there.

'Western territory, pardner,' I said.

Chao looked at me.

'Westerns.' I said. 'Films. Bang-bang.'

'Ah, yes.'

'Blimey,' I said, 'where *do* you come from?'

'I told you, you should not ask.'

'No, I shouldn't, I suppose. But you're obviously not American and you do work for us. Where you come from is hardly classified information?'

He didn't reply. 'Look,' I said, 'if I offended you with nasty racial joke, I'm sorry. But if we are going to spend days together in this plane, it's too damn small for bearing grudges.'

He looked hard at me for a moment. 'I'm from Hong Kong.'

'I've landed there,' I said. 'Kai Tak airfield? Very nasty. Mountains and a curly approach.'

He said, 'I was as glad to get away from Hong Kong as you are from San Francisco.'

'As we both are.'

He smiled, stiffly and formally, but he smiled. 'It was overcrowded, claustrophobic. Riches and poverty.'

'I know,' I said. 'It's the contrast that's sickening. In San Francisco nobody's poor, I suppose?'   .

'Not so many.'

I said, 'In Calcutta once I felt ashamed to have eaten. I don't remember Hong Kong was anything like that.'

'It isn't,' he said.

That was as far as the conversation went, because as we climbed through eleven thousand I pushed the mask at him. He looked at it a bit dopily.

'Oxygen,' I said.

'For me?'

'Yes.'

'But not you?'

'I don't need it yet,' I said. 'You do.'

'We Chinese—' he began.

I said, 'For God's sake, I've spent a lot of time up here. Wear it. You need oxygen as much as anybody does, Chinese or no.'

'I'm sorry. I did not know.' It took the tension away.

The little Tiger clawed her way up to seventeen thousand and I levelled off and set the radio, watching the Nevadas beneath us, picking out Yosemite National Park, and the blue of Mono Lake and noting that we were heading towards a little place called Manhattan, Nevada.

The occasional updraught from the mountains booted us about a bit, but it was nothing serious. I'm long past even the possibility of airsickness and Chao Li apparently wasn't susceptible, so I simply sat back and let the Tiger fly itself, more or less, while I looked at the ground below. I'd never realized before how mountainous the US is; for nearly a thousand miles from San Francisco to Denver the whole land mass was over five thousand feet and a hell of a lot higher in lumps. Nowadays we think of overland journeys in terms of two hours of John Wayne, but what it must have been like to take wagons over that kind of country beggars the imagination.

Below us the land turned from brown to purple as the light began to fade and the valleys filled with deep black shadows. It's a magical time to be in an aeroplane, with the sky going into violet and the moon showing clean and cold. There was nothing much to do apart from the occasional glance at the altimeter and the fuel gauge and the regular switch of frequencies as we passed one radio beacon and headed for another, waiting for the abrupt darkness the west to east flyer always gets.

I'd just watched the radio needle flick from six o'clock to twelve as I passed over Hanksville, Utah and set the frequency for Grand Junction, Colorado, when I saw another aircraft's lights two thousand feet below and perhaps a couple of miles back. So far, I had seen surprisingly little traffic considering this was one of the busy airways : a few jets howling through the sub-stratosphere and one or two biggish prop-jets and four-piston jobs, but hardly anything my own size. But what the hell was this guy up to? If he stayed at that height, he had every chance of flying into a mountain; on the other hand, nobody climbs *through* an airway. You approach it at a specified height and speed and *turn* into it.

I looked at my chart. Mount Peale was off to starboard at thirteen thousand, but not that far off to starboard, and we weren't much more than an hour's flying from all the fourteen-thousand-plus peaks in the Rockies. Well, it was his problem and there wasn't a hell of a lot I could do about it, because he had to be flying in lane and under air traffic control. Perhaps, I thought, he was heading for one of the little towns in the foothills. But in that case, why climb to fifteen thousand? I kept glancing down at the little red and green lights skimming through the night below me, a bit puzzled by it all. The next time I looked he'd gone. It seemed to answer all the questions : he must have turned out of the airway.

Shortly afterwards I saw a set of lights coming towards me, a thousand feet down and almost directly beneath. In airways you're banded in alternate directional layers a thousand feet apart so that, in this case, west-east aircraft rode at odd heights and east-west at evens. When you see a set of lights like that, you check your altimeter again. I was okay at seventeen and he must be at either fourteen or sixteen. As he got nearer I decided he must be at sixteen.

It was normal enough; what was far from normal was the way his wing-tip lights suddenly swung through ninety degrees and he banked off to port like a fighter. I gave a little tug on the pole, just in case, and slid the Tiger up a few more feet. If some nut was doing aerobatics down there, I didn't want to know. I watched the plane that had swung so rapidly away: a moment later, he'd resumed station in his lane.

My hair stood straight up. There was only one explanation: he'd been avoiding another aircraft going the wrong way in the sixteen thousand foot lane, and that meant some lunatic was cruising round the sky within three hundred yards of me, in the wrong lane, at night.

I dug my elbow into Chao Li's ribs. 'Look behind us and down. See if you can see anything.'

He pulled the mask away. 'What?'

I said, 'Aircraft. Something's happening up here.'

He turned, staring out of the starboard window. 'Nothing there.'

I was looking to port. It's difficult to see much because most aircraft don't have, or need, rear view mirrors and in our case, there was a dirty great engine housing in the way. Weaving from side to side a little to widen the angle, we tried again. Still nothing visible. But something was there, I knew it was; I couldn't see it, but twenty years of flying develops an instinct or two.

A minute passed, then two, as I banked and turned gently within the airlane, my eyes searching the airspace for his lights. I found myself watching the shadow of a little cloud racing along below me and then realized it wasn't a shadow but an aircraft, and that it was flying without lights. No wonder the other bloke had been playing Richthofen!

'He's down there,' I told Chao Li. 'Flying without lights and two or three hundred feet below us. You tell me: who is it?'

'What do you mean?'

I said, 'What was it Al Capone said? Once is coincidence, twice is something else. The third time it's enemy action. I've had too much the last twenty-four hours to believe this is just Fate having her six-monthly anti-Shaw kick. Who is it?'

He stared back at me. 'I don't know. Nobody knows *I'm* aboard.'

I looked down at the other aircraft: he'd narrowed the gap still more. My hand went to the radio.

Chao Li said, 'No!' sharply and suddenly.

'Look,' I said, 'aside from anything else, air traffic control needs to know about this.'

'Yes. And they'll want to question you when we land. That's right?'

I nodded. 'And they'll find you . . . Okay.' Reluctantly I withdrew my hand from the transmit switch and looked down again at the speeding black shape below. It was near enough now for me to get a good look for the first time. The bright moonlight showed me a bi-plane of a kind one doesn't see too often in Europe, but whose characteristics I knew well enough. She was built and stressed for fast aerobatics.

As I watched, she inched higher. The bi-plane was less than a hundred feet below now and flying almost directly beneath the Tiger. My altimeter showed seventeen thousand dead; I had room to move. With another three hundred feet gained, I looked down again. He had come up after me and was now flying if anything, even closer than before.

Beside me Chao Li said, 'Why?'

'How the hell do I know?'

I was watching, waiting for the bi-plane to edge closer still, but he didn't; he just maintained his station, a hundred feet or so below me, flying literally in my shadow. How much fuel had Newton said I'd got? Two-fifty miles extra? I said, 'We'll see how much speed he's got.'

The Tiger's advertised maximum level speed is two hundred and with the engines wound up to nearly two and a half thousand revs, she was really going. For a moment or two, the black shape slid back, but then as he turned on power, he came steadily back towards me. I throttled back. There was no point in wasting fuel. It was a moment or two before he followed suit.

'That answers one question,' I said, savagely. 'He can beat us for speed.'

Chao Li said, 'What's he trying to do?'

'I don't know,' I said. And I didn't. 'Why the hell would anybody want to fly immediately below me?'

'Could he force you to do anything?'

'No,' I said. 'He couldn't. Wait a minute, though. He could force me to climb by coming closer and . . .'

'And what?'

'He could stop me going down. Just by staying where he is.'

I looked out of the window. Below, the black shape still raced across the moonlit earth, its windows silver in reflection. It seemed to be moving a little to port, climbing a fraction, then a little more, until it was almost level with me. I tore my eyes away, looking at the controls. Beside me Chao Li was half standing in the starboard seat, staring across me at the bi-plane.

'Look out!' he yelled.

I didn't waste time looking; with full right aileron and a big bootful of right rudder, the Tiger whipped round on its wing tip in a tight banking turn that imposed stresses for which it most emphatically was not designed.

'What was it?' I shouted above the roar of the engines.

'A sub-machine-gun,' he said. 'I saw it in the front cockpit.'

The bi-plane must have followed fast. A second or two

later, he was coming at me from the starboard side, having turned tighter and faster than I could. I pushed the pole forward, watching the spurts of fire from the sub-machine-gun's barrel and knowing the bullets were chattering just above me. I was beaten for speed and manoeuvrability; I was in a dog-fight, unarmed. To hell with Chao Li! I wasn't going to be shot down in an airway without letting some-body know what was happening. As the Tiger sped through two hundred miles an hour, I reached for the radio switch.

Chao Li said, 'Remove that hand.'

I turned towards him. 'No, damn you,' I said. 'We must—'

I stopped then. There wasn't much point in talking. Chao Li's hand held a gun.

Sixteen

I hauled the pole back, praying that the wings wouldn't fall off and searching the sky around me for the bi-plane who'd have dived after me and would soon be appearing on one side or the other, pumping bullets at me. He came up to starboard, climbing a little, so I dived away to port and saw him come round in a tight turn across my line of flight. He lost a little height to get at me and I climbed again, staying above him. There's a technique to dog-fighting and I'd learned it at the hands of some of the Battle of Britain men at Little Rissington. But Spitfires and Hurricanes won their dog-fights as much because they were better aero-planes as because the pilots were vastly superior. And my little Stripe Tiger was no match for an aerobatic bi-plane.

I shouted, 'He'll kill us, you know that? He'll kill us.'

I looked at Chao Li for a brief second. His face was pale and set. 'If we die, we die,' he said. 'But nobody must know. You understand?' The gun was steady in his hand.

'Put it away, then,' I said. What I'd told Chao Li wasn't altogether true. I'd back any competent pilot to avoid being hit by sub-machine-gun fire. But collision was another matter and the chances of the two aircraft colliding were very good indeed; if we were to survive, our survival would have to be bought through sheer flying skill.

I switched off my own lights and waited till I saw him coming at me, then turned in to him. Dog-fights, they used to say at the Central Flying School, are games of poker; if the aircraft are evenly matched, it's bluff and bluff again, pilot to pilot. I'd see how strong this joker's nerves were. He shot upward across the Tiger's nose with his motor roaring and I promptly climbed after him. I climbed longer, though, and away from the moon; he was anxious to get after me again and began his turn. He should have looked, first. I came at him from down moon at my full maximum diving speed of two hundred and ten miles an hour and almost sat the Tiger on his upper wing. He hurtled to port after me, but I was already climbing and it took him time to get in position. When he did, I went away again on a big bootful of rudder, snarling across in front of him and damn nearly getting a cabin full of bullets for my trouble. I saw his muzzle flashes but felt nothing.

It did give me an idea, though.

I managed to get above him, then climbed down moon and, while he was still throttled back looking for me, I came down at him in a low, banking turn that meant the Tiger was approaching him at an angle of thirty degrees or so from head-on. I narrowed the angle to about fifteen, then slid away to port, climbing. I was taking a hell of a chance with the Tiger's tum exposed to him at close range. I waited tensely as we flew past but nothing seemed to have hit us; there was no smack of metal on metal to say a bullet had struck the aircraft. Once again, skidding for grip, the Tiger slewed round and up.

Lurking up there, down moon, I watched as he looked for me again; the bi-plane's vision, fortunately, was even more restricted than mine. Then, as he spotted me and began to turn and climb, I pushed the pole forward and swung down at him, praying I'd get the angle right. This wasn't the kind of trick you could pull more than once and I was banking on the fact that the sub-machine-gunner probably wasn't a pilot. Again I came at the bi-plane from a thirty-degree angle, but this time I narrowed it more. He opened up, from that front cockpit, as I had hoped he would, and kept his finger on the trigger as I tore at him. The muzzle flashes pointed towards the Tiger like flaming fingers in the night sky : as we howled closer and the angle narrowed, I felt and heard two of the bullets smacking into the cabin floor.

To say that I waited is absurd; things happened in microseconds. But I was judging my moment, leaving it to the last foot before dragging the pole towards me and tearing over him. The shots screamed towards me and I could see the man's head and forearms well clear of the open cockpit as he strained to hit me. I could imagine, too, that the pilot must have realized in the last fraction of a second, exactly what was happening. He was too late, though and communication between open cockpits isn't easy. The guns of old-time fighter aircraft were synchronized to let bullets pass between the revolving propeller blades. There was no Constantinesco Interrupter Gear here, though. As I tore across his nose I saw the muzzle flashes swing after me. Then they stopped and he dipped. He had shot up his own propeller!

The bi-plane literally fell out of the sky. These special aerobatic aircraft have all the natural inherent gliding capacity of half a brick. With no engine power to keep his nose up he simply stalled and went : I didn't see him after the first few seconds or so. Minutes later, though, I saw the flash of flame as he hit the ground.

Lathered in sweat, I sat back in my seat, breathing hard. Beside me, Chao Li was still holding the gun : I could see the moonlight glinting dully on the metal.

'If you don't put that bloody thing away,' I said, 'I'll throw it out, and you out after it.'

'I suspect that was a very clever piece of piloting.'

I said, 'It was a lucky piece of flying, that's for sure. Bloody lucky!' I could feel anger burning inside me now that the tension was over. It mushroomed until my body trembled and my head ached with rage.

'What is it about you?' I shouted. 'What have you done? What have you got? Why? Why? Why?'

He just stared back at me with a calm that made me feel almost homicidal.

'To hell with you, you bastard,' I snarled at him. 'When I get this thing down at Denver, you can bloody well start walking. That's what I'm going to do. I wouldn't fly with you again if— You can all get lost: you, Lennox, the whole bloody lot. Do you hear?'

The gun was in his left hand. Slowly he transferred it to his right.

'Mr Shaw.'

'What?' I shouted. 'What now?'

As I swung round in my seat to face him, he slapped me hard across the mouth. 'You are like an hysterical girl,' he said contemptuously.

If I had taken my hands off the wheel, I swear I'd have killed him, but I'm a pilot and my instincts and reflexes have been conditioned by years of flying.

'Hysterical what! Listen, when I get this aircraft down, I'm going to get out and then I'm going to pawse you off your stocking-tops. D'you hear!'

There was silence.

'I said, Do you hear?'

'It is no longer of any importance. You are no longer hysterical, Mr Shaw. But I suggest you put on your lights.'

My anger had evaporated quickly as it usually does and I was grinning to myself at the little so-and-so's indestructible cool. Since I'd met him at noon, we'd been chased out through the Golden Gate, he'd damn near drowned and now, an attempt had been made to shoot down our plane. All the time, I'd been the one with the things to do : boats to steer, planes to fly; he'd been the one with nothing to do but suffer. Amazingly, he seemed unaffected.

I did as I was told and put on the lights. 'Mind if I use the radio now?'

He met sarcasm, properly, with silence.

'Golf Alpha Lima Zulu calling Grand Junction.'

A pause, then : 'Grand Junction. Go ahead, Lima Zulu.'

'Lima Zulu. I thought I saw an aircraft crash a few minutes ago,' I said.

'Your position, Lima Zulu?'

'I was about fifteen minutes past Hanksville on the Grand Junction beacon.'

'Did you see any lights, Lima Zulu?'

'No,' I replied truthfully. 'He didn't seem to have lights on. I saw a black shape falling, just for a few seconds, then, a bit later, the flash. It may have been a bi-plane. Not sure, though.'

'Okay, Lima Zulu. Thanks. Your heading, please?'

'Lima Zulu. I am flight-planned into Stapleton Airport, Denver.'

'Grand Junction. If we want you, we'll talk to you there.'

'Roger and out,' I said. 'Okay?'

Chao Li said, 'They will come out at Denver?'

'No,' I said. 'I'll get a letter in a few days, asking for a formal report on what I saw, but that's all.'

'Good.' He began to grin and I was startled for a moment until I realized why. I lifted the oxygen mask to his face.

'Come on,' I said. 'I couldn't bear it if you passed out now.'

Half an hour later we passed over Grand Junction and I switched frequencies to the beacon at Kremmling, Colorado. We'd been in the air nearly five hours and I was beginning to feel just a microscopic little bit exhausted. All I wanted in the whole wide world was the nearest hotel room to the airport. I didn't even care whether or not it was sound-proofed. Thinking about a bed, a big soft, squashy warm bed, I flew on towards Kremmling and Denver, up the valley of the Colorado River. Ahead I could see snow-capped mountains to left and right, towering to more than fourteen thousand feet, but the air was clear and flying was smooth. Not much more, I thought, than half an hour to Denver. A whiff of oxygen would help a bit. I reached be-hind, took one of the oxygen bottles from beside the cabin tank, connected the mask and took a few breaths. My mind promptly began to function again and I realized with a real feeling of horror that I had been responsible that day for a lot of death. In all my life, I had never killed or injured anybody. Now, in one day, how many? The people on the fast cruiser who'd hit the fender of the Golden Gate Bridge certainly hadn't survived in the icy water and the bi-plane had contained at least two more. Five, probably. Five dead men!

I slipped the mask away. 'Chao Li. Tell me what the hell all this is about?'

He looked at me. 'Two things. One is that you are flying me to Britain. The second is that you became involved, fool-ishly, in smuggling drugs.'

'Foolishly? Inadvertently is more the word.'

Chao Li shook his head. 'Nothing is inadvertent, Mr Shaw. You were used because you are the type of man to be used.'

'Spare me the philosophy.'

'Certain things are inevitable.'

'Only death,' I said. 'The rest is people. Who's likely to know I've got you aboard?'

'Nobody. Unless I was seen at the airport. Who *could* know?'

I rubbed my eyes. They were beginning to feel as though

somebody had emptied the ashes in them. 'So it's still the drugs people?'

'Who else?'

'God knows. But they must be pretty damn desperate. Five dead men and I haven't even *got* any drugs!'

Chao Li said, 'I should try not to think about it, Mr Shaw.'

'Thanks!' He was right, though. I went back to flying the ship, examining the instruments and the airspace. The little Tiger was droning happily along and the fuel gauge still showed half-full. It must be in error, but it was indicative of nice, economical performance and I liked the way she handled. It's not every light aircraft you can treat like a fighter.

We passed over Kremmling and came under the Denver controller's firm and formal hand. Apart from us he'd only got about fifty big jets howling round in the stacks, so you'll imagine how thrilled he was to hear my voice.

'Okay, Lima Zulu. Your fuel state, please?'

He was going to shove me in a stack somewhere. 'Fuel gauge may be defective,' I said. 'It's difficult to judge.'

'Thank you for your help, Lima Zulu. I'm sure United and TWA won't mind. You are cleared for a straight-in approach for runway twenty-nine right, QNH one zero one seven. Wind velocity two-eighty ten, call three miles.'

I was never so glad in my life to be getting out of the air, sailing in over the Denver approach lights at a nice conservative seventy while the 707s and DC8s and Coronados waltzed around above.

'Lima Zulu. Thank you,' I said.

'Not at all, Lima Zulu. Just do us a favour. Get that fuel gauge fixed. Did you say Golf Alpha?'

'Yes.'

'You're a Lim— You're English?'

'I am,' I said sweetly, 'but the aircraft isn't. Nor is its fuel gauge.'

'Okay, Lima Zulu. Taxiway nine, please.'

'Thank you.' I obeyed orders and turned off quickly to leave the runway open for all those blue uniforms and gold braid queued up behind. 'There's an old flying joke,' I said to Chao Li, 'that there were originally three Wright brothers, but the third one's still stuck in the stack at Kennedy.'

He was begging my pardon and I was never minding when the radio crackled. 'Uh, Denver tower. Have you a Mr Shaw aboard?'

'Lima Zulu. Yes.'

'Will you please have Mr Shaw call San Francisco. Message from a Mr Hayes. The number is Gateway One, seven four nine nine.'

'Thank you, Denver tower,' I said. 'Roger and out.'

Parking the modern light aircraft is a bit like parking a car. You switch off, lock the door and leave it. I will plead guilty to the satisfaction I felt at leaving Chao Li inside, curled up across the two seats, safely out of sight. I hurried across to the terminal, found a telephone and put through the call to Rafer Hayes. The phone buzzed only once.

'Hayes.'

I said, 'It's John Shaw.'

'Anything happen tonight?'

'Anything happen? Somebody tried to shoot me out of the sky.'

'Any notion who?'

'Not a clue. No lights. No idea of the make.'

'What happened?'

'He tried to rough me up, flying close. Then he started shooting. Finally he shot up his own propeller.'

Rafer said, 'Does the name Wong Peng something mean anything to you?'

'Yes. And to you. He's the rough one who gave me the going-over.'

'You'll be interested to know, then, that he hired an aircraft today at Ignacio, from an advanced flying club.'

I said, 'It was a bi-plane built for aerobatics, right?'

'Right.'

'He's had a little trouble,' I said. 'I don't suppose you'd want to look, but he's thirty miles or so out of Grand Junction.' Knowing who it was eased my conscience a little.

'I'll get it checked. There could be evidence. Did you go out in a boat on the bay this morning?'

'Yes.'

He said, 'They want you pretty bad.'

'I gathered that. But who the hell are they?'

'Chinese. Powerful, I think. I only have suspicions but I'm working on them. If I'm right, it's very big.'

'Keep it, Rafer,' I said. 'Tomorrow I'm going a long, long way away. I want to leave it all behind.'

He laughed. 'Okay, John. You earned it. Just one more thing.'

'For you, nothing. What is it?'

'You *have* told me all of it. Left nothing out?'

I thought of Lennox and British Intelligence and the agents who killed policemen; of Chao Li now hiding in the Stripe Tiger, the man I was whisking out of the reach of the law that Hayes represented.

'No,' I lied. 'You know the whole thing.'

Seventeen

I said, 'Golf Alpha Lima Zulu, flight-planned San Francisco to Gander, Newfoundland. May I have my clearance?'

'Stand by, please, Lima Zulu.'

The cool silence of Stapleton Airport in the early morning was shattered every couple of minutes as the business boys jetted away to their conferences and sales meetings. Between roars, I looked around me and listened. I expected any moment to hear the sound of a police siren and to see the cops scurrying towards us.

I waited, thinking about the woman. Why hadn't I just walked by and left her to it? Anybody else would have done, why hadn't I? Up to that moment, everything had gone so beautifully. *Come on, come on. Give me clearance*!

The night before I'd used one of the free phones on the airport concourse to call a local motel and we'd travelled out there in the motel's courtesy car, obtained sandwiches and coffee from machines and slept in a cabin detached from its neighbours. I'd paid the bill with my credit card as I registered. It had all been done with marvellous anonymity; I don't think anybody in the place knew Chao Li was Chinese, even if they knew he was there, because he'd stayed quiet and in the shadows.

How he'd slept, I don't know; I had just dived into the big, black pool and stayed down, warm and snug and needing it, until our six-thirty call came through. Then I slid out of bed, showered, wished the motel gave away free razors with its free blades, and went out to get some breakfast from the slot machines. When I was coming back with a handful of bacon sandwiches and two cartons of hot coffee, she came out of one of the other cabins: about fifty-five, I'd say, and bony, with hair scraped back and sharp eyes behind the glasses; a teacher, at a guess, or somebody's tough old secretary. She gave me a formal good morning as we passed, then walked over to a Buick that was parked across from her cabin.

Twenty minutes later, when Chao Li and I had eaten and fixed with the desk to be driven to the airport, we came out of our own cabin and she was still there.

'Oh, I wonder—would you mind?'

'What is it?'

'I have a flat and I don't seem to be able to—' She was one of those women who never finished sentences. 'I wonder if—'

I looked at my watch. 'I'm in a bit of a hurry.' I was getting almost as tired of punctures as of Chinese.

'If you'd just show me—'

Chao Li by this time had about turned and gone back to our cabin. In my shoes he'd have told her to get lost.

'All right.' I opened the boot and got out the tools and a rather bald spare, jacked the Buick up and changed the wheel. By the time I'd done, the courtesy car was standing in front of the reception office.

'Why that's awfully kind of—' she said. 'I really do—'

'Pleasure,' I said. Back in the cabin I washed my hands. 'Come on.'

We walked out together. She was still sitting in her car and as we walked past, she came bounding out. 'I've been thinking about your—You're from England, aren't—? I wanted to tell you that I do appreciate your—' She was looking at me, but then her eyes flicked to Chao Li and her face sort of set for a moment, then her expression began to shade across towards puzzlement.

'Yes, I'm English. Sorry, madam, but I must go. The car's waiting.' I made myself very English indeed and we skipped across to the courtesy car. When we were in, I looked across at the woman and she was still staring after us in a bony, puzzled and, I suspected, slightly suspicious way. Had she recognized Chao Li?

Come on, tower, let's have that clearance!

If she had recognized him, we were desperately easy to pick up. The motel had my name from the Diners card, the courtesy car had taken us to the terminal. Two men, one Chinese, one English, and the British registration letters GA eighteen inches high on the booms. I kept my fingers crossed as the fuel tanker pumped petrol into the wings and Chao Li sat with the big sunglasses on, pretending to be absorbed in the Tiger's technical manual.

'Sign here.'

'Thanks.' I signed.

Then it came. Lazy voice. 'Uh, okay, Lima Zulu. You may begin to taxi now. Take up position behind a Boeing seven-three-seven of Braniff Airlines.'

I slackened with relief. 'Roger, Denver tower.'

I still had to start the engines, which is no way to go about matters. Fortunately, though, they fired at once. I eased the power, took the brakes off and taxied forward.

'Uh, Lima Zulu. One moment.'

I turned and looked at Chao Li. This was it, I knew it! This was it! 'Well. Do we make a run for it?' He stared back at me, eyes a little wider, but still cool.

'Is it possible?'

I said, 'This thing could get off tidily in a hundred and fifty yards. It's possible.'

'Then go. You must go!'

My hand went to the levers to bang them up to maximum boost.

'Lima Zulu. You reported a defective fuel gauge on arrival. Have you effected repairs?'

For a moment I was speechless.

'Lima Zulu!'

'Yes,' I said. 'Oh yes! It was just the setting.'

'Okay, Lima Zulu.'

I throttled back again and the Continentals stopped screaming as we fell in behind the ghastly pop-art livery of the Braniff Boeing. My mind was, at that second, composed of similar multi-coloured whorls and swirls. Had I checked the petrol gauge!

'Nice to know they care, isn't it?'

'Is it defective and have you checked it?'

Chao Li was beginning to remind me of a couple of sergeant instructors I well remembered.

I said, 'It is slightly defective, and I have not checked it. Nor, for the moment, shall I. I want to get away from here.'

'You think the woman recognized me? It is unlikely.'

'Don't forget your face has been on television and probably in every newspaper across the country.'

'No. All Chinese look alike. She may have wondered, but she would do nothing.'

'I wish I shared your optimism.'

The Boeing turned to the runway, wound up its engines and vanished, leaving the air behind it full of black smoke and death. I sat waiting.

'Why do you not move?'

'Three minutes, yet,' I said.

'Why? I thought you wanted to get away from here.'

'Because if we take the Tiger up now into Uncle's slip-stream, the turbulence will very likely wash us out of the air. It takes a long time to disperse.'

I waited, watching the second hand of my watch as it made three slow circuits of the face, then I worked the engines up to take-off power.

'Lima Zulu to Denver Tower. Take-off?'

'Okay, Lima Zulu. Clear take-off—starboard when airborne.' Two minutes later we were at six hundred feet and climbing. 'Lima Zulu, climb to flight level one one zero then on Victor Eight to Des Moines, Iowa.'

'Lima Zulu. Thank you, Denver.'

We kept climbing. It was seven-thirty and the air was open for us clear across Newfoundland. Below, the land was already falling away as, with the Rockies receding, we eased across the sky towards the great plains. We still had the tail wind we'd had the night before, but at eleven thousand it was not ripping along so smartly. Twenty knots, perhaps. I reckoned on a ground speed of about one-sixty. With chart and the ruler out, I made some rough calculations on time and distances. Three hours, roughly, should see us to Omaha and another three to Milwaukee. The way the flight plan diverted us north round the Great Lakes made Ottawa about another six. Allow half an hour for food, fuel and functions at Milwaukee and we'd be in Ottawa about eight p.m. We'd have to do something about the Customs and immigration problem at Ottawa, of course. Sleep a bit, then fly up to Gander in the morning: seven hours Ottawa-Gander. After which, heigh-ho for the long crossing! It would be a hell of a long day, but with a night's sleep at Ottawa, possible.

We stayed on Victor Eight across the flat lands clear up to Des Moines then swung smoothly on to Victor Two-Nine-Four to Madison, Wisconsin and, finally, Milwaukee. Nothing happened either. Not one thing happened. After the day before it seemed unbelievable. I brought the Tiger in at Waukesha county airport, Milwaukee, where we re-fuelled both ourselves and the aircraft, then took off again, flying up the western shore of Lake Michigan on Victor Seven to Green Bay. I'd bought a newspaper at Milwaukee, wondering whether the woman at the Denver motel had decided to talk to the police or not. There was no mention of us on page one and that's where it would have been. By the time we'd passed Iron Mountain and Marquette, with the immensity of Lake Superior stretching to the north, and turned on to Victor Three-One-Six for Sault Ste Marie, I was feeling decidedly happier than I'd done since I left London. Finally, I watched the massive locks at Sault Ste Marie slide away beneath us.

'Okay, buster,' I said. 'We're in Canada.'

'And tonight?' Chao Li asked.

'Is a problem. It's the only problem we've got left. But it's a problem.'

'What do you mean?'

'Customs and immigration. It's our first landing in Canada after leaving the States. Unless we stay in the Transit Area, we'll have to go through Customs and immigration.'

'So?'

I said, 'Just how powerful is the name of Sidney Lennox in the Dominion of Canada?'

'Out of the question. The instructions said no one must

know. In any case, the Canadians and the Americans are hand in glove.'

I took my passport out of my pocket. 'Look, it's okay by me. I can go through and have a damn great steak, then crawl into bed and digest it. The problem is you.'

'If we were just passing through, would we have to go into Customs?'

I said, 'No, but we're not. And there's nowhere else to go on to. Or at least, there's nowhere else we wouldn't have the same problems.'

'Nowhere? What about the little airstrips?'

'You'll have heard of radar? They're watching us come in. If we divert out of lane we attract attention. They might even scramble a fighter to inspect us.'

'Then I stay in the aircraft.'

'You'll freeze to death,' I warned him. 'The nights are cold in Canada.'

'I'll be all right.'

I looked at him doubtfully. If there'd been an alternative I'd have taken it, but there wasn't. If I tried finding some backwoods airstrip and was caught I'd be in pretty serious trouble and I didn't forget I had a living to earn in the air long after this trip was over.

Chao Li nodded confidently. 'Newspaper insulates. I'll wrap it round me.'

'All right,' I said. 'If that's the way you want it?'

We flew steadily on over Sudbury and North Bay and came down at Ottawa on the button at eight o'clock, San Francisco time. I set my watch three hours forward. When I'd got the fuel in, ready for the morning, I went across to the transit area and spent my last dollars on a small bottle of rum and an Indian blanket at the duty-free shop and a container of soup at the caféteria, then marched back to the Tiger and handed them over.

Immigration really wasn't worried about me and the

Customs man knew I had nothing to declare, but he asked me all the same. 'Not a thing,' I said. 'I only came here to sleep.'

He gave me a threatening look. For two pins he'd have had my trousers off as punishment for levity, but I must have looked tired and appealing because he waved me through. Half an hour later I was showering at a nice cheap motel near the airport and wondering whether to have a fillet steak lightly grilled or a socking great plate of gammon. While I was wondering, I switched on the television set in my room and caught a newscast.

Half-way through, my mouth went very dry. '. . . San Francisco police are trying to discover whether there is any link between the murder, on the Berkeley campus last Sunday, of Patrolman Kowalski, and the discovery in the Pacific early today of a private yacht, drifting and damaged, with the body of a beautiful Chinese girl on board. So far, there has been no identification.' The announcer moved on to another story.

Rafer Hayes knew damn well I'd been aboard that boat; knew, too, who the beautiful Chinese girl was.

I'd lied to Rafer and now he'd know that I'd lied. He'd even given me the chance to change my mind when he asked if there was anything I hadn't told him. On the other hand, I *had* saved his life!

I sat for a minute or two, trying to work out how much danger there was that some great hairy policeman would come barging in through the door of my room. The boat had been found early today, so maybe Rafer didn't know yet. Or if he knew, hadn't said anything. I looked at the telephone. I was desperately tempted to put through a call to Rafer in San Francisco and find out what the score was; the only snag was that, if Rafer had discovered somehow that I had told him less than the truth, the call could be traced and I'd be held by the Canadians pending an extradition application by the United States. I would just have to take the chance and sleep here. No man could continue on up to Newfoundland and then take on the Shannon trip single-handed and without sleep.

So instead of the steak or gammon, I had a hamburger in a bun and a cup of coffee, asked for a call at four a.m. and went to bed. Three and a half hours later, and it seemed like minutes, the telephone awakened me. I knew the sleep had done me good, even if it didn't feel as though it had. I dragged on my clothes and went back to the airfield. Soon the engines were singing and the cabin heater was on and Chao Li was beginning to thaw out a bit. I'd found him draped awkwardly across the two seats, wrapped in newspaper and blue with cold, but he still had that compelling calm, in between shivers, and was anxious only to be off.

It was seven minutes past four when the Tiger lifted off the Ottawa runway and a quarter past seven when we passed over St John, New Brunswick. At ten thousand feet we had thirty knots of favourable wind, so the fuel ought to be okay. If you have any sense, you don't take chances anywhere when you're flying, but the trip over Nova Scotia and into Newfoundland gives you the sort of view that makes you run mental fingers over belt and buttons. I looked at the fuel gauge again and decided I'd go down and top up. The Bay of Fundy and the Cabot Strait seem from the air to consist entirely of massive rocky cliffs, deep lakes and loneliness. Just short of an hour later I came in at Halifax, filled the tanks, signed the chitty and flew away. Two hours after that I dropped down like a flea on the concrete hide of the vast white elephant that is Gander. I didn't feel as fit as the flea, but I didn't feel too bad, either. All I now needed was breakfast and off.

Gander presented, as ever, a dismal picture, with fine snow blowing in little whipped swirls off the empty tarmac and the grey and forbidding waters of the cove assuring you that this was a bleak and blasted spot. I radioed for the petrol tanker.

'To the top,' I said. 'And when you've filled the wing tanks, there's another one in here.'

The fuel loader grinned at me. 'Shannon?' He was obviously used to the idiots who came here in midget aircraft to hop the Atlantic.

'Unfortunately,' I said.

He shrugged. 'Your neck, buddy. What's she make? Tiger, ain't she?'

I said, 'Yes she is. One-forty true. I'm hoping there'll be something pushing up there.'

'Another guy went about seven,' he said.

'In what?'

'Grand Commander.'

I said, 'Now you're talking.' I was listening to the fuel as it flowed into the big, square, galvanized, hundred-gallon tank that was bolted to the cabin floor behind the seats. With that full, the Tiger would turn into a pig, wallowing rather than lifting off the runway.

'Sign here, please.'

I signed.

'Thank you, sir. Good luck.'

I watched the tanker roll away among the snow flurries. 'The condemned men breakfasted well,' I said. 'Come on, I'll buy you some bacon.'

'And coffee,' Chao Li said. 'Don't forget the coffee.'

Gander is one of the saddest places I know, a massive airport built at enormous expense to handle transatlantic flights. For years passengers poured into Gander's lousy facilities and complained, so the new airport was built. At that moment, more or less, a Comet flew the Atlantic non-stop one way and a Boeing 707 the other, and Gander quite suddenly wasn't needed any more. So it sits there, handling local traffic and a few odd flights plus the occasional diversion. When I'm there, I always feel as the only man staying at the Hilton might feel: there are shops and restaurants and all the rest, waiting to serve you, but there's only you and you can't be in all of them at once.

Our footsteps echoed on the modernistic tiling of the big hall in the angular, warm terminal building as we crossed to the restaurant. We sat drinking coffee and looking out at the emptiness outside, which matched the emptiness inside, and waited while the bacon sizzled and the eggs fried. At that point the Tannoy came on with a click.

'We announce the arrival of flight four-zero-one from Havana, Cuba, due to land in a few minutes. This flight continues to Copenhagen and Moscow. Passengers joining this flight at Gander will be called shortly before take-off.'

It was a brave little announcement in its way, for there was hardly a soul in the terminal. Four-zero-one wouldn't be picking up any new passengers at Gander. I chewed steadily through the meal, watching the sky, interested to know what kind of aircraft Cuban Airlines flew.

'Ilyushin, I reckon,' I said.

'I beg your pardon?' Chao Li's capacity to be formal was extraordinary.

'The aircraft. It will be a Russian Ilyushin.'

'Oh?' he said. He was more interested in the toast and marmalade, and I suppose I wasn't doing much else but make conversation. I still stare up at aircraft, just as the kid in that recruiting ad did. When I saw it, I felt the little spread of satisfaction we all get when we've just demonstrated our brilliance. 'See,' I said. 'An Ilyushin.'

It wasn't though, it was an old Britannia, probably ex-BOAC and looking a sight less elegant than it must once have done in BOAC's majestic navy, white and gold. She taxied round in front of us, and the truck-ladder went forward. When the doors opened, passengers poured out and I swear you never saw anything like it. The crew looked as though they were about to get on horses for a Mexican scene in a Hollywood Western: all droopy black moustaches and bandy legs. The passengers were of distinct types: first came hairy male imitations of Fidel Castro, all wearing olive green denims; then some clean-shaven Slav types in baggy trousers; and finally three or four who—

'Come on,' I said to Chao Li. 'We're leaving.'

'Why?'

'Those characters out there,' I said, 'off the Cuban Britannia, are Chinese!'

He looked up at me. 'So?'

'So I've seen enough to last me. Finish that coffee—we're leaving now.'

'This is pointless.' He got up protesting, but he got up. I hurried out. I had still to check the weather.

I had a feeling something was wrong, badly wrong. I didn't know just how badly.

Eighteen

'Good morning.' The usual meteorological pessimism was absent; at Gander visitors are welcome.

'Morning. How are things for Shannon?'

'Fine,' he said. He was a big, fair-to-ginger man with glasses; fiftyish, cheerful. 'At least, it was earlier. Let's have a look.'

He walked away and came back with the latest North Atlantic weather map and plonked it down in front of me. 'See for yourself. There's a big high four hundred miles or so east of Greenland. See? You did say Shannon?'

'I said Shannon.'

'Yeah. Well, it's all right. Better if you go Great Circle. That high is generating nice winds. From fifty to fifty-five north you should have sixty-plus tail winds.'

I must have been smiling: the news could hardly have been better. I'd expected lows out there, with towering fronts climbing from sea level and packed with the murderous anvils of cumulo-nimbus on which small aircraft get beaten to death. 'Thanks,' I said. 'That's great. How long will it last?'

'As long as you need it, I should think,' he grinned cheerfully. 'With sixty knots behind you, that won't be long. In fact you may do even better. Up to seventy perhaps.'

'And no problems?' The feeling I'd had when I saw those Chinese coming out of the Britannia still lurked.

'Not a thing. Not if you're going to Shannon or the Azores. Bluie's a bit hairy.'

I said, 'It's always hairy.'

'Today's a bit worse than usual. This high's skimming all the muck and rubbish off Labrador and Baffin. But you're okay. What are you flying?'

'Stripe Tiger.'

'Push-pull?' he said. 'What's she like?'

The Tiger is an unusual aircraft. The cabin has an engine forward and an engine aft; one pulling, one pushing. Instead of a normal tail set-up it has twin booms like the old-time Lightning. It's been nicknamed the Mixmaster. This however was not the time or the place for long elaborate comparisons of past and present flying equipment. I wanted to be away. 'She's nice,' I said. 'Known better. Known worse. *Comme ci, comme ça.* You know.'

'Yes.' He sighed a little ruefully. I'd be in Ireland tonight and he'd still be here, waiting for somebody to talk to. It must be a lonely job.

'Thanks very much,' I said, meaning it.

'Good flight.' He smiled and raised a hand.

I clattered down the stairs and looked round the hall for Chao Li. He was waiting by the exit doors with a big Thermos.

'Clever old you,' I said. 'Coffee?'

'There's rum left, too.'

'Excellent.' I was beginning to feel a bit happier, though

that feeling still persisted somewhere in my guts. 'Let's get this thing into the air.' I held the door open and we stepped out of the heated air and broke into a trot that became a gallop as we realized just how cold it was. Together we sprinted across to the Tiger, climbed into the cabin, shut the door and fastened our lapstraps.

I turned to look at Chao, sitting calmly in the starboard seat. 'Ready?'

He looked surprised that I should ask. 'Yes, I'm ready.'

'Right.' I reached and started the engines.

'Golf Alpha Lima Zulu calling Gander Tower. Bound for Shannon. Cleared for take-off please?'

'Okay, Lima Zulu. You are clear taxi runway zero-nine-zero, QNH one-zero-zero-seven.'

I took the Tiger round to the start of the runway and began to wind the engines up. With the kind of weight we'd got on board, I was going to need every bit of power I'd got just to lift her off the runway.

'Lima Zulu clear for take-off.'

'Roger, Gander Tower. Thank you.'

'Good luck, Lima Zulu.'

I watched the instruments as the twin Continentals blasted up to two and a half thousand revs. The Tiger was shaking a bit as I let off the brakes and she began to roll forwards. The graphs said she'd need a speed of eighty-five to lift-off, but as the needle hit the figure I knew she wouldn't do it, so I waited, building up to ninety-five knots before I pulled on the pole a little. The Tiger's nose came up one reluctant millimetre, then dropped again and we bumped on the tarmac. I held her steady and waited as another hundred and fifty yards went by. My God, but this one was a cow, fully-laden! Very gently, I lifted her again. Those little wheels really didn't want to leave that runway, but eventually they detached themselves and we groaned into the air an inch at a time. In the first airborne mile we must have climbed all of thirty feet.

I came round a little to port, adjusted the heading and let her climb.

'That was not a good take-off,' Chao Li said judiciously.

I turned to look and he was frowning at me. 'Not good at all,' I said. 'Bloody awful, in fact. She doesn't want to be an aeroplane, you see. She wants to be a car. Let's hope,' I added fervently, 'that she doesn't want to be a duck.'

The Tiger struggled upward and I felt a bit sorry for whoever had bought her. Admittedly that cabin tank was heavy: an extra eight hundred pounds of fuel plus twenty or so for the tank itself. But that, after all, was only the weight of four men and she was supposed to be a six-seater. I wondered whether the engines were developing all the power they should, then stopped wondering because happiness doesn't lie that way when you're on a long hop across water.

The coast of Newfoundland lay almost directly below us now, the coves and inlets looking harsh and hostile with the light mantle of snow and the rocks showing their noses through it. Ahead there was only the Atlantic.

'Wind down the antenna,' I said.

Chao Li bent and turned the handle that unwound the wire of the trailing antenna from its spool. The normal Radiomobile installation wasn't designed for long-distance work like this and I had an RCA job for this trip: ten thousand dollars' worth in a little box bolted under the bulkhead. With the long aerial streaming behind us, this radio would have the range and power.

'Lima Zulu calling Gander Tower.'

'Come in Lima Zulu.'

'Radio check.'

'I hear you, Lima Zulu. Strength nine and clear. Good luck.'

'Now, Chao Li,' I said. 'Take your last look at land for a while. There's only water now for about nine hours.'

'Only water.' He sounded solemn and I didn't blame him.

It's a pretty sober thought.

'For eighteen hundred miles.' I've made the crossing from Gander a few times, all ways about, but I've never done it without thinking of Alcock and Brown who did it fifty years and more ago. I knew how they must have felt standing on the airfield at Torbay, looking out at all that water; then heading out over it. It's a strange sensation, a gambler's feeling : you're scared stiff but oddly excited.

I reduced rpm and boost to climb power. The Tiger clawed for height and gradually won it, using fuel at a high old rate but getting up until the individual waves of the Atlantic merged together into the endlessly changing, moving, black-and-gold sheet that is the pilot's ocean. There were a couple of beetles on the surface : fishing boats, probably, coming back from the Grand Banks. We'd made probably fifty miles and that was the odd thing if you thought about it : we'd be in Shannon almost as soon as the fishermen reached St John's.

Eventually another look at the altimeter showed ten thousand and I levelled off, reduced rpm and boost to maximum continuous and adjusted the trim. 'We're there !' I said.

Chao Li looked puzzled. 'Where?'

'Our economic cruising height at our economic cruising speed,' I said. 'All I do now is to throttle back to sixteen hundred revs and we'll find out if the old bag falls out of the sky.' As I did it, Lima Zulu seemed to bounce as though she were on the end of a long piece of elastic.

Chao Li said, 'It is noticeable.'

I grinned at him. 'Isn't it, though.' And I thought, privately, you're scared, you cold-hearted little bastard, you're scared !

'If you gave the engines more power?'

'It's a funny thing about fuel,' I said. 'The more you use, the lighter you get; the lighter you get, the farther you can go. Sweetness, you see. And light. However, the lighter you are, the less fuel you have and the sooner you must come down. Happy medium, ten thousand feet, one-forty knots, sixteen hundred revs. As long as the engines hold out, Bob's your uncle and Charlie's your aunt!'

'What happens if one engine goes.'

'That's right,' I said.

His lips tightened.

I said, 'It's okay. We stay up.' It wasn't fair to frighten him. 'The aircraft's built to fly on one. A bit more slowly, of course, but we'd manage.'

'Ah.' It wasn't so much a comment as a sigh of relief. 'Nine hours.'

'To Shannon, yes.'

'Where is Shannon?' He said it with elaborate casualness, but he was scared all the way through. Some people are, in aeroplanes.

'Ireland, I'll get the chart out and show you.' I half turned in my seat to reach behind me into the chart pocket on the cabin wall. Holding the pole steady, I turned to look, found the North Atlantic chart and was about to face the front again when I noticed the blanket. It was the Indian job I'd bought at Ottawa and it seemed to be filling almost the whole space between the fuel tank and the cabin wall.

'What the devil?'

Chao Li turned quickly towards me. 'What is wrong?' There was a tremor in his voice.

'The blanket,' I said.

He turned, reached down, grasped a handful of the thick material and pulled. I'm not sure which I saw first as the edge of the blanket slid forward: the girl or the gun.

It was a long time before anybody spoke. When my instincts and thought processes unscrambled themselves, I realized that I'd changed the flying attitude of the aircraft and we were two hundred feet higher and flying the way crabs walk. When everything was straightened out and we were in level flight again, I half turned to look at her. The barrel of her automatic pistol was pointing at me, about the middle of my back. The girl was white-faced but her eyes were wide and bright, glittering with determination. She was also beautiful, but it was not a moment for judging beauty. She was dressed in Cuban Airlines uniform.

'Don't tell me,' I groaned, 'that you're hi-jacking *me* to Cuba!'

'No!' She said it vigorously. 'Not to Cuba. To America!'

It's not that I'm brave, but pilots have advantages in situations like this: nobody shoots the pilot purely on impulse; they may do it, but not until they've given the matter the thought it merits. I turned in my seat and resumed my normal flying posture, then glanced at Chao Li who was engaged in easing his own pistol from the pocket of his coat. The girl couldn't see what he was doing because the back of the seat was in the way.

I said, 'No, Chao Li.'

'What?' He looked at me sharply, angrily.

'Not now.'

'You are a fool!'

'What is this?' the girl said. Her fear was audible in her voice.

'Nothing.' Chao Li's hand was still easing the gun clear of the material.

'No,' I said.

He ignored me. In another second he'd have it clear and be blazing away. I waited, watching him out of the corner of my eye. When it was on the point of coming out, I smashed the side of my hand down on his wrist.

He gave a little exclamation of rage as the gun fell to the floor, but it had tumbled near me, my boot was on it and by that time the girl was saying, 'You fly me to America!'

'No.'

There was a silence, then I turned to look at her. The wide eyes were even wider and the fear in them was clear to see. She was determined, though. 'If you do not fly to America, I shall kill you.'

'That's three of us,' I said.

'You should have let me shoot her,' Chao said beside me.

I kicked the gun towards him. 'No shooting,' I said. 'No shooting by anybody. That big grey thing is a petrol tank. I don't want bullets flying about in the cabin. I don't want bullets severing control linkages or breaking glass. I don't want wounded and dead aboard. So don't fire your bloody guns, either of you.'

She said, 'Give me your pistol.'

I glanced at Chao Li. He was scowling in chagrin like a child ordered to return an iced lollipop.

She went on, 'If I read in your eyes that you are to shoot, you will die. Hold the gun by the muzzle and give it to me.'

Slowly, he obeyed, then turned and stared angrily forward.

'You will fly me to America.'

'Not me,' I said. 'I'm going the other way. Europe.'

'Where?'

'Shannon. Then London.'

'I go to Miami. You fly me to Miami.'

'No,' I said.

'You will bring the aircraft round in a hundred and eighty degree turn and head for the United States.'

'No.'

Her voice was suddenly very cold and I turned to glance at her. 'I shall count to ten. On ten, I shoot. One, two, three—' She meant it. She had steeled herself to shoot and she would.

I said quickly, 'Why do you want to go to America. Europe has a certain old-world charm.'

'I want political asylum. Four, five—'

'And only America will give it?'

'There are many Cubans there. Six, seven, eight—'

I said, 'If this man returns to the United States he will

be in very great danger. Do you understand?'

'I understand. Now turn the aircraft round. Nine—'

Desperately, I said, 'I will take you personally to the United States Embassy in London. You can seek asylum there. Or in Britain.'

'Turn the aeroplane round,' she said. 'Do not doubt that I shall shoot.' The barrel of her pistol was cold on my neck and the muzzle trembled. There's no combination quite so lethal as determination mixed with fear and firearms.

'One hundred and eighty degrees,' I said wearily. I felt weary; there seemed to be no escape from trouble. Everywhere I turned, there it was.

'Before you make your turn, tell me your heading.'

I leaned forward to look at the compass. 'Two seven eight,' I said.

'Now turn.'

I started to bring the Tiger round in a wide, shallow, hundred and eighty degree turn.

'Read off the figures,' she told me.

I did as I was told. At eighty-two she stopped me. 'Hold that course.'

'Aye, aye, ma'am,' I said.

'How many hours to America? she demanded, a few moments later.

'Seven or eight at least,' I said. 'We may have to touch down in Canada.'

'We are only two hours out of Gander, why?'

'Powerful tail winds. We had the equivalent of a jet stream behind us.'

'Hold your course,' she said.

'You stupid fool!' Chao Li raged. 'You stupid, stupid fool. I could have shot her and you stopped me. Now see . . . !'

'Tough,' I said. 'It's tough all round. On me, too, I got you out once before and I'll get you out again.'

The girl said, 'You are not friends?'

'No,' I said. 'I don't think we are. Tell me why you're running away.'

She hesitated. 'Because I am afraid.'

'I see.'

'No. You are a man. You do not see at all.'

Which made it clearer. 'It's a man you're afraid of?'

'Not a man,' she said vehemently. 'A pig. He put my brother in prison and my brother died. Now he want me.'

'Surely he can't—' I got no further.

'He is powerful. For me it is that, or prison. Or this.'

'And your family?'

She laughed bitterly. 'Two cousins only, now. In Miami.'

'All right.' At that moment there wasn't a lot I could do. I said, 'For the sake of knowing who is who, I am John Shaw, from London. James Young is the angry gentleman on my right. He's from Hong Kong.'

She said, 'My name is Maria Martiñez.'

An hour ticked reluctantly by. Then she said suddenly, 'I wish to smoke. Is it safe to smoke?'

'You're sitting next to a hundred gallons of aviation spirit. I think not.' Mention of the cabin tank reminded me that I ought to switch to it. It was much better to use that fuel while there was still petrol in the wing tanks, just in case. I reached forward to operate the pump switches.

'What are you doing?'

'Switching to the cabin tank,' I said. 'When it's empty, maybe you can smoke.'

'Thank you,' she said. I smiled to myself. Thank you, indeed! Being tough didn't come very naturally to Maria Martiñez.

'Don't thank me,' I said. 'I'm not doing it for you. In any case, it should last four hours or so.'

I moved the switch and the engines roared on. It's always a nasty moment and I was congratulating myself that it had passed when they began to splutter and misfire.

Within ten seconds both engines had cut. There was nothing I could do as the Tiger's nose tipped down and she began to dive towards the Atlantic two miles below.

Nineteen

Rapidly I stabilized the Tiger in glide trim. We'd ten thousand feet. At two thousand a minute loss, that gave five minutes or so in the air. I reckoned she'd be making a hundred knots now. I'd switched back to the wing tanks as soon as the engine cut, but whatever was in the fuel line had to be cleared before fresh clean fuel could flow to the engines. If it was a blockage in the fuel lines we really were finished. I fined off the pitch a bit to turn the engines over faster and give the whirling props a better chance to clear the engine.

'What is it? What's happened?' Chao Li's voice was shaky.

'How the hell do I know,' I said savagely. 'Either it's a blocked fuel line, in which case we all die a couple of minutes from now, or it's something in the fuel. Water, maybe.'

I checked the trim. It was pointless, really, because when an aircraft is trimmed for maximum glide there's nothing you can really do to help. The forward propeller whirled in front of me and I hoped, no, I prayed, that it was whirling unspent fuel from the engine and sucking clean fuel in.

Behind me I heard the girl muttering, '*Ave Maria gratia plena Dominus tecum . . .*'

The altimeter needle slipped back and I watched helplessly, switching my eyes from the whirring prop to the airspeed indicator and back again to the altimeter. We were down now to six and a half thousand.

'Come on,' I said. 'Come on!' but it was no use talking.

We could only wait and hope as the Tiger slid on and down in that long, slow glide. The Continentals are magnificent engines and I had to give them the chance, if they'd take it, to spew out whatever had stopped them, and to fire on good fuel.

At three thousand feet with a minute and a half to go, I knew we'd had it. I'm an optimistic man, but now I knew. I'd been on a jinxed trip from the start and this, chaps, was it. It's strange what you think about at that kind of moment: my own mind went back nearly twenty years to Charlie Farrell, dying at nineteen in a Gloster Meteor, saying, 'If anyone can hear me, goodbye.' I clearly remember wondering if I might meet Charlie again where I was going.

I switched on the radio . . . two one eight two kilocycles. Distress frequency. 'Mayday, Mayday, Mayday. Golf Alpha Lima Zulu . . . I am ditching approximately fifty-two twenty north, thirty twenty-six west. Repeat, Mayday, Mayday . . .' By the time I'd said it a few times, we were probably too low to be doing much good.

'Lima Zulu. Weather ship Alpha. I have your position on radar and D/F. Will notify.'

'Thank you, Alpha. Position approximate. Repeat, position approximate.'

'Understood, Lima Zulu. Good luck.'

I shouted to the girl. 'There's a rubber dinghy stowed behind the tank. You two work it forward.'

'Is there a chance?' Chao Li asked.

'At the speed we'll hit,' I said, 'there's about one chance in a million. All the same, get it ready. When we hit I'll try to ditch level. Get the door open straightaway and kick the dinghy out. Keep the door open and follow it, even if we're underwater. Remember!'

'*Ave Maria gratia plena Dominus tecum* . . .' the girl's voice droned on behind me.

'Praying's precious little use now,' I said. 'Just get that dinghy forward. The Lord helps those who help themselves.'

We were down to fifteen hundred. Five hundred yards below us the surface of the Atlantic boiled and heaved and nowhere in sight was there a ship or an aircraft. I could hear the girl and Chao Li trying to drag the heavy dinghy out of its place, grunting with effort, breath hissing as knuckles, knees and elbows were barked.

The sound, when it came, could have been a shoe scraping against the cabin wall, or a sudden cough. But when it came again, I knew that it wasn't. Cough . . . cough . . . cough . . . cough . . . cough . . . cough . . . cough . . cough . . cough . cough. Suddenly the after engine caught and roared!

Inside my chest somebody started banging my heart with a dirty great hammer. Twelve-fifty feet on the altimeter . . . I eased the pole back again, levelling her off, increasing rpm and boost. Slowly we came out of the glide. I could barely grip the pole with my sweating hands, but I'd got her now and I held her. At least we weren't going to dive straight in. A minute later, the forward engine coughed and spluttered, then fired.

I started to say, 'Put the dinghy away,' but there was a frog in the dry depths of my throat and he came up to stop me and I had to start again.

'Weather ship Alpha, Weather ship Alpha,' I called. 'Lima Zulu calling weather ship Alpha.'

'Go ahead, Lima Zulu.'

'Engines restarted. Not ditching, not ditching.'

'Well done, Lima Zulu.' The operator's voice held real relief. 'Give our regards to God while he's still with you!'

'Lima Zulu, replanning flight. Stand by.'

'Okay.'

The girl said, 'You see. I kept praying. You tried to stop me, but I prayed and we were saved!'

'What's that about replanning the flight?' Chao Li said sharply.

For a moment I didn't answer. I was trying to calculate

how much fuel there might be in the wing tanks and thumbing through the Pilot's Notes for single-engine performance figures. After a minute or two, I swung the aircraft round and looked up. 'Right,' I said, 'it's decision time and I've made it. We can't go on. We can't go back. So we have to divert. There's only one alternate we have a chance of reaching.'

They both started talking at once. 'We are near America,' the girl said. Chao Li's quiet voice was drowned by hers, but it was fair to assume he didn't want to go to Gander.

'Shut up, both of you,' I said. 'And listen. I'll tell you where we're going and why we're going there. The possibilities open to us are : one, to ditch beside the weather ship. One, two or three of us would almost certainly drown and the aircraft would sink. Secondly we could try to go back to Gander, which is possibly the most sensible thing to do.'

'I would die before I would go back,' the girl's voice shook with determination.

'That could be what it means. Gander, or die.'

'Why?' Chao Li demanded. 'What is wrong?'

'I'll explain later. The third is to try for Goose Bay, Labrador. Goose is military. It reeks of radar and secret installations of all kinds. If we put our nose anywhere near Goose without permission, they'll put us inside first and ask questions afterwards.'

'So where do we go?' the girl asked. 'Shannon?'

I said, 'We couldn't get half-way. No, we're going to try for Bluie West One. Greenland. And I doubt whether we'll make it.'

I spent the next half hour going over my calculations again and again, until they were as right as they could ever be. The trouble lay in the imponderables : the petrol gauge I hadn't had fixed, the drift that might have occurred.

'Listen,' I said, 'as far as I can tell, we're here.' I jabbed my finger on the map forty or fifty miles north of the position I'd given to the weather ship. 'And we're trying to get to here.' I pointed to Bluie in its ghastly lair deep in that icy fiord. The distance is approximately seven hundred and fifty miles and we have fuel for—I think—four hours' flying. With luck, there ought to be a bit of tail wind helping to carry us up there; twenty or twenty-five knots.'

Turning in my seat, I looked at them. They looked as I felt, pale and serious, eyes wide with the knowledge that death was very near.

'We get there, yes?' the girl said. As she spoke, she seemed very young, very innocent, very trusting.

'Pray a bit,' I said gently. 'That might help. But the answer is no. I don't expect to make it.'

'But why? You turned thirty, forty minutes ago,' Chao Li said. 'Four hours' fuel.'

I said, 'First, I didn't go about.' I turned to the girl. 'When you wanted the heading I gave you the wrong heading to see if you knew what you were talking about. You didn't.'

She was almost pleading. 'But you turned the aircraft?'

'Sure,' I said, 'then bit by bit I brought her back again, so now we're flying on one engine just below the revs where fuel consumption rises steeply. I've switched one off. Four hours' fuel would show one-forty miles by four, normally. With one engine it's more like one-fifteen, but we use only about seventy per cent of the fuel. That would give us, theoretically, about six hundred and thirty miles' range.'

Chao Li said, 'And how far to—what is it? Bluie?'

'Bluie West One, they call it,' I said. 'It's seven hundred miles, maybe more.'

'Then how?' the girl asked.

'Tail winds could make it just possible. At low consumption on one engine, we've five hours' fuel. Five hours of a twenty-five knot tail wind is a hundred and twenty-five miles.'

'So we shall get there?' she said, her face shining in a

tiny moment of hope.

I said, 'If everything is exact in my calculations. If we *have* that much fuel. If we *are* where I think we are. If we make *exactly* the range we ought to make. *If* all those things happen, and *if* my navigation is perfect—' I stopped and looked at them—'then we shall be coming into the most dangerous airfield I know, in foul weather, and using the very last drops of our fuel.'

Twenty

We weren't going to make it; I knew damn well we weren't and I'd known for some time. With all the weight we had aboard: the three of us and eight hundred pounds of useless fuel, I was requiring too much power from the one engine. When I'd worked out the equation at first, there had been a chance, a tiny one, but a chance. Now there was none. As sure as God made small green apples, we were going to drop into the sea and drown a hundred miles or so short of Greenland. In front of me the forward propeller, fully-feathered, contributed its quota of drag to our slow march; behind us the after engine roared healthily, holding us up, pushing us forward; ready to go on bearing our weight until it stopped. I was cold and angry and totally helpless. Over and over again I asked myself how it had happened, who had sabotaged the cabin tank? I never doubted for a second that it *was* sabotage. Somebody had put something in the tank with us in mind. I thought of Airflo Inc and Don Newton, sitting in his temporary executive office; of the Airflo mechanics who'd bolted the tank in; of Marion Capote, with whom the whole nightmare had begun. Was Capote the pivot? Had the spares I brought him been spares? Or drugs? And why should everybody be crazy to kill me? Because I'd taken drugs into the United States by accident? Surely not. This kind of desperate planning and pursuit had to be for other reasons. Chao Li, perhaps. But nobody knew Chao Li was aboard. Newton might have seen *a* man get aboard, but that was after the fuelling and he couldn't know it was Chao Li, even if he knew who Chao Li was.

No, it was me they wanted to kill, and they had succeeded too. Or in three more hours, they would have succeeded. I'd just like to know why before I went!

Marion Capote was rich, anyway, and an air maniac; not the kind to muck about with drugs. Newton, though, with his hypertension and air of impermanence was a very different kettle of fish. And Newton had said he'd taken the Tiger up himself. It had to be Newton.

I looked at the galvanized cabin tank. So Newton had sabotaged it and there was something in the fuel. But what? My mind leapt on the question with a kind of desperation and began to rip at it. What could Newton have put in, easily, while he was in the aircraft?

I tried to get into his mind. He'd left the wing tanks alone, because we had to fly a respectable distance before we crashed. So they'd used two approaches, a belt and braces job. If the gunner didn't get me over land, the cabin tank would, over the ocean! But brother Newton wouldn't leave it there. Brother Newton would worry about things going wrong, inquiries by competent inspectors and engineers. He could have put sand in the tank. Or he could have put sugar. What else? Water! Of course! Sugar turns to carbon and blocks the jets. Unless we crashed in the Atlantic, either sugar or sand would certainly be discovered, and he couldn't be sure. But not water! If the bi-plane got us, the tank would explode on impact and the water be dissipated.

'Young.' That was the name I'd used. He'd have to learn to answer to it.

He jumped a little. None of us had spoken for some time.
'Yes?'

'Have you ever flown?'

He shook his head.

'You?' I asked the girl.

'No. The pilots let me hold the controls sometimes. You
know. But not flown.'

'But you *have* held the controls?'

'Oh yes.'

'Get in the back,' I ordered Chao Li, 'and let what's-her-
name—Maria—get into your seat.'

'Why? What's—'

'Never mind talking,' I said. 'Get!'

When she was safely installed in the starboard seat, I
showed her how to maintain an attitude. It's not difficult
and she soon had enough control for my purpose. I climbed
over the back of my own seat and made Chao Li take my
place. Then I began to inspect the tank and my heart sank.
The mounting was bolted firmly to the floor. I'd hoped it
might be standing on a plinth that would lift it a little clear
of the floor and that there might be a drain plug; if there
was, it was under the floorboards. I got the emergency lamp
off the bulkhead and shone its beam down into the tank.
Somewhere down there, there should, I thought, be a stack
pipe, possibly two, but I couldn't see them. Impatiently I
jiggled the beam about and finally I thought I saw them.

Chao Li said, 'What are you doing?'

'If somebody put water in this tank,' I said, 'it would be
at the bottom. Right?'

He nodded.

'Why?' I said.

'Water is heavier than petrol.'

'Right,' I said. 'And I know there's ninety odd gallons of
petrol in there because I saw a Shell tanker put it in. There
can't be much water. A couple of gallons, five at the outside.'
Five, when I thought about it, was the likely figure. A jerry-

can full. Newton must have gone out to the aircraft with a jerrycan of water in the van or jeep, or whatever it was, and simply tipped it into the cabin tank.

'Now,' I went on, 'The way this fuel system is rigged, fuel can go to the engine either direct from the wing tanks, or from this one!' I glanced at the girl and at the radio compass : we were slipping into a port-wing-down, nose-up attitude. 'Maria,' I said. 'A little forward, a little to the right.'

She corrected with a frown of concentration. And accurately. I was beginning to think this was quite a girl.

'The fuel,' Chao Li said, 'not the girl.'

'Simmer down. If we could get the water out of the bottom of the tank,' I said, 'we could begin to use the petrol.'

'Can we not use it off the top?'

'No. We've no way of pumping it to the engines.' I got down on my knees and tried to find where the floorboards came up, but of course, they didn't. The Tiger, like most small aircraft, was designed for servicing from the outside. I could just see where the stack pipes vanished through the floor and that finished it. 'Forget it,' I said heavily.

'Why? If you have an idea, why forget it?' the girl said.

'Because the drain plug must be under a hatch on the underside,' I said. 'That's why.'

'And you can't get at it?'

'No.'

She thought for a moment. 'I once saw two men standing on the wings of an aeroplane while it flew.'

'No.' I said. 'It's impossible.'

'Are you sure? If we are to die, it is worth being sure. No?'

She made it sound humorous. God knows how, but she did.

I managed to smile. 'All right. It's worth being sure.'

Swapping seats with Chao Li was awkward, but we managed it. 'I have control,' I said, taking the pole. Maria had

170

done a good job holding the controls; we were level and steady.

I throttled back, slowly, and trimmed her to increase the angle of attack. I wanted to see how slowly the Tiger would fly and still remain fairly easy to control. Stalling speed was sixty-three miles an hour, and it's possible, of course, to fly below that if you use a lot of power and the lift of your wings is augmented by deflected prop-wash, flaps down; but the girl wasn't a pilot. I settled for eighty. 'Hold her like that.'

The wind almost tore my head off as I stuck it through the window and looked down and back along the outer wall of the cabin. The diagrams of the aircraft had shown me where the hatches were located, but diagrams look easy and the reality, at fifteen hundred feet and eighty miles an hour, looks very difficult indeed. The hatch I wanted was located about two feet below the cabin floor and about the same distance to the rear. It looked as though it might be held in place by screws rather than a catch, but the manual didn't say.

With my head back in the cabin, ears tingling and hair blown, I checked the trim again.

'Okay?'

'Fine,' I said. 'You'll make a flier yet. Can you keep her like that?'

She nodded. 'I think so. I can try.'

'No sudden movements,' I said. 'None at all. If trouble's developing, yell for help.'

She smiled. 'I will do that.'

'Now,' I said to Chao Li. 'I'm going to tie my feet into that seat harness, then hang out. I want you to lower me an inch at a time.'

With the door lock unfastened, the door still lay flat against the fuselage, held in place by the slipstream. I had to push like hell to get it open and when I stopped pushing it flew back into place with a tremendous bang. If a hand or a foot were trapped with that kind of force, it wouldn't be much use afterwards.

'I need something to wedge it open,' I said.

There's not much loose in the cabin of a light aircraft, but Chao Li finally handed me the blanket. 'Force it where the hinge is,' he said.

'Thanks.' Again I forced the door open and rammed the thick edge of blanket into the acute angle between door and cabin floor. It held the door open, but the extra drag swung the Tiger sharply to starboard and I had to correct the trim before I could do anything else.

Sitting on the starboard seat, I mucked about with the seat straps until I'd got a good strong loop of webbing round my ankles. The pressure my muscles could exert in that awkward space and posture was limited, but it seemed solid and ought to hold me.

'Right,' I said to the girl, 'watch out as I hang out. There may be a bit of extra asymmetric drag to correct, but do it with rudder and aileron, otherwise you'll get in a tangle.' She nodded, solemn and serious, concentrating hard.

I did a sort of clumsy handstand on the seat, pushing my legs back. Because the harness stopped them the effect was to push the upper part of my body forward. I looked up at Chao Li.

'Do not worry,' he said. 'I have strong arms.'

'I hope so. For God's sake hold tight.' I eased my body forward, turning on to my left shoulder and holding on to the door frame with my right hand; reaching down with my left. As my hand left the shelter of the door, it felt as though icy water were racing over it and I knew that whatever I had to do must be done quickly. Pushing with my legs, I eased my body forward again, feeling with the tips of my fingers at the cold, smooth aluminium sheeting, searching for the little ridge that would indicate the hatch was under my hand. Still I could not reach, so easing forward again, I brought my head below the level of the cabin floor, felt the sudden change of equilibrium and tasted vomit. For now the greater part of my weight was outside the aeroplane. Fifteen hundred feet below lay the rough, icy waters of the northern Atlantic.

'For Christ's sake hold on,' I shouted. Chao Li's grip tightened and the seat-belt braid bit hard against my ankles. I stretched my left hand out and down, still gripping at the door frame with my right. My fingers, more numb with every second that passed, searched the smooth, painted metal for the crack at the hatch. Then raising my head and straining my stomach muscles, I managed to glimpse the hatch two or three inches beyond my grasping fingers and eased myself forward again. An inch, an inch and a half—I stretched and strained but I couldn't reach it. My right arm was at full stretch now; to reach the hatch I would have to let go, and that meant hanging by the ankles in space. Staring down at the foaming surface of the ocean beneath, I was afraid, deeply and desperately afraid : my mind played over to me, like a film, the feeling of falling endlessly and helplessly into space and my own last, uncontrollable screams of terror.

Hanging there, I swallowed bile, feeling the sweat icy on my forehead. Unless I went soon, my left hand would be useless, too numb with cold to do anything. Grimly I looked down at the waiting, moving Atlantic, ready always to welcome more to the thousands, the millions it has swallowed. It would swallow us, too, unless I could force myself to go against all my instincts, to relax the grip of my right hand, and to reach.

'Hold me,' I bellowed. 'Hold me!' Consciously I forced myself to relax my fingers, to loosen their grip on the door frame. I felt the metal slide beneath my hand, knowing that once the grip was loosened I would not be able, alone, to regain it. It was fingertips only, now . . . my whole being seemed concentrated in the tips of my fingers, the left reaching, searching, hoping; the right slipping inexorably now, over the cold metal. Then I touched the crack at the edge of the hatch cover and slid my numb fingers over its surface, searching for a thumbhold, a spring clip, some easy means of releasing it. But the surface was smooth apart from the tiny, rounded heads that my fingers could only just distinguish and which must be either rivets or screws. Were they screws? Three lives now depended on my finding out, but there was almost no feeling in my fingers now and they slipped and slid over the tiny heads. My nails, they were the answer! If I could feel the shape of a screw head, I'd know. Bending my fingers, I felt carefully at the heads. Was there a driving slot? Was there? Certainly there was a little irregularity, but it didn't reach across the whole head. Then did another one bisect it? I felt, and hoped, and when I knew the answer, I could have wept.

'Up!' I shouted. I tried to wriggle backward as Chao Li heaved at my legs, but didn't seem to be moving. 'Up!' I shouted again. 'Pull me up!' I could feel his hands tugging at my legs but I stayed where I was. 'For God's sake—pull!' I shouted. Bending at the waist until my stomach muscles quivered with tension, I struggled to get my right hand back as Chao Li heaved at my legs. Then I touched the frame. 'Again. Again.' At the next heave I got a grip and seconds afterwards, I was back in the cabin, nursing the frozen, nerveless block that was my left hand.

'Well?' Chao Li asked quickly. The girl was staring at me, eyes wide, afraid of the knowledge, but knowing already from my appearance what the answer was.

'Useless,' I said disgustedly. 'Philips screws, six or eight of them.'

'Philips?'

'The slot is like a cross,' I said. 'You need a special screwdriver. There isn't a hope. Not a hope in the bloody world!' I sat staring at my hand as the blood flowed back and the pins and needles began. It might just as well not bother, I thought: an hour or two more and it would be congealing anyway. Then we searched the cabin, looking for anything that could be adapted into a Philips screwdriver, but there was nothing. It was like looking for something that could be adapted into an elephant.

'Turn out your pockets,' I told Chao Li and turned my own out too. There were coins and my keys but they were Yales or variations on that theme; they wouldn't turn anything.

'Are there such things inside the cabin?' the girl asked and I looked around. The whole thing was covered in Philips screws.

'All around you,' I said. 'And we couldn't unfasten a single one if we wanted to.'

'I think,' she said, 'that there is a file. A fingernail file. In my handbag. It is back—'

Chao Li was reaching for it before she had finished, ripping it open.

'I think it's in—' she began.

'Give it to her,' I said, 'let her search her own handbag.'

In a moment she produced it: a wicked-looking thing about nine inches long and whippy. All we needed now was something to shape and enough time to shape it. But what? Nobody had any idea. We searched the cabin again but there was nothing. What? What? What? I needed a rod of aluminium, or mild steel, whose tip could be filed to the cross required. I'd have cannibalized anything, including the aircraft, to get that tool, but there was nothing. The throttle levers were too thick, and chrome steel anyway, and there seemed to be nothing else. Minutes dragged by as we all racked our brains; we knew, all of us, that it was over, that in a little more than two hours we would probably be dead. One of us might make it into the dinghy, but it was unlikely. The sea would be cold. And if we did get in, the wind would freeze us to death.

Moodily I looked at the handbag. It had held the file; what else might it contain? We searched it, looking at the lipstick case and the key ring, the odd coins and the powder compact. Nothing doing. I was about to toss it down when I realized suddenly that it had a metal frame. The bag was plastic, but metal held it together.

'Sorry, Maria,' I said, as I began hacking at the stitching with the file, my excitement growing as I uncovered a frame made not of brass but of iron or mild steel. 'Where did you get this?'

'Russia. At GUM in Moscow.'

'Thank God they haven't got round to instant obsolescence yet,' I said. 'This was built to last.'

With the plastic cut away, I examined the frame. Along the top, on each side, ran a bar of mild steel which carried the fastening clips. It was roughly three-sixteenths thick. If I could only shape the ends . . .

I broke it away and began to file. With the tiny teeth of the nail file it was desperately slow, finger-aching work, but they did, slowly and gradually, make an impression. First I cut four channels in the sides of the rod, then filed in to let them meet across the end. The edges of the little file grew smoother and smoother and made less and less impression, but I rubbed away, counting each little shiny particle of metal scraped away as a victory. Then, with the flat surface of the file, I began to shape the end. Occasionally I had to break off to straighten out the Tiger's attitude as it slipped beyond Maria's control, but she was doing beautifully.

An hour went by, then another quarter. Time was becoming tight and precious. If I didn't finish it soon, Nature would finish us. I sawed desperately at the iron, testing it now, every minute or two, on a screw head on the cabin wall. At last, it fitted! Not perfectly; not even well, but enough to turn the screw. I bent the rod to a right angle and tried it, left-handed, on one of the screws that held the lining to an interior stay. And it turned! Slowly, and awkwardly, but it turned.

'Right.' I looked at my watch. We had probably about

thirty minutes' fuel left. More or less. It could, I realized sickeningly, be a good deal less; there was no way of knowing.

Chao Li said, 'Would it not be easier if I went out and you held me? You are bigger, stronger.'

I shook my head.

'Then let me do it,' Maria said. 'I am not a fool. I can unfasten screws. You are needed to fly. I am light. He could hold me easily.'

I smiled at her. 'You're not dressed for it.'

'I'm not—! You, you—man!' she spluttered. 'You are so stupid. Of course I am the one who should go.'

'No,' I said. I meant it. God knows, I didn't want to hang out there again with the icy wind blasting at me and the Atlantic waiting, patient and threatening, below. But nobody else could do it.

'Why not?' Maria demanded.

'Because you don't know what a drain plug looks like,' I said. 'For that matter, I don't know what this one's like, but I hope I'll recognize it when I see it. Now, hold on tight, James Young. We haven't much time.'

I knotted the webbing round my ankles again, shoved the door open and rammed the blanket into the angle, then slid awkwardly out. My left hand, holding the home-made screwdriver, slid across the plating as I eased my body out of the cabin until my hips rested on the sill, then forward again. I had to tell myself that what mattered now was to do it, not to avoid discomfort; to force myself to allow my body to hang in space, to reach and to ignore the cold. My muscles ached as they strained to hold my body close against the aircraft's side and I manoeuvred to get the tip of the screwdriver into the first screw head. Finally, with the wind ripping at my clothes, freezing my face, my neck, and my hands, I managed the first contact. I took a breath, pressed the driver as hard into the slot as I could and began to turn. Nothing happened. I tried again, praying that it wouldn't slip, strip the screw slot or damage the makeshift driver. Still nothing. Again I urged my aching stomach muscles to bend me into position, praying that the man at the factory, tightening the screws, hadn't put his weight behind it.

Then the first one moved . . . and moved again. As quickly as I could, I turned the driver with my freezing fingers until the screw came into vision, sticking half an inch clear of the plating. Now the next. That was easy, turning first time. Two, now. I prayed the others would be as easy. There were, I now knew, six altogether. Number three was awkward, but I got it, then number four came free quickly. Number five I couldn't shift at all, perhaps because the strength of my muscles was ebbing and I could no longer find the purchase; perhaps because my numb hand no longer had the strength to exercise a strong grip. I moved quickly to number six and strained to turn it, but it wouldn't give. I strained and strained again, then felt my breath surge in relief as it turned a fraction, then a fraction more. I'd got it. Quickly I unscrewed it all the way.

That left only number five; the rest I could flick away to the ocean below. One big effort now, I told myself; just one last big effort.

I put the tip of the driver into the cross slot . . .

At that moment the Tiger gave a sudden convulsive lurch. What it was, I don't know : an air pocket, a sudden over-correction of aileron or rudder. Whatever it was, my body flicked sideways in a whip-like motion against the cabin side and the driver went spinning from my grasp.

Twenty-One

Helplessly I watched it spinning away to the ocean a quarter of a mile below. Disappointment flooded into my throat like

178

sickness. There was nothing to do, now, except wait and die. For the want of a screwdriver, an aircraft was lost! I watched that driver fall until I could see it no longer. Then I turned. 'Haul me up.' I shouted. As I struggled to climb backward to the cockpit, I stared once more at that hatch cover, now held by just one screw. Just one. It might as well have been a hundred. I wriggled and strained backward, scraping knees and thighs as I went, wrenching my body round for a grip with my right hand.

Then I saw the door.

The door! Was the hatch made like the door? If so, I might be able to prise it loose, bend the metal, do something at least. 'No.' I bawled. 'Leave me, leave me.' I slid forward and down and clawed for a grip on the hatch, trying to find a place where the screwless holes allowed the cover to slip down. If I could just get a grip on the edge, get my fingers underneath! But I couldn't; try as I might, I couldn't exert any leverage. It may sound silly, but hanging there upside down over the Atlantic, I began searching in my trousers for a coin, a big coin for preference: fifty cents, or a ten; it didn't matter which.

There wasn't a big one, though: just a few small American coins that weren't big enough to give any leverage at all. But then my fingers touched leather: my keys in a little folding leather case. I dragged them out and pushed the end of one key under the edge of the flap, then levered. The hatch cover moved, just a little! The key also bent. I put two keys together into the slightly enlarged slot and levered again. It opened a little more. Transferring the keys to my right hand, I felt with my left for the edge of the cover and just managed to get my fingertips under it. Now, bending and pulling, heaving with all my strength at that square foot of braced aluminium, I managed to force it open another half inch or so. And there it stuck. No strength that I could exert would move it a millimetre and my strength was, in any case, going fast. I would, I knew, have difficulty just getting back into the aircraft.

Desperately I tried one final time to lever it open; every ounce of strength I had was concentrated into downward pressure on that cover. If it didn't work, I was done. The cover moved a little, but not downward. Instead, pivoting on that one screw, it turned, opening a narrow gap through into the space behind the hatch. I tried to slip my hand through, but there wasn't room. Another push failed to move the hatch any more. But an idea came.

Now, summoning the last reserves of my fading strength, I twisted my body so that Chao Li could hear me call. 'Gun,' I shouted. 'Gun. Pistol.'

'Why?' He shouted back. I could have killed him.

'For a lever,' I yelled.

My heart lurched as I felt one of his hands loosen its grip on my legs. I'd known it would happen, but I felt, all the same, in the instinctive way we animals react, that I was about to fall. I know I screamed. With the wind ripping at me, half paralysed by fear and cold, I fought for self-control, trying to think of some way he could give me the gun without releasing his grip on my legs and without my having to climb back to the cabin. Then I thought of a way. If he slipped it into my trouser leg at the ankle, it would slide down the leg and I could pull it out at the waist. Two minutes later I had Maria's Mauser-type pistol in my hand and was pushing the barrel into that gap, levering downward on the butt. The metal creaked a bit and gave. Slowly, but it gave. The gap grew to an inch, then wider as I moved the barrel to a new position and levered again, each time for new purchase. Now, at last, the hole was big enough for my hand.

With the gun in my right hand, I reached my left in through the bent hatch cover, feeling among the control wires and stays. Would I recognize the damned thing if I touched it? I'd never be able to get my body into a position where I could see! A minute or more must have passed as my searching fingers moved over the assorted metal surfaces in the dark recesses behind the hatch. All the time my body was coming further and further out of the Tiger's cabin and Chao Li's ability to hold me decreased with every movement. Now I was held by the webbing straps alone and they were biting into my ankles excruciatingly. Then my probing fingers found a round plug with a knurled edge, perhaps an inch and a half across. I gripped it between finger and thumb and tried to turn, but my hand was now too numb for a proper grip. Somehow I had to warm that hand. I opened my mouth and put in both forefinger and thumb—try it, you'll almost choke as I did—but I also felt the warmth transferring from tongue and cheeks to the nerveless, cold flesh. In a minute or so, the pins and needles began and became painful. Another minute. Now it was time : I reached into the cavity, gripped that knurled cap and twisted desperately . . .

And it gave. I twisted again and again until I felt cold moisture on my hand, then quickly tightened it again while I examined the fluid on my fingers, touching it with my tongue and then turning my hand so that the drops flew away on the wind. There *was* water, I was sure of it, running in microscopic drops on the oil film the petrol made on my skin. So again I unfastened the plug, letting the contents of the tank flow down over my hands and out into space, carrying, thank God, clear of the red hot exhaust of that roaring after engine.

There was no way of knowing how much had gone. In my mind I was trying to work out how a couple of inches of water in the bottom of a tank would flow out with the pressure of the petrol on top. I couldn't though, and there was certainly no way of checking. I twisted my body upward. 'Young.'

'Yes.'

'Unscrew the filler cap inside. When it's down six inches, let me know.'

'Okay.'

I hung there like a lump of meat in an air pressure freezer, watching the fluid flow, keeping my hand on the plug the whole time in case it loosened under pressure and followed the screwdriver down into the Atlantic. How long it took to dribble out, I don't know and didn't care; when I got the word, I would screw that plug back and I wasn't thinking beyond that. The problem of getting back into the aircraft was too brutal for my battered mind, as it would probably be too much for my tired and weary body. Twice I screwed the cap back for a moment while I tried to decide whether the fluid was all petrol or a petrol and water mixture. I couldn't, though. That six-inch drop in the level of the tank was the only safe way. I hung, waiting . . .

'Okay.' Chao Li was shouting above me.

'Right!' I tightened the plug for the last time, gave it one final nasty twist with my aching fingers and let my body sag away from the side of the aircraft.

I breathed deeply a couple of times, taking great punishing lungfuls of the icy air that probably did more harm than good, then twisted and grabbed for the door frame. After two fruitless and painful attempts, I knew I couldn't make it, and Chao Li, tugging at my legs, hadn't a chance : a ten-stone man trying to lift a fourteen-stone one in that kind of situation has an impossible task. Once more I tried, straining and reaching, but I couldn't make it; I knew it, and I was exhausting myself trying. I hung for a second, thinking. Was this how I was to die; hanging upside down from an aeroplane and freezing to death in unsuccessful acrobatics? *Acrobatics*? Acrobatics!

'Hey!' Even my voice was weak.

'Yes.'

'Tell her . . . tell the girl, when I shout, to twist the wheel sharply to the left and kick the rudder bar hard with her left foot. Do you understand?'

'Turn the wheel to the left, kick the rudder with her left foot?'

'Right.' I tried to gather myself for one effort. 'Now!' I yelled.

The Tiger stood suddenly on its left wing tip, flinging me upward with a shock that felt for a moment as though it would break my back. When the instant flash of pain vanished, I realized it had worked: the open door was below me, not above. I fell heavily, half into the cabin, half against the roof. The gun spun away into space. Two seconds later I had scrambled inside and was rapping out instructions.

'Get these straps off my legs, Young!' Then, while he fiddled with the knots, 'Maria, ease the wheel round . . . no! not too sharply . . . now the rudder . . . just straighten her out, now the wheel . . .' By that time the webbing straps were free and I could grab the wheel myself. My hands and feet were aching and numb, but they behave instinctively on rudder bars and joysticks and I got the Tiger level and trimmed in high old time.

Chao Li didn't need to be told about the door: he reached across and dragged the blanket out, then snicked the safety-catch on the door lock.

'Rum,' I said. He got it out and I took a big swallow, feeling the harsh warmth bite at my throat then spread through my body. If we got to Bluie, maybe they'd get me for flying under the influence.

Maria said, 'I think you are one brave man.'

I grinned at her, but there was more hysteria than bravado in it. 'I think you are one good girl pilot,' I said. 'Now, the question is: when do we find out if that petrol is petrol?'

'How long before the other is finished?' Chao Li asked.

I looked at my watch. 'Now. Five, ten minutes. Any time.' I turned from one to the other. 'There may still be water in the tank. There will certainly be water in the pipes. The moment I switch it over, the engine's going to cut, because the feed pipe water is going to have to work its way through.'

'And our distance from land?'

'Who knows now?' I said. 'Hundred miles . . . seventy . . . could be anything. We haven't exactly been flying with great precision this last couple of hours.'

'But the gauge,' Chao Li said. 'It still shows the tanks are one-quarter full.'

'You forget. That gauge is faulty. Just like all fuel gauges are faulty. The makers calibrate them as best they can, but they can't do more.'

'I think you must switch,' Maria said. 'It is important to find out now. To sit and wait is stupid.'

'All right,' I said. I sat for a moment looking round the Tiger's cabin, listening to the roar of that one Continental. It might be the last time I'd hear a healthy aircraft engine. I stared down at the surface of the ocean. Away to the West the sky was darker with the muck and rubbish the Gander met man had promised; soon we would be in snow. My mind and body felt leaden, ready for death, unwilling to struggle any more. If the fuel flowed properly and the engines ran, I still had to fly into Bluie and in the kind of weather we'd be in then, my chances of missing the fiord walls weren't good, radar talk-down or no radar talk-down.

First I unfeathered the forward propeller and switched on the electrics: two engines would suck the water through from the feed pipes faster than one. With a roar she was away, healthy and powerful.

'Now's the time for prayers,' I said. I looked at Chao Li, pale as a ghost, teeth tight on his lower lip, and at Maria in the port seat, eyes closed and already murmuring her Hail Mary. I wondered how long it would take, in Castro's Cuba, for Lenin to supersede the opiate of the people.

Beneath my fingers, the switch felt absurdly small and unimportant. It was strange to think that it could kill us all; that in moving it I became a kind of executioner. And then

184

it was done, the little lever flicked over almost unintentionally. How long before anything happened? A few seconds? A minute? We sat there watching the clear blue that was the tip of the forward prop, listening, too, waiting for the first missed beat in the healthy roar of the engines.

Slowly the seconds ticked away and still those two Continentals roared on, beautifully on song, generating power with wonderfully smooth precision. We waited, sweating. At least, I was. Sweat itched in my hair, gummed my shirt against my back, slicked my hands, and still the engines didn't falter. Not a missed beat, not one tiny squirt of water into one of those twelve cylinders. It didn't seem possible, but it began to look as though we might have got away with it; began to look as though we could hope. Maria sensed my glance and opened her eyes.

'Is okay now?'

'Dunno,' I said. 'It looks—'

At that moment the nose engine cut out. It didn't cough or splutter; it just died.

We waited tensely as the rear engine roared. Chao Li's fists were clenched tight, his knuckles white, his black head lowered. He was doing what I was doing: willing the fuel to flow along those pipes!

Then the rear engine cut.

It was not silence, for the two propellers were driven to turn by our forward motion and they clacketed on. With each turn, I knew, water was being injected into the cylinders, the sparks fed to it, then it was being sucked out again. Or most of it was. A healthy engine can take a certain amount of water, spew it out and fire again when clean fuel becomes available. But we hadn't much time and we hadn't any guarantee that the fuel *was* clean. The Tiger's nose tilted down once more and I let her fall a few feet before trimming her to glide. The seconds ticked and with each tick we lost height—a hundred feet, two hundred, three, four, five. I fined off the propeller pitch to revolve them faster. Beside me Maria began for the tenth or twelfth time, *'Ave Maria gratia plena Dominus tecum . . .'*

At eight hundred the Atlantic waves looked huge; they also looked terrifyingly near, rearing up hungrily as though to lick at our feet, and still there was no sign from the engines that fuel was being burned.

I switched on the radio. 'Mayday, Mayday. Golf Alpha Lima Zulu, ditching in the North Atlantic approximately seventy miles south of Cape Farewell. Mayday, Mayday . . .' Cape Farewell was well named.

Behind me Chao Li was wrestling the dinghy forward again; I could hear the rubber scuffing across the cabin floor. The surging Atlantic was only five hundred feet below us now, white foam on angry black waves, and still the Tiger plunged downward. I kept talking into the radio, getting the Mayday away continuously to whoever might be listening, hoping to give them time to pinpoint the signal on D/F.

Two hundred feet. I remember looking at myself at that moment; at my healthy body that was warm and fed and reasonably efficient and would soon, in minutes indeed, no longer be mine and be on its way to becoming a part of the rolling ocean. Still we dropped.

I said, 'I'm sorry. It doesn't seem to have worked.'

Neither of them said anything; there wasn't really anything to say with the ocean coming up at us with that chilling, monstrous inevitability. I felt a touch on my arm and turned. Maria was looking at me, holding out her hand.

She said, 'Please.'

I reached across and took it. It was small and warm.

Then the forward engine coughed. Just once. One cylinder fired once and was silent. My heart hammered in my chest; a second ago I had been resigned. But that was hope! Another cough, then one from the rear engine! Maria's fingernails dug into my hand. Again the coughs, the firing of occasional cylinders in no sequence. It was like being tortured to death, this hope at the last second, given and withdrawn. Both engines were spluttering now, trying to expel the last of the useless water and breathe the pure fuel, but it was almost too late. The engines fought for all our lives as the Tiger slid down towards the rolling, straining ocean. And suddenly, unbelievably loudly, with a desperate, shattering vroom of sound, the rear engine exploded into its firing sequence. I turned on revs and boost to take-off power and tilted the aircraft's nose up, praying that the spirit was now clean; that this new hope was not to be smashed; that more water wasn't passing down the pipe to cut the motor again. Was it even hope? We were at about fifty feet and on one engine we'd probably have to crawl along at that height.

Then my seat moved against me with that unmistakable little shove a powerful engine gives one's body, and my eyes flicked to the rev counters. Now I had two, clamouring away! I also had seventy-five or so gallons of fuel. Joyfully I hauled the pole back and set the Tiger climbing away from the greedy ocean.

All I had to do now was get into Bluie West One.

Twenty-Two

For the second time I'd broadcast a Mayday distress call; now for the second time, I withdrew it. 'Golf Alpha Lima Zulu. Engines have restarted. Now okay. Making for Bluie West One.' I said it again and again, imagining all the cursing skippers, in the air and at sea, who had changed course to come to my assistance, and feeling like the boy who kept on crying wolf. Then Bluie came back at me: 'Weather conditions Bluie West One bad and deteriorating, wind velocity forty knots gusting fifty with blowing snow. Visibility down to three repeat three hundred yards and closing. Divert. I repeat, Lima Zulu. Divert.'

'Negative, repeat Negative,' I said. 'Bluie West One within range. No others.'

'Possible alternates at Frobisher, Baffin Island; Goose Bay, Labrador,' Bluie urged encouragingly.

'Negative,' I repeated. 'Am coming on. Request positional fix.'

'Very well, Lima Zulu. Stand by.'

He came back in a couple of minutes with the co-ordinates. 'Radar reports your position forty-six degrees twelve minutes west, forty-nine degrees thirty minutes north. You are approximately sixty-five miles from Cape Farewell. You will be talked in on Ground Control Approach.'

'Roger, Bluie,' I said: 'Airspeed approximately one-seventy, height one thousand feet.' Thank God their radar was serviceable!

'Lima Zulu. Have you flown into this airfield before?'

'Affirmative.'

'Good luck. We will help you all we can.'

'Roger,' I replied. 'And thanks.'

'Is it really so dangerous?' Chao Li asked.

'You mean with talk-down procedures?'

'Yes. Do they not say: now you are here, now fly there?'

'They do. Look—' The pair of them might as well know they'd escaped the frying-pan of the ocean for the fire of Bluie. 'Bluie is murder.'

'Why?' Maria said softly. 'Why do they fly there if it is so bad?'

'Because it's the only tenable airfield in the whole area. The only bit of flat ground. And it's difficult to get in. In this weather it's very difficult indeed.' I pointed to the west where the grey snow clouds hung on the sky like dirty washing. Soon we'd be among them.

'But why impossible?' she persisted. She was inclined, this one, to believe in miracles. She'd just seen me performing something very close to one, and now she was seeking deliverance via another.

'It's just Bluie,' I said. 'I can remember hearing a guy called Hughie Green describe it perfectly. He's an entertainer, but he's been around the North Atlantic for thirty years and he knows Bluie well. He said: Imagine you're flying along a street in a big city with high buildings on each side, and when you come to the next crossroads, you've got to bank to the right and fly down another street. Or crash. Cake the whole setting in ice and snow and toss in a nasty wind. That's Bluie.'

'I see,' she said.

'No. You don't see at all. Until you've actually seen Bluie for yourself, you can't imagine.'

Twenty minutes later we were approaching the entrance to Bluie fiord in blowing snow that built on the windshield. I had the Tiger's speed down to about seventy and once I was in the fiord I was going to fly a sight slower than that, way down below stalling speed, in fact, and hope my reflexes would help get us in.

The tail wind was still there and now, far from being a friend, it was a very dangerous enemy. By dropping the tail and so increasing the wings' angle of attack on the air, I'd got the speed down to probably fifty miles an hour and the Tiger was literally hanging in the air on the power of the engines, prop-wash blasted at the flaps. It would have been easier, much easier, in a headwind, but the air revolving round that high was blowing straight into the fiord. With the screen wipers on I stared forward, looking for the towering walls at the entrance to the fiord.

'Lima Zulu to Bluie. Have you got me on approach radar?'

'Affirmative, Lima Zulu. Approach controller speaking. Your height, please?'

'One thousand.'

'Ten degrees left, Lima Zulu. Hold your height at one thousand. Carry out vital actions for landing.' That's to remind you to lower your wheels. You've no idea how many idiots try to land with their wheels retracted. The Tiger's undercart, however, was fixed. No problem. At least not there.

Another voice. Thank God! They'd got me on PAR. 'Lima Zulu, this is your final controller. How do you hear?'

'Loud and clear,' I said. 'Very loud and very clear.'

'Good. We have you on Precision Approach Radar, and you are entering the fiord on the centre line. Do not acknowledge further instructions.'

I've no idea what visibility was, partly because I was glued to the instruments and partly because it was never the same for two consecutive minutes: the swirling clouds of snowflakes rolling one moment into a vast, opaque cloud, then lifting, suddenly and magically, so that the rock walls seemed to loom at us and instinct had to be fought because instinct demanded correction and instinct was wrong. Slowly I felt my way along that fearful place like a fly buzzing carefully along between two flypapers.

'Okay, Lima Zulu, okay.' The controller's voice went on soothingly. 'Five degrees left . . . two degrees left . . . okay . . . okay . . .'

'Open the cabin windows,' I said. There was a tiny pause of incomprehension, then Chao Li opened the door window and Maria the port one. Snowflakes raced into the cabin on the icy wind. 'Now get your heads out,' I said. 'Watch those bloody cliffs. If one's coming near, tell me. Understand?'

'Yes,' said Chao Li.

Maria nodded.

'But gently. No shrieking. Just tell me we're getting near; don't shriek "Look out" or anything like that.'

We crawled forward. Those rock walls climbed to nine thousand feet; they're like all those pictures of the North Wall of the Eiger, but they're worse. You can't turn; you can't really climb. Once you're in the fiord, all you can do is keep going, keep hoping and above all keep your wits about you and your eyes skinned.

For long moments snow swirled in tight skeins before us, blanking out vision; then it swung away and as the towering walls marched forward, I made the tiny corrections to aileron and rudder that moved us away. I was flying as though my hands and feet were eggshells: just obeying. Over-correction would be as fatal as no correction: it would simply swing us away from one rock wall to smash us into the other and we would join all the fliers whose bodies and machines lie at the bottom of Bluie fiord.

'You're two degrees left, Lima Zulu. Okay now.'

With the screen wipers cutting quadrants in the windshield snow and two extra pairs of eyes staring out to port and starboard, we gradually won distance, but all the time we were getting nearer to that right-angled turn up the corridor.

'Okay, Lima Zulu. On the centre line.'

'Thank you, Bluie.' I stared forward at the black water below and the white sky above and the vast rock walls on either side; I was looking for the turn like a man in a thick fog trying to find the right street corner.

A tiny nudge from Chao Li and a nod at a huge rock buttress that reared out of the wall: a tiny correction to the controls to move the Tiger twenty or thirty yards towards the centre of the gorge.

'Okay, Maria?'

A moment to look, then 'Okay.'

'Lima Zulu, you are approaching the corridor turn, still on the centre line. You're doing well, Lima Zulu. Very well. One mile to the turn. Repeat, one mile.'

A mile! Less than a minute before I must judge that turn perfectly—or pile against the rock wall, one tiny plume of flame against the grey-and-white vastness. I found myself trying to swallow but failing because there was no moisture in my mouth. My eyes were on the monolithic wall to starboard, watching for the break. Ahead, snow swirled in a tight, racing cloud that spun and boiled within itself, then hurled its opacity at me.

'You are approaching the turn into the corridor now, Lima Zulu,' Bluie's final controller murmured gently. It was a soft, soothing voice like a well-bred undertaker's. Desperately I stared round me, trying to discern, through the snow flurry, the angle in that great wall. But there wasn't an angle there; nothing but millions of flying white specks that flashed endlessly by. Back to the instruments!

'Lima Zulu. Flying blind in heavy snow flurry.'

'Lima Zulu, I shall instruct on turn to starboard. You are now approximately four hundred yards away . . . keep coming . . . you are on the centre line . . . keep coming . . . on the centre.'

The seconds ticked by as I peered alternately at the instruments and into the flying snow, waiting for the order to bank the Tiger. Snow can and does do strange things to radar and I was praying that theirs was modern and the green dot on the oscilloscope was a nice clean one, not a spreading blur of confusion.

'Begin your turn now, Lima Zulu,' Bluie said. 'Ninety degrees and a tight turn. Okay now. Okay. No, Lima Zulu, to port. To port!'

It was my own fault. I'd been so mad keen to make that turn a full ninety degrees and to make it good and tight that I swung the Tiger through more than ninety. I corrected frantically, my eyes on the compass. While I was doing it I felt a nudge from Chao Li and glanced up in time to see the snow whisk away like a curtain flicked aside and the massive rock wall looming at me.

I booted the Tiger to port so hard that Chao Li was flung across the cabin and crashed into the opposite wall, but there wasn't time to think about him; Greenland was poised to swat the Tiger and I had to get her clear. Slowly she came round; desperately slowly. She was in the worst possible trim for rapid turns: nose high and tail down, trimmed for a widened angle of attack. I felt sweat break out all over me! The starboard wing tip, swinging through a wide arc, couldn't possibly miss. It couldn't! It was going to hit! I watched, leaden, as it came round to its inevitable impact, swinging, swinging, swinging, until, unbelievably, it must have passed the wall . . . swinging until Lima Zulu was clear once more, heading away from that monstrous mountain of stone.

'Five degrees left,' the controller said. 'Well done. You are now back on the centre line, Lima Zulu. Now down to five hundred feet and hold your course. Approach path is dead ahead. I shall begin to talk you down but the final approach should be visual.'

'Thank you, Bluie,' I changed the trim and moved forward more easily, more confidently, listening and obeying. Now that we were round the corner, the snow was thinner, moving more slowly. Five minutes later, as my wheels touched on the runway at Bluie West, I heaved a massive sigh of relief. Everybody does. Everybody always heads for the Bluie bar, too, where the sign says, 'Please note : every piece of ice used in your drinks is at least a million years old.'

As I taxied towards it, I felt even older.

The Danish Government man looked at me narrowly. His expression wasn't exactly disbelieving, but it showed he had listened to me with a degree of surprise.

'So this gentleman, Mr er—'

'Young. James Young,' I said. 'British passport.'

'Mr Young threw his passport out of the aircraft?'

I said patiently, 'No, I did. The passport was in his case and when we were trying to lighten the aircraft, I threw it out.'

He nodded. Immigration officers the world over think much the same way : passports are their universe, precious as rubies. 'He did not try to stop you?'

'I shouted to him,' Chao Li said, 'But you see—'

193

'He was too late,' I said. 'By that time, the case was twenty feet down and dropping fast. There wasn't a great deal I could do.'

'Very careless,' he muttered. 'Very careless indeed.'

'Perhaps,' I said, 'you'd prefer that I'd chucked him out and kept the documents. More orderly!'

He scowled at me. 'And the girl?'

'Stowaway,' Chao Li said. 'Hi-jacker.'

'Ah,' the immigration man brightened. 'Her uniform. What uniform is it?'

'Cuban,' I said. I turned to look at her. She stood there, pale, defiant and naïve; a nice girl who'd taken a lot of risks and was now at the end of the road.

I don't know why I said it. I could have got rid of her there and then, so easily. It must have been something to do with the items listed above and the way she'd kept her nerve in the crisis. 'She's not a hi-jacker,' I said. 'I invited her aboard.'

'You are a fool,' Chao Li said. He turned to the immigration man. 'She boarded the aircraft at Gander and hid until we were out over the Atlantic.'

The immigration man's lips tightened. 'You are the pilot, Mr Shaw. Yours is the responsibility.'

I said, 'Agreed. I told you. She was aboard by invitation. My invitation.'

'Three people. Two seats?'

'Look,' I said. 'She's seeking asylum. Not in Canada, where she quit. Or here or in Denmark. She's seeking asylum in London.'

Chao Li said, 'I do not understand this. She had a gun. She ordered Mr Shaw to fly to Miami.'

'A gun?'

'No gun,' I said. In my mind I could see it still, spinning off towards the Atlantic as I tumbled back into the Tiger. I nodded towards Chao Li. 'He's had a tough time,' I said sympathetically. 'We all have.'

'This gun,' the immigration man said.

'She had it.' Chao Li was coldly angry. 'She brought it on board the plane. It was an automatic pistol of Chinese manufacture.'

'Please,' I said. 'We only want transit facilities anyway. Food, sleep and off. That's all.'

'Hi-jacking is an offence of extreme seriousness.' The immigration man looked at Maria.

'Agreed,' I said. 'But have you ever heard of a hi-jack *away* from Cuba?'

'You require transit facilities only?' He looked at Chao Li, at Maria, at me, his eyes switching coldly along the line and back. 'Your route?'

'Keflavik and Prestwick,' I said.

He nodded and I thought how familiar this kind of scene must be to him. A staging field like Bluie must get a hell of a lot of traffic that is, to say the least, informal, and there wasn't really much this guy could do except look threatening. He could deny us permission to leave transit, but we didn't want to leave anyway. He could possibly order us off, but if I pleaded lack of sleep, he couldn't insist. He could, I supposed, clap us in irons for any one of a dozen reasons, but if we intended to leave as soon as possible, there wasn't much point in that either.

'Very well.' He handed my passport to me and Maria's to her. To Chao Li he gave a rather elegantly ironic shrug.

'I tell you,' Chao Li said again, 'that she is a pirate. She should be detained and charged.'

He got another ironic shrug.

'Thank you,' I said. 'Come on!'

Outside Chao Li said, 'Why? Why did you do it? She could have been left here.'

I said, 'Because I like the colour of her eyes.' While we'd been arguing with the immigration man, the light had gone. I was grinning, but I doubt whether Chao Li could see it.

'You are a fool,' he said. 'An irresponsible fool. I shall

report this to Lennox. The girl is dangerous.'

I said, 'Don't be a bloody idiot. If I'd handed her over and laid charges here, we might both have been kept as witnesses until the hearing. And *you*, chum, are on Danish soil, from which our American friends could and would extradite you. Your feet, as we used to say, wouldn't touch.'

He stopped and stared at me for a moment, his dark eyes calculating. In that light he'd be able to see precious little, but he must have been half-satisfied. 'Very well, Mr Shaw.'

'There's one more point,' I said.

'What is it?'

'I'm handing her over personally, when we get to Britain. I said I'd do it. And I will.'

'Very well,' Chao Li repeated. 'It is my belief that you are irresponsible and that our mission is being endangered by your behaviour. I warn you that I may need to take action.'

He stalked away across the airfield and I watched him go. I wondered what action he meant to take. I couldn't help thinking about the cop at Berkeley and about Jasmine Yang.

'Mr Shaw.' Maria's voice was low.

'Yes.'

'I am sorry. You are in much trouble because of me?'

'I was in much trouble long before I met you,' I said.

'I do not understand.'

I was still watching Chao Li. He was among the lights now, crossing to the dormitory huts. 'What don't you understand?'

'You. I threaten to kill you, yet you speak for me against your friend.'

'Don't worry,' I said. 'I told you you'd get the chance to seek asylum and you will. Now off you go. I'll see you in the morning.'

I watched her walk away towards the huts for women transit passengers, then I turned and hurried back to the Tiger in her parking bay. The cabin tank had been drained and hosed out with compressed air before it was refilled. The wing tanks were full. All was well again.

Except that I couldn't find what I was looking for. I shrugged and went to the Met room.

Twenty-Three

About six hours later, the thing I'd been looking for was pressed against my neck, just below the ear. I woke with a nasty shock in my little cubicle in the transit dormitory at Bluie to find Chao Li bent over me, gun in hand.

'Get up,' he said, softly, 'and get dressed.'

'Don't be bloody silly,' I said, 'and put that thing away.'

'Get up,' he said. 'We're leaving now.'

'Not on your life,' I said, a bit smugly. 'You're not leaving without a pilot and I'm not going yet.'

Chao Li looked at me. 'There are other pilots in this hut. If you refuse I can take one of them. *Any* one of them.'

I said, 'They wouldn't take you.'

'At gunpoint? The first one might not, but the second would, when he saw the first one die. Get up and get dressed.'

I began to climb out of bed. Why the hell hadn't I followed up last night when I'd found the gun was missing from the aeroplane! I'd known he'd got it, but I suppose I hadn't thought he'd go this far. Or I'd been too tired, too lazy to think. 'What about the girl?'

'Quiet!'

I bent to lace my shoes and saw his feet step smartly back. He stood in silence as I finished dressing, then gestured with the gun barrel; I led the way outside.

'All right. Where now?' I asked as we stepped out into the bitter night air.

'To the aircraft, naturally.'

'Why? And what about the girl?'

'You are a sentimental fool, Shaw. Because she is a pretty girl you will let her ruin our mission. You were instructed that no one must know about me. Now she knows and the authorities here know.'

'Only that you're James Young.'

'It is too much.'

I said, 'For God's sake, there are six hundred million Chinese.'

'You refuse to acknowledge that this is necessary,' he said, 'although your orders were absolutely explicit. That is why I am doing it.'

'So what happens to her?' I said. 'She's still in transit here. She hasn't been admitted. Unless she's lucky she'll be on the first plane out. She may even be sent to Cuba and that means imprisonment or death.'

'So?' he shrugged.

'And what about the weather. We don't know if it's fit for flying.' I was stalling, wanting time. Given time I'd find some way to get her out. I was surprised I cared at all; perhaps it was the old business of action and reaction : Chao Li wanted to leave her, so I didn't.

'Look at it.'

It was cold and dark with the stars bright in the velvet black, and a clear moonlight. 'You're mad,' I said. 'It may be okay here, but we aren't staying here. We need to know what it's like between here and Keflavik. It's all right going up, but we need to know we can get down.'

'You'll get down,' he said. 'And you'll learn about weather from the radio.'

He walked alongside me all the way, the gun out of sight. When we got to the Tiger, he reached up and opened the door. 'In first.' I climbed across the port side seat and fastened my seat belt as Chao Li got into the cabin and took the starboard seat and slammed the door. I sat, waiting.

'The weather,' he said.

I switched on the radio and asked. Air controllers are courteous and helpful people and I've always been grateful for it. This time I wished the controller had said what I'm sure he wanted to say: 'Get your idle legs over to Met!' Instead he asked me to stand by, then came back chattily. I suppose it made a change in the middle of the night. The weather was reasonably healthy and thanks to that high, it was clear across to Iceland. 'You can get to Shannon if you like,' he said. 'If you've got the range.'

I thanked him and started the engines.

'Lima Zulu to Bluie control, clear to take-off please.'

'Okay, Lima Zulu. You may begin taxiing.'

It was all so easy, I thought, bitterly. Just get a gun and go where you like. Shove it in the pilot's back and help yourself! Perhaps I had been a bit tricky about the girl, but' what the hell! She wasn't likely to do either Chao Li or Lennox any harm.

'What a bunch of bastards you are,' I said. 'You and Lennox.'

Chao Li said nothing. As we bumped round the perimeter to the end of the runway, he sat still, the gun steady in his hand, watching me.

The radio crackled a bit. 'Lima Zulu clear take-off.'

'Roger,' I said. I wound up the revs and the Tiger growled forward under her weight of fuel, picking up speed slowly but steadily and then, with all the easy grace of a drunken nanny goat, becoming airborne. I turned her on to the line and headed out along the fiord which, in the still that's so common in the wee sma' hours, looked scenic and dangerous instead of just dangerous. We didn't have much height and I didn't try to gain any: just skimmed above the water a couple of hundred feet up, turned left at Oxford Circus, and flew away. Soon afterwards we came out of the mouth of the fiord and set course for Keflavik.

'Put it away,' I said. He still held the gun so that its muzzle pointed at me.

He didn't move.

'For God's sake,' I said, 'what do you imagine I'm going to do? Go back? You want to go to Britain. I want to go to Britain. We're going. Put the gun away.'

Finally, he did. He put it where he could reach it, though, in the little cubby-hole in front of his seat.

I said, 'Are they all like you in Lennox's outfit?'

He didn't respond.

'He's a bastard himself,' I said. 'And I've met one or two others when I've been flying for him. Where does he find you all? He must have to search pretty hard.'

This time he looked at me.

'Go on. Tell me,' I said. 'Does he have little exam papers and Bastardy Quotients determined by how ready you are to cut out granny's guts?'

'You are a fool,' he said. 'You cannot see the big things for the small. It is a matter of great importance, international importance even, that my journey should be secret.'

'And the hell with everybody?'

'Fly,' he said.

'No. Come on, explain. Don't people matter at all? When it comes to intelligence, how many people are worth one fact? Come to that, how big is the casualty list? Per annum will do.'

'It is simple,' he said. 'It is like war. It *is* war. This war does not end.'

'And you enjoy fighting it!'

'Enjoy? It is necessary.'

'Yes.' I was making a mental note that after this trip, Lennox could look elsewhere for his chauffeurs and that as soon as I got to London I'd tell him so. At length and pleasurably. I began to think about the words I'd use . . .

At ten thousand feet I levelled her off and reset revs and boost for max/continuous. With a seventy-knot tailwind, the Tiger would gobble up the Greenland-Iceland hop then I'd take on more fuel and swing south for Prestwick.

'When do we reach Iceland?' Chao Li wanted to know.

'Another three and a half hours or so. We'll be at the PNR in an hour or a bit less.' It was nice to make him ask. A tiny little, mean little, bit of my own back.

'PNR?'

'Point of no return,' I said. 'That's when it would take longer to go back than go on. We've got a dirty great chuff wind so we must be making two-ten. By the time we've flown an hour and twenty minutes it would take us four hours to fly back. Easier to go on.'

The minutes and the miles went by. I was navigating by the stars for a while, until I hooked on to the Keflavik long range radio beacon, and even with Chao Li beside me, I was enjoying flying through the night towards the dawn, with the black velvet below and the grey-blue velvet above, pierced with stars.

The milestone came. 'PNR,' I said. A moment later, I was saying in amazement, 'What the hell—?'

Maria was grappling with Chao Li across the back of his seat, trying to reach the pistol. He'd been too quick for her, though. He'd got her arm in a lock of some kind with his left hand and the pistol was in his right hand before I knew what was happening.

'Get back,' he said. 'Sit on the floor.' She obeyed slowly. 'Now understand this, if you make one movement of any kind, I shall shoot you.'

'Do you know what he did, this one?' Maria said. Her tone was cold but fear vibrated in it. 'He came into my room in the women's huts. But I was not in my bed, was I? Ha!' She seemed about to spit at him.

'Be silent,' Chao Li said.

'He came in,' she said, 'with a gun in his hand, and he walked over to the bed pointing it. He would have shot me!'

The sound of the shot blasted our eardrums in the little cabin. I swung round with difficulty, held firmly down by my seat strap, and saw Maria huddling away from him, clutching at her arm and trying to stay in the shelter of the fuel tank. Chao Li was already climbing over the back of the seat.

'Leave her,' I shouted. I reached out to grab his arm, to try to hold him; but he shook my arm away. In another second he'd fire again. It must have been the grip of my seat belt that gave me the idea. A second later Chao Li was tumbling back, clawing for a hold as his body smashed into the door. I'd taken a big bootful of starboard rudder and starboard aileron and shoved the Tiger's nose down for good measure. Something heavy crashed into the back of my seat and grunted. It could only be Maria and she must be wounded, but Chao Li had to be neutralized before I could do anything about her. I hauled the pole towards me, tearing the Tiger into a climbing turn. The G was tugging at me, even strapped as I was into my seat; the other two didn't have a chance. Chao Li was catapulted out from beside the door and flew with a crash into the fuel tank and I heard the agonized grunt of his impact. The gun, though! Where was the gun? Desperately I tried to see whether it was still in his hand, but he was draped across a corner of the by-now-almost-horizontal tank. Again I swung the Tiger round, praying that she'd stand up to the treatment, and this time Chao Li fell backwards against the cabin wall. There was a smack as the side of his head hit the spot where floor and wall joined, and he seemed to go limp.

'Maria!' She didn't reply. 'Maria!' I listened, watching Chao Li. He didn't move. I must have knocked out both of them. Straining round in my seat I could just see that she appeared to be wedged between the rear wall of the cabin and the back of the tank. But where was the gun? And where was the petrol coming from that made the cabin suddenly reek like a garage forecourt? I saw its dull sheen on the tank metal by the filler cap and realized that it had been forced out by the pressure of sudden movements of the aircraft.

Chao Li was beginning to stir and groan and I had only seconds to get that gun. If he fired it again, in this vapour-laden cabin, we'd all vanish in a blue and yellow flash. I ripped at the clasp of my seat belt and flung myself backward over the seat. I knew what would happen and it did! The sudden extra weight tilted the aircraft back and the elevators uncontrolled now, moved naturally to adopt the new attitude, tail down. I slid to the back of the Tiger's cabin in a heap, smashing into the unconscious Maria; but as I slid down one side of the cabin, Chao Li was carried down the other. I forced myself across the tiny space between the tank and the cabin wall, reaching for where the gun lay in the angle, but as I did so, she stalled and dropped the port wing, catapulting me back. Chao Li's hand came into view at that second, reaching slowly, weakly for the gun. As the Tiger slumped round into a wing-down, slow spin I hurled myself at the gun, but his hand got there first and his fingers closed slowly over the butt; I did the only thing I could do, making a ball of my fist and hitting hard at his wrist.

The gun flew free and I grabbed it, lurched back as the aircraft spun, and began to try to slide to my seat before the Tiger could twist off its tail assembly. My left shoulder smashed into the steel tubing of the seat frame, but I'd still got the gun in my right. Awkwardly, I climbed over and got my hands and feet on the controls. A glance showed the wings and wing struts vibrating like a jews' harp; God knows what was happening to the booms and the tail. Any second they could go, and especially under the strain of pulling out of the spin.

Even the sound of a spin is terrifying, but this wasn't my first or my hundred and first. I'd practised spins in my time till my toenails grew twisted, but that was in aircraft stressed for maximum all-round performance, not a layabout's lightweight conveyance like the Tiger. It's one of the things you never forget, like the first lesson on the Bren, and somewhere at the back of my mind my ginger-haired flight-lieutenant instructor, Martindale, said, 'Full opposite rudder.' I kicked the rudder bar, hard. 'Pause,' he said. 'A nice—long—pause—' I waited, itching. But he was right and I knew it. 'Stick forward.' That's the bit that frightens you to death. You're hurtling down, spinning like a belly-dancer's tassels, and you move the stick forward.

God! What would this do to the Tiger's wings? Could they stand this strain for more than a few seconds?

'Wait for it, Shaw. Wait, lad. A nice long wait.'

I waited, sweating, thinking about the wings. The spin was easing, easing, easing, but they'd drop off soon.

'Centralize controls!'

My hands and feet moved, automatically almost, keeping everything nice and straight until the Tiger came out of her spin into a simple dive and I felt the old familiar tugging at my guts at the bottom of the curve.

I got her level at seven thousand feet and looked behind me. Chao Li lay in a heap forward of the tank and Maria lay to the rear of it, held there by its bulk. I looked at the gun, opened it, removed the bullets; put them in one pocket and the gun in the other, then got us straight on the Keflavik beacon.

I opened the windows to disperse the vapour. The blast of icy air did the job in about three seconds. There was nothing else I could do. I wanted to get back and see how badly Maria had been hurt, but if I left the controls again, I'd simply be repeating the murderous strain on the tail. It was doubtful whether it could stand it again; after all it had been through, I was surprised the tail was still with us: Stripe Aircraft's advertised top speed in a dive obviously contained a substantial safety margin!

The gun came back into my hand again as I heard Chao Li groan. From this moment, I was going to be master of this ship and my own fate. I waited, looking round from time to time as he moaned. Finally he sat up and looked at me. The look became a stare, and animosity was its major component.

'Get back there,' I said savagely. 'And bring the girl forward. And be careful.'

The flat, level hatred of his stare altered slightly as he raised a hand to his mouth, then examined the bloody saliva on his fingertips. 'You fool,' he snarled at me. 'What do *you* know? You let your stupid, animal instincts get in the way of things too big for you to understand.'

I let the gun pivot a little in my hand. 'Bring her forward.'

'Shaw, you must be mad. She must die! She knows, so she *must* die.'

'She may be dead already,' I said, grimly.

'No. I hit her in the arm. The bullet went through the wall. See?'

I looked. There was a little hole in the padding. 'Get her!'

He eased himself along to the rear of the cabin and dragged her forward.

'Sit her up with her back against the tank.' He obeyed. The bullet hole was a tiny mark in the fabric of her jacket, and the wound, when her jacket had been removed, was simply a deep-cut channel across the surface of her arm, from which blood flowed slowly. I tore the first-aid box off the bulkhead and watched while he dusted it with penicillin powder and taped a big square of gauze over it.

'Rest her on that blanket,' I said, 'and then sit in that seat and do up those straps.' When he'd fastened them, I reached across and pulled them as tight as they would go. Who cared if they stopped his circulation?

I said, 'Now keep still, very still.'

'Very well, I suppose I must tell you,' Chao Li said suddenly.

'Not me. I only drive the bus.'

'It is imperative,' he snapped.

'Then I'll know and you'll have to kill me too?'

He shook his head. 'The detail: it is the detail that is vital. But the scheme . . . it is a decision by the extreme right, both in Western Europe and America, to write off a generation.'

'To what!' I said. 'You must be mad! You're talking about millions of people.'

Chao Li nodded. 'Millions. More than Hitler and Stalin killed. *Now* do you see why it is important?'

I shook my head. 'It's impossible! A conspiracy of the extreme right—who d'you mean?'

'Big men. Important, rich men with vast resources. Men who own huge companies in petro-chemicals and distributive industries. They have the will and the resources.'

'All right,' I said. I didn't believe a word of it. It was like the ravings of a madman. 'Why?'

'Because,' Chao Li said, 'the generation is not theirs to control. It has slipped away from them.' He said it slowly, carefully. 'They set the targets for people to strive after: things that are always newer and always more costly. And each succeeding generation has acquiesced and dreamed of bigger cars and more things of every kind. But now they're threatened. Do you see? The students, the hippies, the flower people of a year or two ago, they aren't so interested in things. They are interested in ideas and concepts. The big men do not like it.'

I said, 'I can see why business doesn't love the hippies. But how are they going to do it?'

'When I said they mean to write off a generation, I was being less than precise. They are out to destroy the generation's intellectual élite, at the universities and the schools. Their weapon is—drugs.'

'Drugs!' I thought about a parcel of parts for Marion Capote's old Rolls-Royce that turned out to be a load of drugs. 'Tell me.' I said.

Chao Li looked at me. He was coldly calm, his face and

206

eyes compelling. 'The students, the university people, regard total freedom as an absolute right. That includes freedoms of every kind. One is the freedom to smoke cannabis, take amphetamines and morphia. It is through this freedom that they will be reached.'

'Go on.'

'Many of these men are in positions of great power and influence, formulating policy. They are often, for example, in the governing bodies of universities. So, for them, it is simple. They ensure that the régime is repressive, that the young are always on the edge of revolt. They do that with one hand. With the other, they keep vast quantities of harmful and addictive drugs flooding into the schools and campuses. Soon there will be a generation of addicts. It has started already.'

Rafer Hayes. The words echoed all that Rafer had said, except that Rafer hadn't known where the drugs came from in such quantity.

'You do not believe me?' Chao Li's voice was low and regretful. 'Think about this. You know, unless you are blind and deaf, that pills of all kinds are freely available—the so-called pep pills, Black Bombers and Purple Hearts and many others. You know that.'

I nodded.

'Some of these are synthetics, yet manufactured drugs require expensive research and plant to produce them. Have you never wondered why so many are made? Why thousands more are made than are ever prescribed? Why they are sold in almost every city and so easy to obtain that schoolchildren can get unlimited supplies?'

'Deliberate over-production?'

'Precisely that. For every one that is needed, fifty are made, or a hundred.'

'It is horrible!' I turned in surprise. Maria was conscious; obviously she had heard.

I said, 'Yes, it's horrible, but why is it necessary to transport you in such secrecy that you're prepared to kill Maria? Why?'

'Because I know who these men are,' he said softly. 'Not all, but many. They know *who* I am, but thanks to Lennox and to you, they do not know *where* I am. If they find me, though, wherever I am, I am finished. That policeman I stabbed : he was not controlling a riot, he was coming to kill *me*. Do you think I wanted to kill him? These men control police forces, they control political organizations of many kinds. I am safe only with Lennox and his people, his organization.'

'I hardly think Maria constitutes a threat to you.'

'No? She is a woman. She will be interrogated. She will talk. Somebody high in government will hear. And don't forget that these people *are* high in government. Don't you realize that the only hope is the professionals? Men like Lennox! They can operate in secret beneath the upper layer. They, too, have facilities, means of fighting. But if the high men know they *are* fighting, then they can easily be crushed.'

He stopped talking and looked at me. 'You understand, but do you believe?'

I stared back at him. Drugs . . . millions of youngsters being destroyed by drugs. Rafer Hayes had said it differently—what was it? A war and we're losing it.

I said, 'I suppose you must be given the benefit of the doubt.'

Chao Li nodded. 'That is why she must die.'

Twenty-Four

The Tiger droned on across the ice-marked waters of the Denmark Strait. Inside there was silence. I had said 'No'

once, explosively. Then I said it again. And again. I had repeated it until there was no point in repeating it any more.
Chao Li had one idea : to kill her and drop her body out of
the aircraft; he wanted her to vanish for ever in the Arctic
seas. My argument—roughly that two wrongs don't make a
right—sounded like feeble logic even in my own ears and
grew feebler the longer I thought about it. All the same, I
wasn't going to connive at this : quite apart from my own
promise to deliver Maria to the US Embassy in London,
I was horrified by the idea of cold-blooded execution. It
obviously didn't bother Chao Li one bit, though. I think it
was the cool assessment he'd made of the need to kill her
that made me resist him so strongly. There were times, as
he argued and cajoled, when I came near to agreeing, but
I always stopped; always tripping over the same thing : why
did he show neither regret nor reluctance?

'Don't you see how absurd it is to weigh her against a
generation?' he demanded.

I winced, screwing my eyes shut to exclude the pictures
and the thoughts. Then I turned and looked at Maria,
whose eyes were wide with fear.

'Don't worry,' I said. I wanted to be reassuring, but
somehow it came out harsh. The poor kid must have been
going through a hundred and fifty sorts of hell, especially
when she detected that I might be wavering.

'But why does he hate me so?'

I said, 'Not you. Not personally. He is afraid that you
might talk too much.'

'No. He hate me. Hate. I know it and I feel it. Why?'

Chao Li shrugged. His face was bland, almost without
expression. He worked at being impassive, I thought; worked
hard at it; he'd been impassive in some pretty hair-raising
situations in the hours since we'd first faced each other
across the body of Jasmine Yang aboard *Sunrise*. On the
other hand he'd shown his share of emotion in flashes. They
were always brought under control rapidly, but they were

there and I'd seen them. I'd seen him angry, disgusted, cold with contempt. He was utterly strange to me.

I said, 'As long as I'm flying this aircraft, you're safe. After we land, I shall try to protect you. In the meantime, I have the gun.'

'Thank you,' Maria's voice was barely audible.

Chao Li turned away and stared out of the window at the sea and the first golden lines of dawn that lay in layers on the eastern sky. Whatever he was thinking about, though, it was not the dawn.

Keflavik looked like being a hell of a problem. Everybody would have to get out of the aircraft for obvious reasons; but everybody would have to get in again, too. Chao Li, if his story was true, was entitled to expect silence both from Maria and from me, even if it was not the kind of silence he'd obviously prefer. The trouble was that I couldn't do a single thing to prevent her disappearance. She could vanish into the ladies' room and howl for political asylum till the cows came home and there was nothing I could do to stop her. And if I were her, that's exactly what I'd do.

When the petrol truck had finished refuelling the Tiger, I walked with Maria and Chao Li across the tarmac to the terminal and kept them with me while we slowly circled the building, looking for the universal signs. There were two doors to the Ladies'.

'I'll be at this one,' I said. 'And Young at the other. If you have any sense, this is the one you'll use.

She nodded and vanished, and so did I. I was in and out of the men's room at a high old speed and pacing up and down waiting for her. Surprisingly, she reappeared. I wondered why. In her shoes, I'd have stayed there and hollered for Icelandic assistance. She looked pale and frightened, but there was an air of determination, too.

'I argue with myself,' she said. 'And I say, Mr Shaw is

brave and he is wise. He does not believe that I am a danger to him. He will protect me.'

'I'll try,' I said. 'But—'

'And perhaps this James Young, perhaps he too will say : "See she came back. I have nothing to fear." '

'Perhaps he will,' I said. 'Listen, when we get back to England, maybe even before that, while we're in Scotland, I'll try to give you the chance to get away. Once you're actually in Britain, things might be easier with the Americans. Okay?'

Chao Li, of course, when he joined us a moment later, made no observations at all. He might have looked a little surprised to see her, but that was all.

I took them with me to Met and learned that the winds on the perimeter of that high would still be assisting us, right down to the Scottish coast. They'd be a little abeam of us now, of course, but they ought to give us about a thirty-knot boost, which would mean Prestwick in about five hours. I set my watch to GMT and did a couple of rapid mental sums : we ought to make Prestwick at twelve-thirty and Elstree, therefore, about two and a half hours later. I'd call Lennox from Prestwick and let him have our ETA and leave the rest to him.

Everything for the next five hours was uneventful. We took off, we flew and we landed. The tower relayed a message. Would I ring Lennox? I crossed to the transit building.

For openers, he said, 'Where the devil have you been?'

'I've been saving your boy's life. And my own. It seemed that some people didn't want us to get back.'

'Your instructions were to fly Gander to Shannon. Why did you not do so?'

'We'd have had to swim,' I said. 'Look, let's leave the inquest till later.'

'Don't think you have heard the last of this, Shaw,' he snapped. 'I'm not accustomed to disobedience. Now—instead of Elstree, you will fly to Ipswich, Suffolk. You will approach Ipswich from the south-east, passing west of Colchester. There is a disused airfield at Wormingford. Do you know it?'

'I know it,' I said. 'Wartime place. Run to seed now. *Way to the Stars* and so on.'

'Way to the what?' He fired the sentence at me angrily, a burst of words.

'Nothing.' I felt like a naughty schoolboy and resented the feeling.

'The wind will be in the north-east.'

'You've arranged it?'

'Don't be a fool, Shaw. I've asked the Air Ministry. Now —you will be heading for Ipswich, but as you pass over Wormingford you will land, just long enough to let your parcel out. You will then take off.'

'Okay,' I said. 'You're the boss.'

'I am indeed. You will take off from Wormingford and proceed direct to Ipswich. If you do this well, no one will know it has been done. Even radar will not pick it up.'

'Don't be too sure,' I said. 'Is it important?'

'What?'

'That radar doesn't pick us up?'

'It is indicative,' Lennox said in his best explain-to-the-idiot-manner, 'of the efficiency of the operation. If radar doesn't see it happen, nobody else will.'

'And the parcel?'

'Will be collected at Wormingford. Ipswich is open for you.'

He put the phone down while I was observing how nice it was to work for a man who appreciated one's efforts. We took off shortly afterwards, flying the airway south, still flight-planned for Elstree. London Airport is closed, in any case, to Stripe Tigers and anything similar. You have to be a big boy, or have a lot of influence, to get in there in a light aircraft these days.

I told the airway controller of my plan change and he peeled me off for Stansted to fly cross-country from there. It's a stretch of country I know like the veins of my publican's nose : I trained and did a lot of my RAF time in East Anglia. As I slid over Dunmow I was whistling. In a few minutes, a few short minutes, I'd have Chao Li out of the aircraft. And I was all right; Maria was all right; Chao Li was all right! Shaw Aviation Services had successfully completed another contract; the last, I thought savagely, for Lennox. Below us there was the long straight line of Stane Street, the Roman shortest distance between two points.

'Turn left at Coggeshall,' I said. 'And you can't miss it.'

'What was that?' I glanced round. Chao Li was looking at me.

I grinned at him, at that intense, dark, humourless face. 'I was just thinking of my old flying instructor. Half left at Coggeshall and follow your nose. He'd have gone mad.'

'I am not surprised.' Chao Li and Lennox, I thought, shared some characteristics. I dropped low over all those Teys and Colnes down there, looking for the railway line that ran just to the west of Wormingford airfield. A moment later I'd got it and was heading for the runway, hoping that after all these years it contained neither herds of cattle nor a selection of large potholes. The one remaining bit o my contract was the rapid land-discharge-cargo-take-off sequence and any circling over Wormingford could easily have every radar erk from Falmouth to Fylingdales putting down his comic and taking notice.

'Get ready to go,' I said. 'Lennox said no hanging about. He was very particular about it.'

I watched the grey, pocked concrete coming up towards me as the Tiger floated easily down. Flaps, throttles . . . I went through the landing sequence in the usual half-thoughtful, half-automatic way, then brought her down soft as an infant's epidermis.

As the wheels touched, my eyes were searching the runway for obstructions, but the only one I saw was a car which must have turned off the Colchester to Sudbury road and was now coming towards us. I braked. 'Right. Go!' He opened the door and turned, looking at me. Our eyes met for a moment, but nothing else happened; he didn't say thanks and I didn't say goodbye. He just jumped down and slammed the door and stood off to one side, waiting.

A moment later we were roaring forward again as the car came on. How typical of Lennox, I thought nastily, that it should be a grey Mark One Cortina : just about the most anonymous thing there was.

I couldn't really see the driver and he obviously didn't intend that I should, because the sun-visor was down that late November afternoon.

I wasn't, in any case, particularly interested. The less I knew about Lennox, Chao Li et Compagnie, I reasoned, the better. A couple of little things did catch my eye, though. The first was a gaudy crimson and blue badge at the corner of the windscreen; then when Chao Li opened the car door and got in, a collecting box rolled out. It was one of those charity coin boxes with a string handle and a slot in the top for donations. It, too, was blue and crimson. Now with the job almost over, I smiled to myself. I felt I could afford to. Chao Li and charity matched like a terrier and a tomcat.

Looking back as we became airborne, I watched the Cortina execute a U-turn on the runway and go back towards the main road. I didn't watch any longer because by that time I was busy calling up the Ipswich controller, but I glanced across at Maria and grinned. 'All over,' I said.

She smiled back and I laughed. I actually laughed. I said, 'Finito. Fin. Done. Ended. Tout est fait. The show's over.'

But of course it wasn't.

Twenty-Five

As I walked towards the Ipswich terminal building with Maria's heels clacketing briskly beside me, the weight of the world was avalanching off my shoulders, leaving only the normal furniture of chips. Then the doorway into the building was filled by broad shoulders and big, flat feet. If I hadn't, by that time, lost all capacity for surprise, I'd have been startled. He shouldn't have been within six thousand miles of Ipswich airport.

'San Francisco,' I said, pointing roughly westward, 'lies that way.'

Rafer Hayes glowered at me. 'And John Shaw just lies.'

That he knew wasn't surprising. He was bound to know sooner or later. I took Maria's arm and made to move past him. 'It's over now.'

'Not for you. For you it may never be over.' He began to count on his fingers: 'Murder, illegal importation of drugs, theft of a boat, deliberate destruction of an airplane, complicity in the deaths of its passengers. Likewise with the people on the boat. Burglary. Assault. You'll get a million years.'

I said, 'This is England. Magna Carta. Bill of Rights. I'm a British citizen.'

'There are also extradition treaties. One with Uncle Sam.'

'Extradition?' My stomach did a flick turn off a half roll.

'And some of it will stick, believe me, boy. Unless—'

'Unless?' I didn't doubt him for a moment. Hayes was sober, solemn and determined.

He said, 'You're a liar. I'm not sure yet if you're a criminal. That's one reason I flew over yesterday. You saved my life. At least . . . I think you did.'

'Unless what?' I repeated.

'Get into the car,' Hayes ordered softly. 'You may be able to help.'

After he'd been driving for a while, I said, 'How come you know this town?'

'I reconnoitred.' He didn't say any more and I sat in silence, thinking about Lennox, whose sense of loyalty would save me from a lifetime in the California prisons. Lennox's loyalty was quite a thought. He would save me, of course. *Wouldn't he?*

A few minutes later there was a signpost pointing to the docks and Hayes gave a little snort of satisfaction and turned as directed. By this time dusk was deepening and the black river shone with reflected light. The car stopped in front of a two-floor building by the water.

'Come on,' Hayes said grimly.

We followed him towards the double-doors that fronted on to the street. At the other side of the building there'd be a loading bay overlooking the river. A sign said, Oriental Imports, Ltd. Hayes pressed the bell.

'It's Saturday,' I said.

He didn't answer and a moment later a light went on inside, then the door was opened by an elderly man. Chinese, naturally. Isn't everybody?

'Mr Sung?' Hayes's tone was surprisingly gentle.

'Yes?'

'I'm from San Francisco.' The wallet was out, showing the badge. 'Federal Narcotics Bureau.'

Across the old man's cheekbones, skin tightened.

'Please come in.'

We followed Sung into the warehouse and he closed the door and turned to face us, looking carefully from one to the other. Then he said, 'My nephew is dead?' It was a question, but he knew the answer.

Hayes nodded. 'I'm sorry.'

'He was killed?'

'We found his body. This man—' Hayes pointed to me —'and I.'

I blinked. Whose body? The body Hayes and I had found had been in a basket in San Francisco and neither of us knew a thing about it. Except that it was . . . damn it, *except* that it was Chinese! 'From here?' I said disbelievingly. 'From Ipswich?'

Hayes asked gently: 'Would you mind saying his name, Mr Sung?'

Sung looked at him through moist eyes. 'His name,' he said, 'was Chao Li.'

'Chao Li,' Hayes repeated. 'Does that name mean anything, John Shaw? Does it?'

Beside me Maria said, 'He is a devil, that—'

'No!' I stopped her. But it was too late. If Hayes hadn't known already, he'd have known then.

He said, 'I can answer the other question, too.'

'What question?'

'The name of your passenger is—'

'Maria Martiñez,' I said.

'The other one. His name is Chiang Yee. He killed a cop. You saw the film. He was the centre of the drug operation at Berkeley. He almost certainly killed Chao Li to take his place.' He held out a picture taken from that TV film.

I felt as though somebody had kicked me in the stomach; as though I wanted to be sick. I wanted to go away. Above all, I didn't want to think about it. I didn't want to think of the risks I had taken for him, of the way I had thieved for him, lied for him, killed for him. Above all, I didn't want to think about what would happen: Lennox would turn me slowly over a hot fire for a very long time, efficiently and with pleasure. And Chao Li, Chiang Yee, whatever his name was—I'd believe anything of *him*. Anything. Except . . . the train of thought rattled through some points . . . there was something wrong, somewhere. Hayes and the old man were talking but I didn't want to listen. There *was*

217

something wrong and I had to work out what it was. The story didn't fit. There were missing chunks, if I could think it through.

I looked around me, at the goods stacked high round the warehouse on fork-lift pallets. Sung did a hefty trade; there was a lot of merchandise here, most of it from Hong Kong. Water chestnuts, bean sprouts, bamboo shoots, dried fish . . . Suddenly I was searching, reading labels, trying to remember that name I'd seen. As it happened, I didn't need to look very hard. There was a small stack of packing cases in one bay, labelled boldly: 'Preserved Ginger. Produce of O-Joy Canning Co, Crown Colony of Hong Kong.' Beside the stack stood a single case, all by itself.

I didn't touch anything, because I was better unencumbered. Instead I sidled back, slid the gun from my pocket and told them all to stand still.

Hayes said, '*Five* million years. No remission. No parole.' His eyes were very cold.

'Maria!'

'Yes?' She looked at me, almost pleadingly. Her eyes said, won't somebody stop all this!

'In the corner over there. Cases of preserved ginger. Can you bring the one that stands by itself.

I watched Sung's face as she brought it, put it on the floor, opened it. His skin was very pale, like old, thin paper. I bent, took one of the cans out and shook it. The liquid gurgled, so I threw it away and tried the next and the next and the next. The seventh didn't gurgle. Nor the fifteenth, nor the twenty-first . . .

I said, 'Find a hammer or a can opener.' When she opened the can, white powder spilled out.

'Simple, isn't it!' I said. 'Sung imports the stuff. It's flown from Vicarsheath and taken to Berkeley and the Lotus Garden from Travis Air Base. And his nice little nephew was doing the American distribution. Along with your friends and my friends and the entire bloody Chinese

218

population of North America. Three pounds of uncut heroin. Nice little trick if you do it twice a week.'

The old man was trembling and I didn't blame him. I took a step towards him. 'I'm not police,' I said. 'So I don't have to worry about rules. I want the whole lot. I want to know exactly when, where and how often. I want to know who's involved. And if you won't tell me, I'll bloody well choke it out of you.'

I was surprised when the trembling stopped; when he raised his head and faced me. 'I do not *trade* in these barbarities!' He spat the words out. 'They use me. They use my business. I dare not—'

'Why let them?'

'They know about . . .' he hesitated. 'One man is helpless against a government.'

'You're trying to say the Chinese Government is behind this?'

He shook his head. 'No. These are criminals. But the Chinese Government is content with their operations. I think the heroin is processed and canned in China and taken to Hong Kong.'

'And your nephew?'

'He is an agent of the China Society.' Sung corrected himself. '*Was* an agent.' His voice cracked as he spoke. 'It was all I could offer.'

I looked at Hayes and shrugged. Maybe he could sort out the truth in all this, but he'd be a clever man if he could. He stood frowning, lips pursed.

Then Sung said, 'There is a man at the University.'

'Which university?'

'Here. At Suffolk.'

'Go on.' I said.

'He comes here sometimes. To take it away. For the students, I think.'

'Who is he?'

Sung shook his head. 'I do not know. In the stores there.'

Twenty-Six

I tried to telephone Lennox but the Civil Service isn't at its most available on Saturday evenings. I couldn't even get a message to him through the duty officer because the duty officer had gone, no doubt furtively, to dinner. So could sir ring back later? That left the whole mess exactly where it had always been, in my lap. So we went to the university.

I didn't decide to go, any more than a leaf decides to float down a stream. Hayes was going, so I had to go too, in case Chao Li really was the Chao Li Lennox thought he was and needed help. That meant Maria had to go because I wouldn't leave her in the warehouse and she'd nowhere else to go. Which left Sung, and he went because neither Hayes nor I was going to leave him behind to do whatever he might do. There wasn't any question of calling the police, either, partly because Hayes knew they'd take over from him and partly because I didn't dare have the local flatfeet trampling all over Lennox's territory. So we drove out along the Suddingtree road and turned into the University's massive grounds.

I'd flown over the new University of Suffolk often enough, so I knew what it looked like : there's a great ring of car parks surrounding a big natural hollow in the ground that holds a kind of city-the-Martians-built which is the core of the place. It has buildings and footways and plazas and underpasses and bridges and there's a greeny-blue concrete moat, brightly lit, surrounding it. There are also several residential towers. They're black monstrosities umpteen stories high that you could easily crash an aircraft into if the students turned the lights out. And Suffolk has bloody-minded students.

We rolled round the perimeter road until the car's headlights picked out a building contractor's board that said

NO CARS BEYOND THIS POINT. CAR PARK and then we turned slowly to the right between some massive old trees. As the car straightened and nosed forward, a blinding light seemed to explode in our eyes. There was a moment's pause before the car's doors were whipped open and a voice yelled: 'Death is too good for them!'

They were grinning, dozens of them, stamping and hooting, threatening us with pistols and rusty swords, blowing blasts on bugles, shrieking. A skeleton loomed out of the dark to rattle suddenly in front of me and was replaced instantly by a leering green face. As the flash haloes began to fade from my vision I could see pirates and Neanderthal men, tramps and clowns. One pushed his head into the car. 'Immunity badge costs one pound. Should cost two for four of you!'

The rigid hair along my scalp gave a final tingle and began to relax. 'Rag Day?' I asked. A pirate chief snarled assent and then directed me in cultivated tones when I asked the way to the stores building. After that the war party withdrew with a few whoops to threaten sudden cardiac arrest to the next motorist through the gate. As they went, a hand thumped the windscreen and left a sticker attached.

'My God!' I'd said it before I could stop myself.

Rafer glanced across at me sharply. 'What's the matter?'

'Nothing,' I said. But I was looking at that crimson and blue sticker and remembering the pocked concrete at Wormingford and the crimson and blue collecting box that had rolled on to it from the open door of the car that picked up Chao Li. I'd assumed, somehow, that the car had come from London and now I hoped desperately that it had.

We drove round the road again until the underpass forked away to the left and turned beneath the moat's concrete aqueduct and down towards the university's working areas. A couple of levels higher there were bands playing and people jumping about, but down here it was deserted: just plain, brick buildings housing the services. We passed the power control building and the garages. A door said, Maintenance Only. Then we found the stores: a flat-roofed, single-storey building on our left without a light anywhere.

I said, 'There'll be nobody there until Monday morning.'

We rolled past, then Hayes stopped the car. 'Oh, but there will, John Shaw. There'll be me.'

'Listen,' I said, 'it's Rag Day. The students are licensed to go mad today. Anything goes—you saw for yourself.'

'So?'

'So they don't leave doors open and put welcome mats out. That store will be locked tight as the Bank of England.'

Hayes shook his head. 'This kind of night, they'll be distributing. Makes it easy for pushers. The stuff will be in there now. And somebody will have left a skylight open. Somebody always does. So wait.'

He slid out of the driving seat and walked back along the road and I watched as he tried the door then vanished along the side of the stores building. He hadn't any authority here at all, except maybe some moral authority and he was exceeding that by about a thousand per cent, climbing at night into the stores of a British university. Perhaps he thought he'd only to flash that little wallet and the police would fall back in wonder. Or perhaps he was so obsessed by his war against drugs that he didn't care. I wound down the window and stared into the darkness, waiting to see his silhouette appear on the roof. Instead, a minute or two later, I heard footsteps, quick, hurrying footsteps that sounded artificially loud. Then a man appeared suddenly on the road. He must have been coming down one of the concrete stair tunnels that curved from level to level and the tube had amplified the sound. It was like walking inside a trombone.

He moved quickly along the road, hands in pockets, then stopped briefly under one of the overhead lights to examine something.

I felt a hand on my arm, gripping tightly. Sung said,

'That's the man. The one who comes to my warehouse.'

By the time I looked round again, he was heading for one of the two doors of the store block. He stopped there, fitting the key into the lock, turning it, then vanished inside.

'You're sure?'

He nodded. 'That is him. He is Irish. His hair is red.'

Could Hayes be in there already and about to be caught? I opened the door of the car and stepped out. 'Stay here,' I whispered. 'If Hayes comes back, tell him.'

I moved quickly and quietly along the road. If anybody was watching I'd look pretty suspicious, but that risk had to be taken. The black of the door was a distorted oblong against the brickwork: he'd left it ajar! I took a deep breath and eased it open, then peered round. Ahead of me was a corridor maybe a hundred feet long with doors opening off it at intervals. Light came from one, on the right of the corridor, about two-thirds of the way along. At the end, the corridor turned off to the left, leading round, presumably in a U-shape, to the other door.

There I hesitated. Was there any point in going on? Maybe this bloke had simply come back because he'd left behind his cigarettes, or his library book, or his left glove. If I did go along that corridor, would I see anything or find anything? Or would I simply see an innocent man who would promptly, and rightly, howl for the police? A tiny sound made me turn quickly, scalp tingling. Sung was beside me, nodding his head at the corridor.

'It *is* the man,' he whispered.

I had no ambition to be hanged, either for sheep or lamb, and I suppose what pushed me through that door and along the corridor was the desire to get away, once and for all, from the crazy nightmare that had surrounded me now for five days. Placing my feet carefully and soundlessly on the tiled floor, I eased forward towards the room from which light flooded. Once or twice I stopped to listen, but there was no sound at all, not ahead in the lighted room, nor behind where Sung followed, nor above where Hayes must still be searching for a way in.

The door was only a few feet away now, but there was still no sound; nor did the light flicker or vary with any movement there might be inside the room. Something about that absolute stillness worried me, but I inched forward to the door frame, then cautiously peered round. The room was empty! So where the hell was he? Where had the man gone?

A second later I knew only too well. 'This is vitriol. Sulphuric acid,' a voice said behind me. A soft, Irish voice. I spun round and saw the man framed in a doorway on the other side of the corridor. 'If you move suddenly I will throw it. Go slowly into the lighted room.'

There wasn't any option. I walked into the empty office. A little card on the door read: 'Mr P. Donovan, Scientific Stores Controller.' I turned to face him, Sung did the same and we stood very still, watching the tiny movement of the fluid in its glass beaker. He stood well away from us, in the doorway. A flick of this man's wrist and we'd never see again or want to.

'Ah.' He drew the word out. 'I see.' His eyes moved from me to Sung and back again. 'I thought you were burglars, but you're not. Not with Sung here.'

Sung said, 'I had to come to warn you. The police have been to the warehouse, searching.'

'What did they find?' Our captor's eyes were hard.

'Nothing.' I looked at Sung, who seemed all eagerness to please.

'And this man?'

Sung shrugged.

I said, 'I think there has been a misunderstanding, Mr Donovan.'

'You can read?' The acid swayed from side to side in the beaker as he laughed softly.

'The whole operation is in danger,' I said. 'They know about O-Joy.'

'What!' The smile vanished. 'What do you mean?'

'They didn't find anything, but they looked. In the cans.'

He flared suddenly. 'You damn fool,' he shouted at Sung. 'You have led them straight here. They'll have kept a watch, followed you.' He glanced round. 'Christ, they'll get us!' His hand was shaking a little as his anger grew.

'Quick, then,' I said. 'We've got a car outside. We can help you get the stuff away.'

'We can't,' he said. 'It's all ready for distribution tonight. All in packets. Look—' he pointed to a side table where rows of small pay-packet envelopes stood. 'If that's not distributed round the university he'll go—' There was a sudden sharp crack and the sound of glass breaking and I turned quickly to look at Donovan. His knees were bent and he was leaning backwards from the waist in a strange, folding posture. As I watched, his body slid to the floor among the broken glass and the spreading pool of acid. From the corridor came the sound of running footsteps and I sprang past Donovan's body to the door, just in time to see Rafer Hayes hurtle through the outside door and into the roadway.

In that moment, it all fitted. Hayes had killed him—and I knew why! Donovan had been about to tell us something and Hayes had killed him before he could. This wasn't, after all, the first time a policeman had turned out to be a crook and it wouldn't be the last. A narcotics agent would be of infinite value to any big drugs organization. He could keep them informed, could help them and hunt the opposition.

Now at last the whole thing was clean and clear. Hayes had come over here because he knew I'd got Chao Li. Yes, that was it! My mind raced back to the conversation we'd had when I'd telephoned him from Denver and he'd wanted to know if I'd told him the whole story. Now I understood.

Chao Li, or Chiang Yee—or whatever his name was, Lennox's boy, anyway—was on to them, so Hayes had to get him. And I was his only lead. Everything had been stage-managed. He'd been taken to the funeral parlour but he hadn't been harmed. Whenever the real trouble had happened, Rafer Hayes had been absent and Chao Li and I had been together! He'd shot Donovan to stop him giving too much away!

But why take me to Sung's? The answer, like all the answers, was easy now I had the key. I was out of things when I got to Ipswich. He had to involve me again, because I remained his only lead.

I tore down the corridor after Hayes, ran out into the roadway and stood, looking, listening, seeking some hint by sight or sound of the direction he had taken. The cold night air was still, apart from the clamour outside the dance and that was far enough away for my hearing to separate it from the sound pattern.

I looked at the curved, concrete stair and its twin up above. That was the likeliest way. Indeed, with the roadway deserted, it was the only way for Hayes to run : up there, in the confusion of Rag Night, he might hope to slip away. As I ran into the open mouth of the stairway, the concrete funnelled a sound to me : the scuff of a shoe, followed by the sound of quick steps on stairs. I raced up, out of the mouth of the concrete tube and stared round helplessly. The floats of the Rag Day parade were massed in the quadrangle; crowds of youngsters were milling about.

I looked at the buildings. The big hall was open and the music suggested a dance—inevitably the Rag Ball. The other buildings opening off the quadrangle were all in darkness, big doors firmly closed. Could he have gone into the dance?

I decided not. He'd prefer to know about the exits to a building before he used the entrance. There was a low wall beside me, enclosing a couple of lonely trees and I jumped up to survey the crowd. The line of floats stretched back across the bridge that was the only entrance at this level and I realized Hayes could move along that line, staying in shelter, until he could cross the bridge into the ring of darkness. Working along the line, I examined each float in turn, the first half dozen cursorily but after that with more care, and glancing up every few seconds to look at that bridge. I was pretty sure he couldn't have reached it yet and when he did he'd be clearly exposed for a second or two.

It was all so damned crazy, this hunting among cardboard battleships and articulated plastic dragons, the comedy cows with udders labelled Mild & Bitter, the windmill and the airship. All had been built on the backs of lorries and all were now abandoned: the parade was over and the dancing had begun. I hunted along the line, peering beneath the trucks, searching the tableaux, but there was no sign of Hayes.

I climbed on to the next float, the ritual operating theatre scene that's in every Rag procession: big bloodstains, saws, hammers and chisels. The plug-ugly nurses and sadistic doctors would by now be swaying and jerking to the pounding, amplified beat of the dance. I turned to jump down, but something caught my eye. At the far end of the float, a man crouched low in the shadows, hidden from the square's bright lights by the bulk of the float. The pale glow from the perimeter lights illumined dark skin and a head whose shape I knew. I took a silent step nearer then launched myself at him in a flying dive that rolled him out of his hiding place and smashed him down on his side on the concrete.

He didn't move. I must have cracked his head on the floor as he fell. Luck, for once, I thought savagely. I pushed a hand inside his jacket to get his gun, and found it, but my hand felt sticky and when I brought it out the stickiness was blood! I pulled the jacket back and found myself staring at blood that welled from a deep wound in his side. It was a wound I had not made; a wound I couldn't have made.

A minute ago I'd thought I understood: I'd thought everything was clear. Now all my ideas were in ruins again. Who the hell had done this?

Twenty-Seven

I was still bent over Hayes, trying hard to think, when I heard the rasp of breath above me. Sung leaned for support on the side of the float, gasping. He couldn't speak but was gesturing anxiously, pointing the way he had come. I shook my head uncomprehendingly and he puffed and panted, trying to find the breath to speak. 'Girl,' he managed at last. 'Girl!' He held his hand, thumb and finger cocked to make a gun. 'Girl!'

Maria? I stared at Sung. 'Maria! Where?'

He was still gasping, still pointing, his whole body tense with urgency. Then he managed to find another word, or rather two. He said, 'Chiang Yee.'

I didn't stop to think, I told Sung to get help and then took off across the square, shouldering people out of the way until I reached the parapet beside the tunnel stair and could look over and down at the deserted roadway. One door of the car hung open. Where, then, was Maria? Where could she be? Four of the tunnel stairways climbed away from the roadway below and she certainly hadn't climbed the one beside me. That left three. One started in the roadway and curled round to a rooftop plaza below me; I dismissed that. The second stairway curled back on itself to the other side of the quadrangle. Could she have used that? But no. Hayes had been chasing Chao Li and that meant . . . I pictured Maria sitting in the car, hearing the shot, seeing Chao Li race out of the stores building and into the tunnel opposite the one beside which I now stood. He must have glimpsed her as he ran: maybe she'd got out of the car at the sound of the shot. Then, after Chao Li had wounded Hayes, he'd returned immediately to get Maria. Which meant he'd gone down the tunnel beside me and Maria, running from him, would have taken the one nearest. And that was the tunnel stair which swung up towards the residential towers.

Following its line with my eyes, looking at the dark fingers that reared from the grass into the night sky, I saw her. She was half-way between the tunnel mouth and the tower, running; she kept half-turning in fear and a man was following her, slowly and somehow inexorably. I'd have known *him* anywhere.

I sprinted down the stairway, out on to the road at the bottom and into the other tunnel. A few seconds later, gasping, I raced out on the other side at the top. And in the few seconds it took, the last, lingering doubts vanished. The truth was that I had been unwilling to face the fact that I had been fooled; that the man I had saved was a murderer and worse; that I was the biggest idiot in history. Now, as I looked towards the black bulk of the tower, there was only the stone-cold certainty that Maria would die unless I could do something about it.

She stood for a moment in the entrance to the tower and even from where I stood, two hundred yards or so away, her terror was clear. In the second or two that she stood there, Chao Li moved steadily, menacingly, towards her.

'Chao Li,' I shouted. He swung round and I ran towards him. 'Wait a minute. Wait!' It was a stupid thing to do, but at least it confirmed everything. He dropped to one knee, aimed carefully, and fired.

I flung myself to one side and heard the bullet sing by and then I had something else to worry about; I'd banged my thigh painfully on a stone as I fell. If Chao Li had come for me I'd have had it, but he didn't. Instead he raced after

Maria into the tower. As I tried to drag myself to my feet, I saw him stop for a moment in the doorway; the glass flashed as he went through, and then I heard a scream.

That blow as I fell must have hit a nerve centre or something, for my leg was both excruciatingly painful and completely unresponsive. It took my weight, but that was all, and I limped awkwardly towards the tower, afraid with every step that I would fall. Twice the leg gave under me, flinging me full-length on to the concrete path. Each time I had to force myself to get up again. My body and my mind wanted, more than anything, to lie, to relax, to let things go. I wanted to rest that leg; instead I forced myself up and hobbled ahead because between Chao Li and complete freedom of action, lay only Maria and myself. Others might know he was here, but only Maria and I had seen him, talked to him. As long as we were alive, he was in danger.

Limping up the couple of little steps that led to the doors, I glanced at the empty foyer and lurched in. I was still wondering why he hadn't come back to kill me out there. Then I knew the answer : he intended to kill us both and he knew I'd follow him, that I'd know he intended to kill Maria and that I'd be determined to stop him. He could afford to wait for me, in a spot of his own choosing, and pick us off at his leisure.

Twenty-Eight

To my right stood the doors of the bank of lifts that served the tower : modern automatic lifts that dealt only in 'up' or 'down' and kept you in the dark about which floor they'd reached. I fingered the 'up' button, watched the little rectangle of light outline my finger and waited, ready to spring to one side if any of the doors opened to reveal Chao Li. They didn't, though; in fact quite a time passed before one of the lifts bounced gently down and a little bell rang to reveal its presence. I got in and looked at the buttons.

The question was, where had Chao Li got out? How could I find him? More importantly, how was he intending to find me? The automatic doors whirred and began to close and I was watching them, stupidly, when the realization hit me and I kicked out with my good leg, jamming it between the spring-loaded safety-edges of the closing doors. They bit on it, gently, then moved back again, and I raced away from them looking for the doorway in the lobby, sprinted through it to the stairs and went up them. Buildings like that have the same basic construction. Running upward alongside the elevator shafts there's almost always another vertical shaft to carry the services : water and sewage lines, cables and conduits. There's usually a door leading from the stairs into the service shaft at most levels. There are also hatches leading from one shaft to another so the repairmen can clamber around. At the top of the first flight I found the entry door to the service shaft and whipped it open.

The core was about six feet by five, dimly lit and with a steel ladder running up one wall. The trouble was that I had lost my sense of direction and hadn't the faintest idea behind which wall the shaft lay. I was lucky, though; before I'd climbed more than a few feet there was a white door, covered in red warning lettering. It swung easily towards me and revealed the roof mechanism of a lift cage which must now be standing at the ground floor.

For a moment I looked up the shaft, which climbed until it vanished above. Fear tasted rank in my mouth as I stepped on to the roof of the cabin and gripped the steel cable.

It was hot, airless and dusty in the lift shaft as I waited for Chao Li to make his move. Standing there, clinging to that cable, I found my uncertainty growing. If Maria had managed to get into one of the lifts and get clear of him, she'd be reasonably safe for a while, hiding somewhere, and he wouldn't want to go searching for her because then *I* might be able to ambush *him*. No—he'd wait on one of the lower floors until a lift moved upward, presumably carrying me; then he'd press the 'up' button. Whatever floor I'd selected, I would still stop at his floor and he'd be waiting when the doors opened. But what if I *didn't* set off in one of the lifts? What would he do then? I was hoping he'd begin to get nervy and bring the lifts up one at a time for inspection. I hoped, too, that there were other doors, at other levels, connecting the lift shaft and the service core.

Suddenly, beneath my feet, the cabin roof jerked once, then shot me upward, swaying a little, and I began to have some idea how the astronauts feel with a Saturn V pushing. The white numbers on the lift doors flashed by at amazing speed and then, as abruptly as the climb had begun, it ended. Above me were the gates of the tenth floor, so the lift must have stopped at the ninth; Chao Li had gone higher than I expected.

Now—where was the servicing door? In the darkness I couldn't see one; subconsciously I must have been looking for white paint, but everything here was in almost complete darkness. Below me I heard the lift doors open but it didn't sound as though anybody got in or out. Perhaps there wasn't a door! I pushed and shoved at the wall in growing desperation, knowing that any second now the doors would close and the cabin would race down the shaft again. At last though, I found the dark rectangle against the dull brick-work and tried to open it, but I couldn't feel a handle. It must swing outward from the shaft, as the other had done, but what held it? If it could be opened only from the service core I was done. Ah, there it was: a long horizontal slot in the metal with a spring catch on the other side! The doors began to close below me as I slid my fingers into the slot. The catch was stiff and awkward and wouldn't budge.

At that moment, the floor beneath my feet simply vanished. I was left hanging by one hand from that slot in the door. As the lift hummed down the shaft, there was nothing between me and a long drop to certain death but the grip of one hand on the door. My feet flailed, searching for a toe-hold to take some of the appalling strain from my hand. I managed to wedge a toe in the brickwork but that wasn't going to help for long. In seconds I was going to drop, and I knew it. Away to my left was a safety handle of some kind, bolted to the wall, but too far away for me to have any hope of reaching it. I lunged frantically with the other hand and touched the door slot, but I couldn't grip it and my hand slipped. Another swing—and I knew this would be the last because my right hand's strength was going fast. I heard my own gasp as my fingers slid into the slot and I pushed at the spring lever with desperate, sweating fingers. When it finally gave and the door swung open a little, I was sobbing with fear; it was all I could do to get my knee on to the ledge.

Gasping for breath, I balanced myself on the narrow ledge of masonry between the lift shaft and the service core, then forced myself to step across to the metal ladder. When I'd made it, I clung on for a while until my heartbeats stopped threatening to shake the building down, then found the door that opened on to the stairs. With the automatic in my hand, I edged the door open slowly and peered out at the stairway. It was empty. I hopped quickly out from the core and began to go down. At the bottom, a door with the number nine on it led from the fire stairs to the main landing of the ninth floor. On tiptoe, I moved across to it, wishing there were a pane of glass in it so that I could see out on to the landing. But the door was of the heavy, fireproof variety; you couldn't have seen through it with an X-ray machine.

I stared at it in frustration for a moment, then took the handle and pulled it towards me a fraction, then a fraction more. When there was a tiny opening, I looked through, and all I could see was the wrong wall. I listened, instead, for any tiny sound that might indicate Chao Li's whereabouts, but the whole tower seemed quiet. The spring was a little tighter than I had expected as I closed the door and there was a small but audible thump. I swore and retreated behind the jamb. Did he hear? If he was there, surely he must have heard! But maybe he wasn't there; maybe all my fine anticipation had been back-handed and he was in some other part of the tower.

Time ticked by and nothing happened. This was useless. I'd far better go for the police and let them sort it out. If I did, though, he'd get Maria and the odds were that he'd get away, too, because I was the only one who knew what he looked like and there must be dozens of Malay, Chinese and Burmese students at the new university.

I began to open the door again, a millimetre at a time. This time I would open it far enough to get a good look at the landing. Then, at least, I'd know whether I was wasting my time.

I held my breath as the door opened and more of the landing was visible. Now I could see most of one side and in a moment I'd be able to see . . . I froze! Fifteen feet away Chao crouched, tense and waiting, and for a moment I didn't appreciate why. But then I heard the faint hum as the lift rose. Was it going to stop at this floor? Chao Li tensed and so did I as the lift's hum changed in pitch and the bell sounded. In a moment the doors would open.

He raised his gun slowly, pointed it towards the lift doors, and, as the mechanism whirred, his fingers tightened on the trigger. The doors were opening.

I said, 'Here I am.'

I shouldn't have done it. I should have shot him as he crouched there.

He spun and fired in one movement and there was a sudden agony in my right hand as my pistol flew out of it and clattered away behind me down the concrete stairs of the fire escape. It was a hell of a lucky shot, but lucky shots are as disabling as clever ones and my hand hurt like hell and was probably badly bruised if nothing worse. I just had time to glimpse Stanley Sung half out of the lift and backing into it again before I swung the heavy fire door with all my strength and raced for the stairs. To this day, I don't know why I ran up instead of down; of the two choices, it wasn't the sensible one, but sense didn't enter into it. I was in a panic. He'd got me now. He was only yards away and he had a gun.

Turning the corner on the stairs, I saw the open doorway to the service core and went into it like a rat into a drain, pulled the door closed after me and flattened myself against the wall. Had he seen me do it? His footsteps clattered towards me, then past, upward towards the next floor, and I relaxed too soon, because a second later they stopped and came down the stairs again. He'd realized that I couldn't be that far ahead.

Quickly and as quietly as I could, I shinned up the iron ladder in the core, but either he heard me or he saw the core and put two and two together, because a second or two later the door opened and light flooded in. I tried to tuck myself between two massive fall pipes as, looking downward, I saw the upper part of his body framed in the little doorway, leaning forward and peering into the shaft, across at the lift-shaft safety door. He looked first down, then up and I tried to make myself invisible in the shadows among those service ducts. Then he closed the door. At that moment my foot slipped on one of the iron rungs and I almost crashed down, but I managed to hold on one-handed until my feet scrambled back on to the rung. He'd heard, though; the door was whipped open again and this time he was looking where he knew I was to be found.

It would take him a few seconds to see me: a few brief seconds for his eyes to adjust to the light inside the core.

Then he would pick me out in the shadows. What could I do? What had I that could be pitted against a gun? Mentally, I went through my pockets: lighter, my keys, a handful of change. If I could throw accurately I might buy myself the time to climb a little higher. I shrank back into the shadows and looked about me. Three or four feet up was a small, metal working platform which must give access to junction boxes or switch mechanisms. If I were standing on that, he'd have to climb to get to me.

My lighter went first, dropped carefully down the shaft until, after a second or two, it clouted something fairly hard, bounced a couple of times and went clattering down. Chao Li leaned over, staring down into the shaft. Meanwhile I tried to collect a handful of small change from my pocket without making a sound. By the time Chao Li had decided that perhaps I wasn't racketing about beneath him and that the sound had been caused by something falling from above, I was ready. I threw that handful of coins as hard as I could: a shower of metal flying at his face like shrapnel.

Something must have caught him, too, because I heard a sharp exclamation of pain as I turned and raced up the ladder. Every step seemed likely to be the last: I was an easy target and I seemed to be climbing in slow motion. That cash must have hit him painfully in the face; he had time to shoot me a dozen times.

I scrambled gratefully on to that ledge; now there was a quarter inch or so of steel between me and Chao Li's gun. And then I found there was more than that. My foot brushed against something softer than the steel of the shelf or the fibre casing of the ducts. When I prodded it with my toe, it chinked, metal on metal. Carefully, my back sliding vertically down the wall to keep the target small, I lowered myself until I could feel with my fingers. It was a plumber's bag!

'Shaw!' Chao Li's voice came up to me. 'I know where

you are. I can even see you.'

With the walls pressing in, the sound of the shot reverberated crashingly in the shaft and there was a clang and a jarring sensation as the bullet hit the underside of the platform. Another followed a moment later, zipping past me up the shaft.

I had to try the bluff. I said, 'You might as well give up. We've got you. That gun won't save you.' I didn't think he'd believe me and he didn't.

'To the contrary, Shaw. I've got *you*. Two people know what I look like. You and Maria. Soon no one will know. Come down!'

'Get knotted,' I said.

'You're being stupid again, Shaw. You're tough and resourceful but you're stupid, too.' As he climbed into the shaft and moved across to the ladder, I bent and felt inside the bag. There were spanners, hammers, bits and pieces of all kinds; I picked up a hammer by its wooden handle and dropped it over the edge of the platform. There was a thud and a grunt and a bullet whanged off the metal, ricocheting wildly up the shaft and missing me by a whisker. I threw a spanner down hard and missed, but another, a second later, caught him again.

But still he came on. He might be bruised but there was no doubt what he was going to do: as soon as he got near the platform, he'd take aim quite calmly and he'd shoot me. There was still the bag, though, and it was heavy. I picked it up and risked a glance over the edge that was very nearly the last thing I did: the bullet actually flicked my hair as it went by.

Chao Li was about ten feet below me, coming steadily up the iron ladder, the gun gripped in his right hand as he climbed.

It was all or nothing now. I was loth to drop the bag because once I let it go I'd have nothing. On the other hand, the nearer he got, the less effective the thing would be. I took a deep breath, swung the bag up, and dropped it straight down the shaft, parallel to the front of the ladder. As it went, I leaned over to watch it. Chao Li's hand came up to fend it off—it had to be the hand that was holding the gun because he was clinging to the ladder with the other. He half-succeeded too, but only half; the looped leather handle of the bag flicked over his wrist and the whole weight of the falling bag bent it. No arm could take that sudden and unexpected weight without giving, and his gave. Suddenly the gun went spinning out of his grasp, rattling down the shaft among the cables and the conduits and the plumber's assorted tools. There was a tremendous racket as chisels and bolsters, spanners and flux went flying down. If anybody else was in the tower, they must have suspected the building was falling down.

I looked down at Chao Li. His face showed his fury and he was looking round him desperately for some way out. I said, 'The bloody British. They fight with all the wrong things.'

The look he gave me contained enough explosive hate for half a dozen good broadsides. I suspect that at that moment all he wanted to do in the whole world was to come after me with his bare hands. But he couldn't. He had to think about getting away.

Swiftly he climbed down the ladder. 'I know you,' he called as he scrambled rapidly down. 'I know your name. I can trace you. I will come for you.'

I said grimly, 'First, you'll have to get away.'

I swung myself on to the ladder and began to shin down after him. I'd gone about two steps when Chao Li flung open the door on to the stairs and jumped out. In a few more seconds he'd either be holed up in one of the students' rooms, or he'd have got Maria and be using her as a shield.

I half scrambled, half fell down the ladder after him, but the door was slammed in my face as I came level with it and by the time I'd got it open again, he'd disappeared.

Had he gone up or down? Guessing down, I took the stairs two at a time, tearing on until I'd gone down two whole floors. Then I stopped to listen. There wasn't a sound from below me: no flying feet, no shouts, no nothing. I turned and began to climb back. He must have gone up the stairs. But why? He'd still have to get past me on the way down. But he could do that in the lifts, couldn't he? I tried to hurry up the stairs but I was weary; I ached all over. My leg was still throbbing from my fall; my hand ached like hell from the bruising when his shot carried away my pistol and, in any case, accumulated weariness lay over me like a great, thick blanket.

But those aches and pains made me remember the pistol. It had spun away behind me; could it still be there?

I almost trod on it, just as, a couple of seconds later, I almost walked into Chao Li. I'd picked up the little automatic on the stairs and was heading up from the ninth floor to the tenth when he came backing down. He'd got Maria with him and had some kind of arm lock on her neck.

It must have been sheer weariness that made me late with the pistol. I hadn't even half-raised it when he said, 'Quite still, or I break her neck.'

'No.' Another voice came from above. Stanley Sung was advancing down the stairs, holding a knife. It wasn't much more than a large penknife, but he held it as though he meant it.

'Before you even have your pistol in position to shoot, and before this man can move his knife, I can kill her,' Chao Li said.

Maria's eyes were wide in fright, her body twisted awkwardly as he dragged her with him.

Stanley Sung had stopped and now stood three or four steps above them, cold and watchful, but helpless as I was.

'Out of my way. I am coming past.'

I stepped back and watched, fuming, as Chao Li dragged Maria past me.

'Stay where you are,' he said. He was below me, almost by the shaft door, when she acted.

The guts it must have taken! One small twist of his arm would break her neck and she knew it, but she put her foot behind his ankle and heaved him off balance with her hip.

As they crashed together to the floor, his alternatives were to break her neck as he fell and leave himself without any defence at all, or release her and try to grab her again.

He relaxed the grip, momentarily, then lunged for her again, but Maria attacked too and her heel smashed against his instep. In the brief second the blow gave her, she rolled clear.

Chao Li was on his feet instantly, damaged foot or no damaged foot, and he did the only thing left to him, whipping open the shaft door, leaping in and slamming it behind him.

Sung smiled at me. 'Caught,' he said gently.

I shook my head. 'It could be a trap for him. But it could also be a means of escape. There's an exit from the shaft on every floor.'

I reached for the door and pulled.

'No,' Maria said, holding on to my arm. 'Leave him. Let him go!'

I looked down at her. 'I'm sorry,' I said. 'But no. Not now.'

I pulled again at the door, wrenching it open this time and climbing after Chao Li into the shaft. Now, ironically, our positions were exchanged: he hiding somewhere in the shadows, I with the gun. I stared up the shaft but there was no sign of him. Down: still nothing.

Behind me, Sung asked, 'You can see him?'

'No,' I said. 'He's here, somewhere, but I can't see him. He must be tucked between two big pipes, out of sight.'

'Leave him. Let the police get him,' Maria begged. 'He will kill you.'

'I'm going after him,' I said. 'I think he's gone up. If he

has—' I swung on to the ladder.

As I did so, something caught my eye. I bent and looked more closely. Through the slot in the white door that led into the lift shaft the tips of fingers protruded. Chao Li's feet must be on the narrow ledge of masonry between the two shafts and his body hanging out in the lift shaft. The other hand would be holding the safety rail. It was daring and he'd almost got away with it.

'All right, come out,' I said.

'He is where?' Sung asked.

I pointed with the barrel of my pistol at the fingertips.

Maria said, 'What is behind there?'

'The lift shaft,' I said. 'Come on out, Chao Li. At least we've no death penalty for murder in this country.'

There was no response. Perhaps he didn't believe I'd found him? I tapped his finger with one of my own. 'Out you come.'

Still there was no response, no movement of the door. While I was wondering why, abruptly it flew at me. He must have been gathering his strength and balancing his weight so that he could swing the door's weight at me as it flew open. He succeeded too, smashing me back against the ladder for a moment. But he hadn't bargained for the lack of space for the door to swing into. With my body blocking its way, the door's swing stopped. I kicked it hard, slamming it to. Chao Li was back in the lift shaft.

He must have known it was the end. There was a moment's pause, then he shouted: 'All right. All right. Open the door!'

'Okay. Come out slowly and do as you're told. I still have the pistol.'

He screamed suddenly. 'Quickly! Quickly!' His voice held a rising inflection that spelled pure terror.

I grabbed for the handle to pull it to me, but already I was too late. The humming that Chao Li must have heard a second earlier was suddenly audible to me, too. The lift was coming down!

'Help. Quick! Help me!' he yelled. I tugged at the handle, but that spring catch was jamming. I wrenched and pulled and finally freed it and the door began to open.

'A-a-a-h-h!' There was that one long sound, that unforgettable scream of terror followed by a sharp thud, and suddenly the lightened door was swinging freely towards me! The descending lift had knocked him from his perch on the ledge. Below him there had been nothing but ten floors of empty space.

I turned to Sung. 'Where's Hayes?'

'They took him to the medical department.'

'And?'

'He was unconscious.'

Twenty-Nine

'Duty Officer.' The voice was young; Oxford overlaid on Birmingham.

I said, 'My name is Shaw. It is very important that I speak to Lennox.'

'*Mister* Lennox. He's not here at this time, I'm afraid.' This lad wasn't afraid at all; he was delighted. There's nothing like a good put-down to cheer the arrogant young.

'Then telephone him in his sleepy suburb!'

'What I do is entirely my decision.' His voice was rich with satisfaction. 'You'd better explain.'

'Certainly. He's a man of ill-humour and long memory and I'm very important to his plans. He might tear you open and dance on your tripes or he might be lenient and just ruin your career. That's what I'll recommend, anyway. Tell him.'

'Shaw, you said?'

'Ess . . . aitch . . . ay . . . double you. As in George Bernard. And quick,' I said nastily, 'or you'll be transferred permanently to the pensions office in Blackpool.'

He was back on the line in a few seconds, still holding on to the shreds of his bland manner. 'Can Mr Lennox telephone you?'

I gave him the number, hung up, and waited.

Lennox didn't hello or anything. 'Well?'

'The parcel,' I said. 'It's a dead letter.'

'How dead?'

'You are, or you aren't. I said dead.'

'How?'

'He fell. Incidentally, it was the wrong parcel.'

'Where are you?'

I said, 'The medical department, University of Suffolk, Suddingtree.'

'The body?'

'Here.'

'The aircraft?'

'Ipswich.'

'I'll be with you in two hours. Wait.'

Click. I was expecting it this time. Typical end to a conversation with Lennox. I wondered what his home life was like. And his wife. My God, his wife!

I rejoined Stanley Sung and Maria just as the doctor was doing his grave optimism act about Hayes. The knife thrust intended for his liver had struck that damned enamel badge and merely sliced across the ribs. Hayes had bled like a perforated pig and been knocked out, but it was just this-and-that and the good doctor had sewn him up. 'Painful,' he murmured, giving a wise and balanced judgment, 'and a nasty shock, of course.'

'He can talk, though?'

'Oh, I don't know about that. The shock—'

'Thank you,' I said.

I walked across to a very frustrated young detective-sergeant and told him again that nobody was saying a word until Mr Lennox arrived from the Home Office, after which we might. It all depended.

The lad had two bodies on his hands and I sympathized deeply with his problems, but I wrapped the strength of the Official Secrets Act warmly around me and walked off to take Stanley Sung and Maria into the dining-room. Hayes lay stripped to the waist on a terracotta examination couch, a big white bandage round his middle.

I said, 'You look like a chocolate orange sundae,' and he grinned, winced and grinned again a bit more carefully.

'I hear you were all ready to hunt me down.'

'Next time, don't run away.'

Hayes said, 'I saw him fire the shot. I had to chase him. He got a bit ahead and waited with the knife, that's all.'

Stanley Sung was crossing the room to Rafer's side. 'You will wish to know?'

I said, 'You mean you're free to talk?'

'This time is as favourable as any.' Sung gave me a polite little bow. 'There will be none better.'

I nodded.

'You see,' he said, 'that I have been in England for many years. My business is now quite large. I am one of three largest importers of oriental specialities. One year ago, approximately, I received visit from other man, also Chinese, who know about me. If British authorities know what he know, they take severe action.'

'What did he know?'

'I lied. I was born in Canton. Not Hong Kong. I made false declaration. Therefore I would be deported. Perhaps to China. I thought this important.' He struggled. 'I am old now. How could it be important?'

'Go on.'

He looked at me for a moment. 'You must appreciate that I buy Chinese food in tins in very large quantities? You will also be aware that container port of Felixstowe is very short distance away.'

'We all saw,' I said. 'The stuff comes in O-Joy tins.'

Sung nodded. 'O-Joy is old and respected Hong Kong cannery. Has exported food for many years, all over the world.'

'Just a minute,' Rafer said. 'Where does the stuff come from in the first place. Not from Hong Kong, that's for sure.'

'Have you heard of the so-called Golden Triangle?'

Rafer nodded. I said, 'No.'

'It is area in South-East Asia, northern parts of Burma, Thailand and Laos and as far north as Szemao in China.'

Rafer said, 'All right, that's where it grows. Where's it refined?'

'In China. I believe canning also done in China and cans labelled in Hong Kong. Of neither, however, am I sure.'

'Do you mean,' I asked him, 'that it's coming in by the container load?'

'Not quite. Every container, however, contain many tins heroin. One hundred, one hundred fifty pounds. Sometimes more.'

'Christ!' Hayes said. I looked across at him. His face was drawn into tight, flat planes of disgust. 'Distribution?'

'This distribution is experiment. That I believe. You appreciate that much of this is my own understanding?'

'Go on,' I said. The old man had a mind like a razor. What he understood was likely to be so.

'The heroin uncut. It is supplied to Chinese Restaurants of the Lotus Garden chain. Also to this—this University of Suffolk. One other thing I know. Distributors ordered to supply heroin in standard form of one quarter heroin to three-quarters milk sugar.'

Hayes said, 'That's roughly five times as strong as the usual fix! What about the States? How's it get there?'

'You know the principal answer. It is sent in Military Air-lift Command jets. The labels are removed from the tins and replaced with the labels from tins of evaporated milk. I supply Lotus Garden in London. They arrange transport to plane.'

Into my mind flashed a mental picture of the driver who'd taken me to Vicarsheath. What was his name? Conroy, that was it! He'd been terrified of being late. And there was the other bloke who'd insisted, more or less, that my parcel go in the plane's hold.

'I have an idea how it's done.' I said.

'Let Mr Sung talk.' Rafer spoke gently. 'He's wanted to talk for a long, long time.'

Sung gave him a little smile of gratitude. 'In America only San Francisco area and university at Berkeley are supplied.'

'Why?'

'Because this is Chinese operation. San Francisco is the start. Then Vancouver, Los Angeles, New York.'

I said, 'Are you sure it's just criminals?'

'I think so, Mr Shaw. I believe this operation conducted by gangsters, racketeers. People like the Ho family. The Chinese Government is willing to supply and to earn currency. Also to benefit indirectly from damage done by increasing the drug problem in the West.'

'Chao Li told me—' I began.

Rafer interrupted me. 'Let him go on.'

'No,' I said. 'This may be important. Chao Li—' I saw the pain in Sung's eyes—'I'm sorry. The man I flew here told me about a right-wing plot to supply drugs to students on a vast scale. He said the people behind it intended to corrupt a generation.'

Sung nodded. 'That was the ultimate idea. But the plot was criminal, not political. First they would demonstrate their method : large and easy supplies at universities and in principal cities. Strong dosage means more rapid addiction. They wish to see how fast the snowball grow.'

'It mushrooms,' Rafer said softly, 'it mushrooms.'

246

'That is the system.' Sung sat back.

I said, 'Your nephew, the real Chao Li. Why was he there? And why was he killed?'

Sung sat up again. 'They did not know about him, but Chinese families have strong ties. He made me tell him why I was troubled. Finally he went to America to find out more. He worked with the China Society, trying to destroy the distribution system there.'

'How?'

Sung was an old man and the talk of his dead nephew moved him deeply. He was on the edge of tears, his lips tight with the effort of control. I waited.

'I would know when supplies being sent. Chao Li organized theft in San Francisco. Five large consignments were lost. They became very anxious.'

'And they must have found out about him,' I said.

'No doubt.' He was quite still, but the light glinted on the tears that ran down his cheeks. 'A man was to take another consignment. He was not to know. It was urgent.'

'That was me. Billy Muggins.' Sung nodded.

'There must have been two identical parcels. One of spares. One of cans of heroin,' Rafer said. 'Quick switch the other end. Easy. But why didn't you tell me about your passenger?'

'For the same reason I'm not telling you now.'

He shrugged, winced, then smiled. 'Okay, okay. Your business. It's your country.'

'There's a bloke called Newton I should have a look at, if I were you,' I said. 'Works for an outfit called Airflo at Ignacio.'

'I'll make a note of the name. You know,' he grinned at me, 'for one little Limey, you left a mile-wide swathe of destruction behind you.'

We chatted around it endlessly. Apart from discovering the identity of the dead man in the basket, Hayes hadn't come up with a lot of information in the couple of days he'd been in San Francisco after I'd left. *Sunrise* had been found drifting in the Pacific with Jasmine Yang's body aboard, but I knew that; the black bi-plane was confirmed as having been hired at Ignacio minutes before I took off. One of the two men aboard had been identified as Wong Peng Chi manager of the Lotus Garden restaurant.

We talked and drank some coffee and talked again. It was all polite, pointless and tense. We were waiting for Lennox, who had triggered all the action and would now have to clean up all the bits. Among those bits was my own problem—all those flying regulations I had broken in four countries. Or was it five?

Lennox arrived in well under two hours, and from the look of him it hadn't been a relaxing drive. He came into the room as though he owned it, ignored everybody else and marched over to me. 'A dead letter?'

I stared at him. Hadn't he understood? 'Very. And the wrong letter, too. And there's no point in all the codewords. Everybody knows.'

He said, 'I am surrounded by fools and worse. It was a simple operation and it has been wrecked.'

Stupidly, I began to introduce him to Hayes, but Lennox merely raked his eyes over him and looked away. 'This is British business. Come with me.'

Shrugging, I followed into a kind of reception office and we stood, muttering together, as he took me through the operation from start to finish. At the end he scowled at me even harder. 'This has cost the life of an agent. The one you should have saved. You should realize it.'

'Look,' I said angrily. 'I've had enough of your bloody arrogance. I've damn near been killed myself, every hour on the bloody hour. I'm sorry about your agent. He—'

'She.' Lennox said.

I stared at him.

'Jasmine Yang, you damned fool!'

Everything in me cringed : my mouth went dry, my scalp prickled, my fingers tensed, my stomach muscles forced bile up into my mouth.

'Jasmine Yang?' I stammered.

'She came to the boat, didn't she! You should have protected her. Instead you get her killed. Now get back in there. I must telephone.'

Meekly I obeyed, walking slowly back towards the treatment room door.

'And don't interrupt me here, Shaw. I may be some time.'

I sat and smoked and thought. Jasmine Yang! And it was my fault, my fault alone, that she was dead. I groaned to myself, remembering how he'd killed her and taken her place. The moment came to life in my mind with terrible clarity, running before my eyes like film : Jasmine Yang beginning to speak, and then the knife, and Chao Li.

The others didn't say anything; they'd about talked themselves out and I certainly wasn't going to add my news to the general chatter. Could I have saved her? Could I have known? I went over and over that scene. Then, suddenly I was mashing out the cigarette and hurrying to the door, flinging it wide. 'Listen, Lennox,' I began.

But Lennox wasn't there.

Thirty

'Give me your keys!' Rafer looked surprised, but he reached into his pocket, grunted with pain, reached again and handed the keys over.

'What's the matter?'

'Later,' I said. 'Come on. I'll need witnesses.'

I took Maria and Stanley Sung with me and demanded a police escort from the detective-sergeant as we went by.

'Why?' he asked plaintively.

I snapped my fingers. 'You know this is important. Hurry!'

A couple of minutes later I was stamping on the throttle pedal of the big American car and roaring round the perimeter road. There were enough horses under that bonnet for a dozen Grand Nationals and the acceleration was frightening. At the gate I simply flashed headlights a couple of times, stuck my hand on the horn and turned on to the dual carriageway. This time everybody else could wait.

I tore along that road like a madman. Why the hell wasn't there a ferry! I'd have to go into Ipswich and out again! Grimly I increased speed, noting with satisfaction that the police car driver wasn't any faster. He was having trouble just keeping up.

Just past Whetstead I could see the Orwell: a nice innocent river with massive quantities of drugs floating up it! My God, what a world!

I roared through Ipswich, brakes screaming, horn tooting. Any other time, this kind of sanctioned roadhoggery would have been a pleasure, especially with a police car on my tail; now I wasn't thinking about anything but getting there. Whipping through the roundabouts, I tore out of the town again, foot down, watching the speedo go to ninety, a hundred.

In the distance I saw Ransome's factory coming up on the left, braked and swung the Ford hard over on to the track, raced on to the field and saw her! I wound the window down and listened to the roar as those two Continentals built up, then I gunned the Ford forward.

He'd got her turned into the wind and he'd seen me coming. Now he set her off along the runway. He might be a few revs short, but he'd pick them up on the take-off run.

Under my wheels, the wet grass gave precious little traction and the Ford was inclined to veer wildly as I steered between the cultivated patches, not daring to risk bogging down in the mud.

'Get out fast when I stop,' I shouted.

I braked viciously, flung the door open and shoved Maria and Sung out, then trampled on the throttle without waiting to close the door.

The Tiger was roaring down the runway now, tearing up to take-off speed. Sixty or seventy yards and he'd be in the air. With my foot flat on the floorboards, I raced at him, our paths converging at an acute angle. Forty yards separated us now and I knew I couldn't get in front of him. Thirty, twenty . . . what the hell could I do? I couldn't prevent his take-off, but I bloody well wasn't going to let him go. No, by God I wasn't!

He pulled the pole towards him and the Tiger's nose lifted, but he wasn't quite ready to lift off. In a second, or two, though, he'd soar . . . I raced towards him watching the Tiger come nearer and nearer. There was only a few feet in it now—I was actually beneath his wing tip.

Then his wheels lifted clear of the ground and he staggered into the air. He was going to get away with it! He was! I spun the wheel desperately and the power steering whipped the front wheels round, throwing the car at the Tiger's side. Her wheels were three feet up, now; four . . .

My windscreen smashed under the impact; I'd hit the Tiger's wheel with the Ford's roof. I was showered with shattered glass as I fought to stop the Ford turning over. Then I got her on a straight line and did a hairy handbrake turn just in time to see the Tiger's somersault.

The blow on the wheel must have canted her over, tucked a wing tip down, and he hadn't had enough power, or skill, or both, to do anything about it. Almost in slow motion, the wing turned in the air and touched the ground. Then the action speeded up as leverage flicked the Tiger over and she smashed down on her back.

Now it was a matter of seconds. That big tank in the cabin had been far from empty and petrol would now be flooding all over the cabin. If there was a spark anywhere, the Tiger would simply blow apart.

I braked the Ford to a halt alongside, leaped out and raced across to the door. Already the air was thick with heavy petrol vapour. Wrenching the door open, I found Lennox's limp body hanging upside down from the harness. It might have saved his life in the crash but if there was a fire now, it guaranteed his death. I wrestled with the catch, then dragged at him, feeling his feet slide clear and down. Then his body fell on me. I struggled to my feet, gripped him under the arms and dragged him away. I kept pulling at him until we were well clear. The fact that the Tiger hadn't exploded already didn't mean she wouldn't.

At last, though, I stopped. The police car came alongside and one of the bobbies got out to help.

'Is he dead, sir?'

He deserved to be dead. I felt his heart, but all I could feel was the thumping of my own. Then I got my fingers in the right place. His heart was beating. In fact, he didn't seem much hurt; he'd just knocked himself out. I've known better men who have died in the kind of crash he'd just had.

After a moment his eyes opened and he looked up at me. 'You pulled me out?'

I nodded.

'Why?' He barked the word. There was no loss of attack.

'Firstly because I didn't want you to get away with it. And secondly—'

'Go on.'

'Because without you alive and confessing, they'd probably gaol me—for trying to kill you.'

He looked up at me and began to climb to his feet. The policeman helped him, looking puzzled.

I said, 'I'm making a citizen's arrest, Constable. Please

take a note of it. The charge is treason-felony. This is a conspiracy against the state's well-being.'

All hell was let loose, of course. I had to swear this and that and there was much telephoning. I didn't know how to get on to the security services, but Ipswich police did and suddenly tight-lipped, stolid men materialized and listened and made notes. Finally, and with massive satisfaction, I withdrew my charge and they made theirs.

Just before it was put, when they brought him from the cell that was called an interview room, he caught my eye. 'How did you know?'

'That you were bluffing about Jasmine Yang?'

'Yes.'

I said, 'She knew where I was staying. She told me she followed me. If you'd told her where to meet me, that wouldn't have been necessary. So you must have told *him*.'

'Sidney John Lennox,' the station sergeant said, 'you are charged that on divers dates—'

I looked at the little scene and went out. Stanley Sung had gone home after giving his statement. Maria hadn't. She hadn't anywhere to go. Taking her arm, I led her out into the air of early morning. Considering what she'd been through, she was remarkably cheerful.

'Rafer Hayes will probably help with your application for asylum,' I said.

She turned to me. She was dog-tired, but her eyes twinkled. 'Freedom,' she said. 'Is it always like this?'

'No,' I grinned. 'Sometimes it gets exciting.'

'Then I think I stay here. In England.'

I looked at her and found she was looking at me and something curious happened as our eyes met. This was quite a girl.

'Do that,' I said. 'You do that.'

Postscript

Only that wasn't the end. A couple of days later my phone rang.

'John, boy. Jimmy Pope.' He laughed hugely.

'If you were Pius, Paul and John the Twenty-Third singing in chorus, the answer would still be no!'

'Is that nice?'

I said, 'If they haven't called already, expect a couple of anonymous gents with the smack of firm government all over them. They'll probably have the handcuffs ready.'

'John, John, John. You're a caution! A real caution!'

'You can expect one of those, too,' I said.

The laughter rolled. When he'd regained control of the mechanism he said, 'Not me, boy. Lennox.'

'The parcel,' I said. 'Capote's differential.'

'All good stuff.' He spoke jokily like a stage-Yiddish street trader. 'We're very happy. Especially now they're all inside.'

'Who's inside?'

'Newton. A collection of Chinese gentleman called Ho. Sundry others over there and over here.'

'Ho, ho, ho.'

'No, boy. It's serious. We got the lot, even the cannery in Hong Kong. Everybody's very happy.'

'And one or two very dead.'

'In the long run, we're all dead. John Maynard Keynes said it, of all unlikely people. You'll be working for me, now.'

'Not this chile,' I said. 'I ain't workin' fo' nobody no' mo'. 'Ceptin' me.'

He laughed again. 'If you want to keep your licence, boy. You're in up to your neck, you know. Illegal entry; aid to illegal immigrants; evading customs; malicious damage; manslaughter.' Then he started to cough and splutter and it went on and on.

'What's so funny?'

'Lennox. You could share a cell with Lennox.'

When he recovered, I said, 'We were talking about my licence.'

'We can square things all along the line, boy. Americans, Canadians, Danes, Icelanders—yes, we can square you. But only *if*—'

'It's like that?'

'Sticky clutches, boy. Once in—'

'Never out! Jimmy, there are four things I want to know. Will you tell me?'

'If I can.'

'Jasmine Yang. Who was she working for?'

'China Society. She'd infiltrated. She was the mistress of one of the Hos. Next?'

There wasn't any way I *could* have known, but Jasmine Yang was going to be on my conscience for a long time.

'Next question, boy.'

'Marion Capote. Who and what is he?'

'Classified. You'd better sign the Official Secrets Act this afternoon.'

'I've done that.'

'It's a good habit. Next?'

'This is what really baffles me, Jimmy. The Hos knew I'd got their boy with me, but they kept on trying to kill us both. Why?'

'You don't know?'

'That's why I am asking.'

Jimmy Pope said, 'From the moment they suspected you knew the route the drugs took, your death became more important than your passenger's survival. And you'd talked to Jasmine Yang. You said four things. That's three.'

'Why did Lennox want Chao Li here?'

'First because he'd been seen. Sooner or later the cops or the narcotics people would have got him. Secondly because he was to work here, organizing the whole distribution chain.'

'That simple?' I said.

'Simple? Look boy, Lennox used to ask me why I used you, when you were so stupid. And I said you were resourceful, too. See you at three o'clock.'

He hung up. Just like that.